SARAH McCARTY

A HELL'S EIGHT ADVENTURE

Tracker's Sin

Spice

Spice

TRACKER'S SIN

ISBN-13: 978-0-373-60548-4

Recycling programs
for this product may
not exist in your area.

For questions and comments about the quality of this book
please contact us at Customer_eCare@Harlequin.ca.

www.Spice-Books.com

Printed in U.S.A.

To Vann—the man who makes me laugh no matter how dark the day. May your life be filled with love, sunshine and laughter for all the rest of your days.

1

April 5, 1858

Dear Ari,

I don't know how to start this letter, except to say thank
God you're alive.

So much has happened in the last year. Not all of it good,
but some of it so special, there aren't words to describe
it. I'm married. Happily so, to a man of whom Papa would
never have approved. He doesn't have money, doesn't have
social position, and doesn't care a fig about mine, but he
is everything I never dreamed big enough to desire when
we used to sit under the apple tree imagining the perfect
husband. A heart that knows no limits, a sense of honor
that can't be compromised, and a love for me so rich, I'll
never be poor. He's Hell's Eight, and if you're still living in
the Texas territory when this letter finds you, you know
what that means. If not, you're in for a treat. The men of
Hell's Eight are a breed apart. A standard on which to build
legends, for all they'll scoff at you if you tell them so.

SARAH McCARTY

My husband's name is Caine Allen, and he's the one insisting I write this letter. He believes in family and in my intuition, and though everyone says you're dead, he says my gut feeling is good enough for him, and he's promised finding you will be Hell's Eight's number one priority. He can be high-handed at times, but in the best ways.

I'm sorry I can't introduce you to the man handing you this letter, but you see, I've made seven copies and entrusted them to seven different men: Tucker, Sam, Tracker, Shadow, Luke, Caden and Ace. Like my husband, they're Hell's Eight and I'm asking you to put yourself in their care because each one of them has made a promise to me, one they've sworn to uphold.

They've promised to bring you home, Ari. Home to Hell's Eight, where there's no past, no recriminations, no judgment, just peace and a place where you can breathe easily. After what we've been through, I know it sounds like a preacher's description of heaven, illusive and unreal. But I promise you there is a way out of hell and if you haven't already found it, I'll help you.

Trust no one but them, Ari, because Father's solicitor, Harold Amboy, is the one who arranged for us to be ambushed initially, and he has men hunting for you, too. He intends to control Father's money through one of us. But you can trust any of these men. Absolutely and completely, with everything you hold dear.

I'm crying as I write this. I can't imagine what you've been through. I can't forget how we parted. My nightmares, which must have been your reality. The sense of helplessness as I stare at the night sky, wondering if you can see the same stars, wondering if you're healthy, happy, and most of all safe.

Do you remember the game we used to play as children when things didn't go our way? How we'd find a patch of daisies dappled in sunlight, link our hands in our special way and then just spin until we didn't care about anything else? I so want to see you again, Ari, find a patch of daisies, grab hands and spin until laughter takes over and all the bad falls away. Though it's irrational, because I have no idea how long it will take the men to find you—days, months, years—I have to say this.

Hurry home, Ari. I've planted a patch of daisies and it's waiting.

"So you're going after her?"

Tracker nodded in response to his twin brother's question, then yanked the square knot tight on the rawhide, securing his bedroll to the back of the saddle. Desi's letter to Ari rustled in his pocket, a subtle prod.

Tin rattled against tin as Shadow stuffed his plate and cup into his saddlebags. "We've got a better lead," he said, pointing out the obvious for the second time since they'd set up camp the night before. "The Saransens down Cavato way actually have a blond woman confirmed, living in town."

Tracker looked at Shadow. It was like gazing in the mirror. His twin had the same height, same broad shoulders, the same sharp planes to his face that lent a cruel edge to his expression. The latter came from their father. The only softness in his face was that full mouth, a gift from their Mexican mother. The same deep brown eyes with the cynical edge that came from knowing everything had a price.

Tracker and Shadow had learned young how to blend into the world around them so they'd be invisible to the "marks" their father wanted them to rob. A pity they'd never been able to hide from him. Tracker jerked the knot again, remembering the spew of bile that had rained down in insults and beatings if their father's standards weren't met.

As the older brother by twenty minutes, he'd tried his whole life to protect Shadow from the harshness of their world. He hadn't been successful. Shadow had suffered at the hands of their father. He'd suffered at the hands of the Mexican army that had wiped out their town when they were just boys. He'd suffered in the days after the massacre as he and the seven other orphaned boys had almost starved to death, searching for a place to belong. In the end, they'd made their home together, found acceptance in each other. And in the years since, those eight boys had grown into the most feared men of the Texas plains. Tracker and Shadow had family in Hell's Eight, but any respect they garnered outside the confines of Hell's Eight land they'd earned with their blood. In this country, the only respect a man held was that which he took. And he and Shadow had taken more than their fair share.

"Deep thoughts, brother?"

Tracker shook off the melancholy and smiled as he slid his rifle into the scabbard. "I was thinking that Caine would be pleased with where Hell's Eight has landed."

Caine was the leader of the group that those eight starving boys had become. He'd taken them from outlaws to lawmen, and Caine's wife was the reason Tracker was on the hunt now.

"He always said we'd get strong first and then we'd get even, and damned if he didn't make that come true."

"Hard to believe we're now the ones people call on when they have trouble." Tracker still wasn't comfortable with that. He'd rather stay in the background with no ties, no expectations, handling what needed to be handled calmly and efficiently, without any notoriety.

Shadow chuckled and shook his head. "Yeah, especially since we were so good at being trouble."

They had been that. Tracker had never felt so free as in those early years when they'd ridden outside the law, taking justice into their own hands, slipping in and out of the shadows, doing what needed to be done with an efficiency that would have pleased his father. But things had a way of changing, and now Hell's Eight was the law, bound somewhat by the rules of society. He grimaced. Hell, they'd gotten so damn respectable that it chafed. The bounty they'd just settled being a case in point.

He pictured again the smarmy smirk of John Kettle as he stood before the judge, hearing his not guilty verdict. The man was as guilty as sin. Tracker and Shadow had buried the bodies of the woman and child he'd killed, before they'd tracked him down. In the old days they would have just killed the son of a bitch in a quick dispensation of justice. Instead, they'd followed the law and brought him to the county seat. But while the woman and little girl were still dead, their killer was walking free, because justice had caved beneath the money and influence of John Kettle's family.

Tracker spat. "Things are changing, brother."

Shadow grunted, knowing exactly what he was talking about. "We should have just gut shot the bastard."

"Next time we will." He wasn't a man naturally given to playing by the rules, especially when they weren't working. Things might be changing, but he wasn't. He liked things clean and neat, with no messy loose ends. John Kettle was a loose end, and sooner or later Tracker would have to clean it up. The bastard killed for the pleasure it gave him. That kind of sickness inside a man only got worse, not better. He would kill again. And again. And again. Until someone stopped him.

"Amen," Shadow muttered.

A warm breeze blew up, lifting Tracker's long hair off his neck in a subtle warning. Goose bumps rose along his skin. His senses sharpened and that inner voice that so often saved his ass issued an alert. He traced the breeze's path backward. South. The sense of inevitability that had been haunting him since the day he'd met Caine's wife, Desi, increased. The woman who might be Ari was south. So was his destiny. He gripped the stock of the rifle, letting the familiar feel of the sun-warmed wood anchor him. The letter rustled. Damn, he wasn't sure he was that eager to meet what was coming.

It was too much to hope Shadow hadn't sensed the tension flowing through him.

"What is it?"

Tracker didn't know what to make of the inner prodding, the overwhelming sense of destiny crashing in on him. "A feeling."

Shadow swore. Their whole lives they'd had a strange connection, strange feelings. What happened to one often was felt by the other. It had kept them alive more than once. Shadow finished tying on his saddlebags. "I'm going with you."

Tracker didn't want his twin anywhere near the disaster that had to be his destiny.

"No."

Glancing from beneath the wide brim of his black hat, Shadow said, "You may be twenty minutes older, but you don't tell me what to do."

The hell he didn't. "We made Desi a promise to find her sister."

"Yeah, so? We'll give the Cavato lead to someone else."

"Who would you suggest? Cavato is in Indian territory. It would be suicide for most men to get within ten miles of there."

"I'd say Zacharias and his men, if he weren't still stove up from that run-in with Comanches."

"They could do it."

Zacharias and his vaqueros were from Sam and Bella's ranch. Tougher men had never been bred, unless it was Hell's Eight themselves. Hells' Eight owed them a debt that could never be repaid. Zach and his men had volunteered to sacrifice themselves in a near-suicide mission, standing against Comanches to buy Tucker the time he needed to get his pregnant wife to safety. Everyone thought they'd been killed. It'd been quite a shock to have them ride up, bloody and near death, at their own funeral.

"I'll be glad when Sam's connections get us what we need to put an end to the attempts on Desi's life."

Tracker nodded. "And Ari's."

"Yeah. Amazing what men will do for money."

And Ari and Desi were worth a lot of money to someone back east. From what Sam and the rest of them had deduced, the whole family had been slated to be murdered on their trip west, but the killers had gotten greedy when they'd seen the girls. Instead of killing them, the attackers had sold them to *Comancheros*. Both girls had suffered horribly. Desi's suffering had ended when Caine had found her standing all but naked in a creek, fighting four men with that hellion spirit. But Ari's suffering probably continued.

No one knew if Ari had survived, but Desi's gut said she had, and that was enough for Hell's Eight. They each carried a letter that contained a promise to bring Ari home to her sister.

And no member of Hell's Eight ever went back on a promise. None of the men really expected to find Ari breathing, except maybe Tracker. Perhaps it was because he was a twin himself and understood that strange connection between close siblings that surpassed logic. Or maybe, he admitted only to himself, it was because of something else, something deeper. But he knew Ari was alive, and he knew he would find her. The only thing in question was whether he would find her in time. Inside him a clock ticked, and lately the tick was becoming louder, as if time was running out.

He glanced south again. Ari was waiting and she needed him. He wouldn't listen to anything inside that said more than that. But he still didn't want Shadow anywhere around what his gut said was going to be his end.

"We can't afford to wait for Luke, Caden and Ace to hit the rendezvous points and pick up their messages. If the woman in Cavato is Ari, you need to get there before she's sold or stolen again."

"Yeah." Shadow's face set in that blank way that said he was accepting what he couldn't change. "And if she's not Ari?"

Tracker patted Buster's flank. "I'll do what I think best."

"Tia said if we bring home another mouth to feed who can't cook, we're not getting another biscuit for the rest of our lives."

Tracker grunted. "Then we teach them to cook on the way to Hell's Eight."

Shadow snorted and picked up his horse's reins from where they dangled to the ground. "Says the man who's always ducking the women trailing behind him."

Tracker looped the reins of his roan around the horn of his saddle. Buster lost a bit of his lazy slump. There was nothing the horse loved more than covering ground, and since he had a stride as smooth as butter, there was nothing Tracker loved more than riding him. "I don't want their gratitude."

It made him uncomfortable, made him feel like a liar. He wasn't a hero. There just wasn't much else a man could do when a woman looked at him with hope fading from her eyes as she realized he was there to save someone else, not just give her something on which to hang that hope. A ride to a safe place. A chance to start over. Not all took it, but some did. And those who did he brought home to Hell's Eight. From there they did what they wanted. Went home to family, went off to new beginnings or stayed under the group's protection. Something Shadow knew, because he'd brought just as many women to Hell's Eight as Tracker had. The difference was that the women didn't imagine themselves in love with Shadow. Tracker wished he knew the secret of keeping them at arm's length. He was getting damn tired of being the butt of jokes.

Leather creaked as Shadow swung up into the saddle. "You might as well enjoy it, since you can't escape it."

"No." He wasn't a ladies' man and never had been.

"Women have touched us for less clear reasons."

"Yeah." He recalled the way Desi looked at Caine. The way Sally Mae looked at Tucker. The only greed in either woman's eyes was that of a woman in love who wanted her man. He couldn't remember a time when he'd been looked at with love. Any softness he'd received in his life, he'd paid for. He was damn tired of paying. He was getting damn tired of a lot of things.

Buster tossed his head and snorted impatiently. Tracker agreed. It was time to leave. He swung up into the saddle.

Shadow stopped him. "Tracker?"

He gathered up the reins. Buster pranced with impatience. "What?"

"You don't have to go."

He blinked. "I gave my word." For the longest time the Ochoa word hadn't been worth shit, but now it stood strong. He wasn't going to be the one who dragged it back into the dirt.

"Desi will understand."

"I doubt it. She loves her sister."

"She also loves you."

He shook his head. "It's not the same."

Shadow adjusted his hat against the glare of the morning sun. "What is it with finding Arianna, Tracker?"

"I don't know what you mean."

"You told me once that you had a feeling she'd be the end of you."

"I was drunk." The dreams had been getting stronger lately, coming nightly, yanking him from a sound sleep with a sense of urgency and doom. He'd tossed back the whiskey in an attempt to escape them.

"You never drink, but when the last one wasn't Arianna, you went on a two-day bender."

"I'd been a month on the trail with five women who did nothing but argue. I was just cutting loose."

"You hate drink and what it does to a man."

"Doesn't mean I'm not as foolish as the next when I get off the trail."

"Bull."

He didn't need this from his brother. Not now. "Let it go, Shadow."

"Not if finding Ari means I lose you." Shadow's horse shifted with the tension in the man.

"There's no 'if' about it. I'm going to find her."

"And if it means your death?"

He'd made his peace with that possibility a year ago. It wasn't that hard. The pain in Desi's face as she spoke of the last time she'd seen her sister, the agony in her voice as she'd exposed her guilt, the hopelessness as she'd begged Caine to help her.… Like Caine, he'd do anything to remove that pain from her. Despite all that she'd been through, Desi was the purest soul Tracker had ever seen. An angel with blond hair and blue eyes. An angel who had seemed so familiar the first time he saw her that he'd thought he recognized her, until he'd gotten closer. *So close,* his instincts had whispered, *but not the one.*

And then she'd revealed the existence of her twin, and that sinking sense had come with the loss of inviolability. Then the dreams had started. Arianna called to him in those dreams, begged him for help. And he could help her; he knew that as well as he knew saving her would destroy him. He imagined Desi's face when her sister came home. Going out a hero wasn't a bad way to go. He met Shadow's gaze and held it. He didn't want to leave any doubt that he went to his end with peace in his heart. "Then I'm making the trade."

Shadow shook his head. The breeze that raised the long, silken hair that lay on Tracker's back barely disturbed his brother's. "I'm not."

Tracker couldn't help that. "Your destiny lies elsewhere."

It was a shot in the dark, but the twitch of Shadow's eyelids revealed what he'd suspected. His brother had demons of his own to wrestle with in the dark of night, when there were no distractions.

"Promise me you'll watch your back."

Tracker nodded. "As well as you watch yours."

"That will be damn good."

"Understood."

Shadow wheeled his horse to the west and nudged him into a canter. As one, man and horse blended seamlessly into an easy rhythm. Tracker watched until his brother grew small in the distance before turning Buster south and urging him into his own ground-eating lope. His destiny waited.

His destiny rested in a little run-down adobe house about a mile out of the town of Esperanza. Evidence of past prosperity was all around the property. A barn big enough to house several horses stood just off to the right. Several corrals surrounding the structure were in various states of collapse. Only the fences near the house were maintained. The home itself clearly had been built for a family, and remnants of happier times remained in the faded red paint on the shutters. However, the only people Tracker had seen coming and going from the house since he'd arrived last night were a stooped, elderly Hispanic man, a small elderly woman, presumably his wife, and a blond woman Tracker had seen only from the back, through the window. By the lack of hoofprints around the exterior, he was pretty sure those were all the residents.

He trained his spyglass on the window again, hoping for a better look at the blond woman. All he saw was the back of a wooden chair, a cup on a table and the edge of a black iron stove. Impatience, a foreign emotion, gnawed at his calm. He wanted—no, needed—to see the young woman who lived there. His gut said it was Ari. He needed it to be Ari. He was sick of the dreams, sick of the apprehension, sick of the fairy tales his imagination wove around her. The woman had lost her family to murderers, her virginity to *Comancheros,* and probably her sanity to God knew what else. Whatever he found, Ari wouldn't be a woman who tiptoed into his dreams at the end of nightmares, held out her hand in invitation and looked at him with softness. He'd be lucky if she still had a thread of sanity.

He shifted his position slightly. There wasn't much cover around the house, which was good from a defense standpoint, but was hell on his knees, as it forced him to crouch. There was only so much cover sagebrush could provide a man his size. And only so much strain his twice-busted legs could take without screaming a protest. He forced the growing discomfort from his mind and resumed his surveillance. He needed to know if the woman was a guest or a prisoner. It wasn't uncommon for women to be sold as slaves this far from the law. And it wouldn't be a surprise, based on what she'd been through, if Ari saw that as a step up.

Movement to the left caught his eye. He turned the spyglass on the back door. The old man stepped down into the yard, steadying himself on the doorjamb a few seconds before straightening his spine and heading toward the barn, where the milk cow was housed. An aged hound strode alongside. It was clear to Tracker that the old man was ill, but didn't want the other residents of the house to know. Tracker made a note of the routine and added it to his mental list. From what he could see, it wasn't a violent household. He'd crept close enough to the house last night to hear some conversation. He'd caught only a bit, revolving around the care of the rosebush out front, before the hound had caught his scent and growled a warning. That fragment of conversation had been enough to give Tracker a hint of *her* voice. Soft and sweet, with Eastern overtones. It was hard to tell through the walls, but he thought there was a strong similarity to Desi's voice.

He shook his head and pulled his hat lower against the

morning sun. If he were hunting any other woman, the information he had now would have been enough for him to act. But this was too important, too personal for reasons he couldn't begin to define. For this identification, he needed absolute certainty.

Movement in the window drew his spyglass back around. Disappointment cut like a knife when all he saw was the salt-and-pepper bun pinned atop the old woman's head. But then she moved on and the younger woman came into view. From the back she looked just like Desi. She had the same delicate stature, same hesitant yet challenging way of standing, as if she needed just the slightest encouragement and she could take on the world. More importantly, she had the same blond hair that fell in a riot of curls down her back.

His fingers tightened on the spyglass. *Turn around. Turn around.*

As if she heard him, she did, turning until he had a clear view of her face.

"Son of a bitch."

He'd known Ari was Desi's twin, but somehow he just hadn't been prepared for the impact. Ari had the same big blue eyes set in a round face above a surprisingly lush, red mouth. She even had the same stubborn chin. If the two were side by side, a body would be hard put to tell the difference. He squinted and pulled his hat brim lower, blocking more of the sun's rays. With further study, he discerned some differences. Desi was small and dainty, but as she'd said, her sister was even more delicate. Maybe Ari wasn't as tall or maybe she was a smidgen fuller in the cheeks. Or maybe it was just her spirit that had that delicacy. It was hard to tell anything from this distance. But one thing was sure, Ari didn't have the look of a woman who'd been to hell and back. As he watched, she laughed, tossing her head, sending curls bouncing over her shoulders. Tracker slowly lowered the spyglass, the image of that smile lingering.

Shit.

He took a breath as the ramifications rocked through him. It really was Ari and she really was alive. More than that, she seemed happy. The latter defied reason.

There were eleven of them. And with me gone, there was just her.

Desi's description of the last time she'd seen her sister whispered through his head the way it often did, bringing the fury that came from knowing how easy it would be for just one man to force a woman of Desi's build down in the dirt. How much pain just one man could inflict on such a delicate woman until she gave up all hope and just did what she was told. When he multiplied that misery by eleven, the rage near drove him insane. He couldn't imagine what it'd done to Ari—but not leave a scar at all? That he couldn't fathom.

A bird burst out of the large bush set between the house and the barn. It wasn't the old man who'd startled it; he was still in the barn. The hairs on the back of Tracker's neck rose. The town of Esperanza was expanding wildly because of the rumor of gold in the area, and in the way of growing towns, the disreputable element was growing the fastest. It wasn't hard to figure out why someone lurked in the bushes near this particular house. Blond women in this part of the country were a rarity. Delicate blond women with the face of an angel were a prize. No telling what kind of scum had come creeping around. Looked as if Tracker had arrived just in time to be useful.

He glanced at the house again. The shutters that hung alongside the windows were solid except for the small gun slits cut into them. Obviously, at some point in the past, the residents had had to fight for their survival. But whatever habits they'd once practiced had now fallen to the wayside. Now, the front door was propped open to catch the morning breeze. The man of the house had left his gun behind when he went to the barn. Clearly, the residents had become complacent, at a time when they should be vigilant.

Tracker raised the spyglass again. He could just make out the figure of a man hiding behind the small wash shed. Tracker estimated the distance. More than a hundred yards and not a lick of cover between him and the intruder. That eliminated the hope of a silent attack. He reached for his rifle. There was more than one way to skin a cat. A quick scan of the surrounding area didn't reveal any other signs of intruders. So there was just one. Tracker carefully drew his rifle forward as he watched, keeping it low so the sun wouldn't glint off the dull metal barrel and warn his quarry. He wet his pinkie and held it up. Not much wind today. The shot would be easy.

The intruder moved forward. Tracker trained his glass on the man, swore and then relaxed. Son of a bitch. He was nothing more than a boy. Dark skinned, with shaggily cut black hair and the tan-colored wool clothes of a Mexican. The youth had to have a powerful crush if he'd risk getting caught spying on a white woman. Even here at the edges of the state, there were white men who would kill him for the offense.

The lad wouldn't care about that, though, if he was in love. A boy in love had no sense and no control. Tracker remembered back to his youth, his first ill-fated crush. The only thing that had mattered was getting a moment with the woman of his dreams.

The boy needed manners cracked into his skull, but not killing. Tracker propped the rifle across his knees.

It was no surprise when Ari came out of the house dressed in a nightgown and wrapper, carrying a pitcher. The boy had to be waiting for something. Tracker set his teeth as the sun shone through the layers of cotton and revealed the fine turn of her calves. The adobe house wasn't so isolated that a woman could go about undressed. His woman sure as hell wouldn't, especially in a robe that clung so enticingly to the soft thrust of her unconfined breasts.

His cock stirred in his pants as the material pulled tight across her slender hips for a moment. Her ass was surprisingly full for such a delicate woman. He did enjoy a woman's ass, and Ari's was a work of art. As fast as the thought entered his head, Tracker pushed it aside. A woman like Ari wasn't for him. He knew it and the world knew it, and if he dared to forget, someone would put a bullet between his eyes as a reminder.

Ari went to the well behind the house. She primed the pump with a cup of water from the bucket sitting on the side, and then worked the handle until the water flowed steadily, standing back a bit so it wouldn't splash. He didn't know whether to be grateful or resentful of that. Wet cotton got temptingly see-through. Ari filled the pitcher with water, stood as if listening for something, and headed back toward the house twice as fast as she'd left. What had she heard that put that pep in her step?

The back door slammed shut behind her. The boy glanced at the barn and then the house, and then took off at a run, looking back over his shoulder several times. Tracker knew just how he felt. He'd have liked a longer look at those pretty calves, the soft thrust of her breasts against the robe. He cursed as the seam of his pants cut into his cock. He was too old to be responding like a randy kid.

He inched backward on his stomach until he had the shelter of a small rise between himself and the house, and then he stood. A soft whistle brought Buster trotting over. Tracker packed up his gear, anticipation nudging him to hurry. He wanted to swat at it the way he'd swat a fly. He was a man of calm, a man of patience. He could wait days for the chance of a shot, ignoring cramped muscles, bug bites and weather. Why was it that he couldn't wait five minutes to ride down to that little ranch?

He slid his rifle into the scabbard, then paused before mounting up. He touched the letter in his pocket, the one Desi had written. He'd promised her he'd bring Ari home.

Everyone had assumed Arianne would be grateful to leave whatever hell she was living in for the chance to be with her sister, but she looked settled here. She might not want to leave the older couple to travel across the state. Whatever had happened since the *Comancheros* had sold her, she'd clearly found a measure of peace here. People could be funny about peace. They rarely wanted to leave it.

The letter rustled under his fingers. A promise was a promise. If he had to bring Ari kicking and screaming to Hell's Eight, he would. She wasn't safe here. The attack on Sally Mae had made it clear that Desi and Ari's enemies were still hunting her, and if he'd found her, they could, too. Swinging up into the saddle, he steered Buster toward the ranch. Leaving wasn't an option, so he needed a legitimate reason to stay while he checked the lay of the land. Word in town was the old man was looking for help fixing the place up.

Tracker patted Buster's neck. "Guess we'll go see a man about a job."

2

The old man was sharper than Tracker had expected. He took one look at him outside the barn door and grabbed up a pitchfork.

"*Que quieres aquí?*"

Tracker halted just inside the door, keeping a safe distance between the tines of that fork and his midsection while his eyes adjusted to the change in light. The last thing he wanted was to hurt an old man who'd taken in Ari and given her peace.

He answered in English. "A job. Word in town is you've got one available."

The old man squinted and looked him over from head to toe. Tracker knew what he saw. The scar on his face alone gave people pause. Coming hard off the trail, dressed in black, his hair long and the scar advertising his way of life like a red flag, he looked like what he was: trouble.

The man didn't lower the pitchfork. "I am looking for a handyman."

"I'm handy."

The old man's gaze went to the guns on his hips. "With a hammer."

Tracker didn't bother to smile. It made people nervous when he smiled. "I'm good with that, too."

"I do not need here the kind of trouble a *pistolero* brings."

Tracker's eyes had adjusted to the interior. There was no one else lurking about as far as he could tell, and the hairs on the back of his neck weren't standing on end in warning. That was about as much of a guarantee as he ever got. He relaxed, pushing his hat back from his forehead. "Is that so?"

The old man showed no sign of relaxing in turn. "That is so."

"From what I saw last night in town, it seems to me a man with a pretty young woman on the property could use all the help he can get. With a hammer and other things."

The old-timer took a step forward, the tines dipping to align with Tracker's gut. "You will stay away from *mi hija*."

Daughter? He called Ari his daughter? That was going to complicate things. "Don't have any intention of getting close. That kind of trouble *I* don't need."

It wasn't precisely a lie. He was only going to get as close as it took to spirit Ari safely back to Hell's Eight.

The old man lowered the pitchfork slightly. "No, you don't." He jerked his head toward town. "They would string you up by your *cajones*."

Interesting. "And who would *they* be?"

"*Los gringos* who came to town last winter."

"There weren't any gringos in town last night."

The old man spat. "They come. They go. But when they come it is *muy malo*."

Likely a gang of outlaws who were intent on making the

town of Esperanza their refuge. "Not the neighborly sort, huh?"

The old one stood the pitchfork on the ground. "No."

The cow mooed restlessly, clearly unhappy with having her morning milking interrupted.

"Then I reckon a handyman who's also handy with a gun might be useful." Tracker held out his hand. "Tracker Ochoa."

Not by a twitch of an eyelash did the old man show any sign he recognized the name. Tracker wasn't surprised. Esperanza was very close to the Mexican border. Not much worry a Texas Ranger's rep would carry this far.

"Vincente Morales."

Vincente's hand was callused and worn from years of work. His grip was lighter than Tracker expected. As soon as he felt swollen knuckles that indicated arthritis he lessened his own grip. Vincente leaned the pitchfork against the outside of the stall.

"This getting old, it is not for a coward."

"You looked pretty damn intimidating wielding that pitch-fork." Tracker took a step forward and indicated the cow. "Mind if I finish this up?"

"I would be grateful."

Tracker readjusted the stool near the animal. "She got any preferences?"

"No. Abuelita is a good cow."

Tracker set his hat down and leaned his forehead against the animal's side. It'd been a long time since he'd milked a cow. He hated the damn things, but he couldn't sit by and watch an old man with pained hands struggle with the chore. It took only three seconds to figure out that there were some things a man didn't forget, no matter how hard he tried. Milking a cow was one of them.

Two tugs and the milk hit the bucket in a hard stream. The old hound moaned and looked hopeful. Tracker smiled and squirted in the dog's direction. His aim was a bit off but the hound compensated, licking the milk off his whiskers with slow swipes of his big tongue. Vincente chuckled.

Tracker caught his eye. "Hope you don't mind."

"No. He can no longer hunt rabbits. It is one of his few pleasures."

"A body's got to have his pleasures."

"Sí."

The barn fell quiet, the only sounds being the hound scratching and milk splashing into the bucket. Vincente broke the silence.

"The job does not pay much. A room here in the barn and supper."

Tracker cocked his head so he could see the man. "Your wife a good cook?"

Vincente patted his rounded belly. "Very."

Tracker bent his head and hid his smile. He could see Caine saying the same thing about Desi forty years down the road. Then he chuckled. It'd be worth living that long to see Caine with a belly. "That'll do."

The cow was about dry. She stomped a hoof, signaling the end of her patience. Tucker squirted the last of the milk into the bucket and leaned back. Too late he remembered the other reason he hated cows. Her tail whapped him in the face, the bristly hairs stinging, adding insult to injury.

"Son of a bitch." He jumped to his feet, barely missing spilling the milk. The cow turned her head and stared at him reproachfully, as if he'd done something wrong.

"Don't look at me like that!" He rubbed his cheek. "I'm not the one swinging wildly."

He grabbed the bucket in case she was one of those cows that delighted in making a waste of an unpleasant task by kicking over the container.

Vincente laughed outright and handed him the lid. "There will be danger for you here."

Tracker laid it in place, fitting the notches between the bucket's handles. "From the unneighborly sort?"

"No."

Grabbing his hat, he settled it back on his head. "Nothing new in that."

"Why do you want this job?"

"My reasons are personal." Tracker straightened. "Why are you offering it?"

"Who says I am?"

"Me."

"And who are you that I should care what you say?"

He took a stab in the dark. A sick man with two women to protect had to be nervous. "A man you can trust."

"I do not know this."

Tracker shrugged. "Doesn't change the truth of it."

Vincente stared at him, squinting to see in the low light of the barn. "But you expect I will learn?"

He shrugged. "Most people find me a right handy man to have around."

The old man studied him for a few more seconds and then nodded. "Yes. I think I will, too." He motioned to the door. "We will try you today. You may put that by the back door of the house." He patted the cow's flank. "I will get Abuelita settled."

"Will do."

"Come right back."

Tracker nodded, used to men not wanting him around their womenfolk.

He made it to the barn door before Vincente called out, "I tell you not to linger because my wife has been nervous of late, and she is not such a good shot."

"She the shoot-to-kill type?" Tracker respected that. No one should pick up a gun without being prepared to kill.

"It would be better that she was, but she has a soft heart and bad aim." Vincente smiled. There was a world of love in that smile. "I am afraid she would aim for your foot and hit your heart. I do not want to be in church so much as it would take for her to repent."

Tracker chuckled. "I'll keep that in mind."

"*Gracias.*" The lightness left Vincente's expression. "Later, if I decide you can stay, I will introduce you."

"Then I guess I'll have to work today to impress you."

"Because you don't want a bullet in your heart?"

Tracker shook his head and called back, "Because it's been a long time since I had a home-cooked meal."

The old man shook his head and gathered up Abuelita's lead rope. "It is lonely for a man as he gets older, *sí?*"

Not for Tracker. He couldn't let life get lonely. "For some."

Vincente slapped the cow's rope against his boot, punctuating his mocking tone when he said, "For some, huh!"

The last thing Tracker needed was an old man playing matchmaker. It was bad enough that Tia wouldn't accept reality. "Yes," he retorted. "For some."

"But not you?" Vincente asked as he led the placid cow out of the barn.

"No. Not for me."

"Huh!" Vincente's snort carried clearly as he led the cow to the fenced pasture. "Drop off the milk and we will get to work."

The old man might be arthritic, he might be going blind, but he was a man on a mission, and that mission seemed to be to get as much work out of Tracker as he could. The first job of the day was to get a sizable new garden area ready for his wife, which involved plowing up the hard-packed earth. It'd been a dry spring, and the ground was full of rocks. The only tool the old man had was a weighted plow. With no horse to pull it, the only option was for Tracker to do the pulling. Apparently, judging from the cut-down harness, this had been the system for years.

After one brutal trip down the length of the marked-off area, Tracker was seriously considering hooking Buster's temperamental ass up to the makeshift harness. But the gelding had a fierce reaction when it came to pulling things, and since Tracker wasn't going to be around long enough to replace the plow, he grudgingly slid the harness over his shoulder and dragged the blade back down the next row.

"You sure your wife needs a garden this big?" he asked as he passed Vincente, who was hauling rocks out of the area with a net spread between two sticks tied together. It was an ingenious device that took the stress off the old man's hands.

"*Sí*. Absolutely."

"Going to be an awful lot of canning."

"Yes. She will be pleased."

Was she going to be pleased or was Vincente? Tracker wasn't certain. But one thing a garden this big would ensure was that a woman would have enough goods to eat or trade, whether there was fresh meat or not. He watched as Vincente again missed a rock with the net. Just how bad was the man's vision?

He looked up at the sun. It was going to be a warm day. "Then I guess we'd better get it done before the sun blisters our hides."

Vincente grunted as he dragged a rock over the plowed dirt. "*Sí*. It will be hot today."

After two hours, Tracker was sweat drenched, thirsty and hungry, but the new garden spot was plowed and Vincente seemed happy. From the house came the ringing of a bell.

"Ah! Breakfast is ready. We must clean up."

Tracker shrugged out of the harness, more than ready to be done with the damn thing. "I thought the job came only with supper."

"It does, but twice my Josefina looked out the window and saw you plowing." Vincente took the harness from his hands and tossed it over the plow handle. "Her soft heart doesn't let a man go hungry. There will be a plate for you and she will chide me if you do not eat it."

Tracker could eat a horse, but having breakfast meant meeting the family, and he wasn't ready to meet Ari yet. Wasn't ready to substitute the illusion of his fantasies for harsh reality. His fascination with the woman had to end sometime, but not this morning. "Women can be the bane of a man's existence."

Vincente slapped him on the back. "So speak the young."

It'd been a long time since anyone had called Tracker young.

"When you are older you will see they are the blessing God puts in a man's life to ease his way."

"Uh-huh."

Vincente shook his head. "You young people today have no

appreciation for the way things should be. Trying to change what you cannot, and running away from what you should be embracing..."

Tracker headed up the path to the wash shed and hazarded a guess as to what he should be embracing. "A woman? I've embraced more than my share of them."

"A *good* woman." Vincent put a lot of emphasis on "good."

It was easy for a man who fit somewhere to hold such beliefs. "My father was Indian, my mother Mexican. There aren't many *good* women who want to hitch their wagon to that mix."

"You do not need many. Just one."

"Uh-huh." The old one was up to something. Whatever it was, Tracker wanted to nip it in the bud. "Vincente?"

"Yes."

"Whatever you've got in mind, drop it." The last thing he needed was a half-blind, arthritic old man picking out his love interest.

Vincente huffed. "I merely point out the truth."

"Thanks." Tracker primed the pump as Vincente scooped out some soap from the tin on the ledge. He let the older man wash first. "But I'm happy with what I've worked out."

"You are not happy."

"I'm as happy as I've ever been."

Vincente muttered something under his breath as he finished washing and pulled his shirt back on. "When you are done, come up to the house."

Tracker looked at the little home in the well-tended yard. Smelled the scents of wood smoke and sausages on the breeze. Inside, two women had a table set, coffee brewing

33

and food ready. When Vincente entered, there'd be pleasant conversation, maybe laughter. There'd be love.

Tracker wasn't going within a hundred feet of that house. Not this morning. He felt too raw inside to sit there and watch what he would never have.

"Will do."

He waited until Vincente reached the house before pulling off his shirt. It took only a few pumps of the handle to get a strong flow of water going. Vincente was lucky to have such a rich supply. Tracker dunked his head in the spray. The well water was surprisingly cold. Frigid. But after the initial shock, it felt damn good on his overheated skin. He grabbed the soap and blindly scrubbed, pumping the handle a few more times, letting the water pour over his head and neck, enjoying the moment. When the temperature turned more chilling than refreshing, he stood, flipping his hair back over his shoulders.

A shriek loud enough to split his eardrums spun him around. He palmed his knife as he turned, ready for the threat.

He knew who it was before he shook the soap out of his eyes. Ari stood there in a pretty blue dress, her mouth open, a look of shock on her face.

He reached for his shirt. The plate of food in her hands fell to the ground, spattering her skirt. Ari's gaze never left the knife in his other hand. Her throat worked furiously, but no sound came out.

Shit. She was still screaming, Tracker realized. Screaming for all she was worth, but not a sound passed her lips. He left the shirt where it lay and took a step back. He couldn't go far with the shed wall behind him and her in front.

"You must be Ari," he said in his softest voice, wincing at the deep rasp that made it sound like a growl. "Hello."

His softest voice wasn't soft enough, because she kept up that horrible pantomime of a scream. Tracker tucked his knife hand behind his back. It didn't make a difference.

Tracker cast a quick glance at the house. The back door didn't open. No one came to the rescue. There was just him and Ari and her fear. Shit! Sam should be here. He was much better with hysterical women. Women trusted Sam even when they shouldn't. It was those blue eyes of his and that devil-may-care smile. But he'd met his match in his wife. They'd been to hell and back, but they'd come out together and they were happy.

"Vincente!" Tracker yelled. *"Venga aquí!"*

No response came from the house, but Ari took a breath and launched another one of those soundless screams. He followed the trajectory of her gaze. *The knife.* She was aware he still held it behind his back. He didn't want to speculate on why, but he couldn't help a quick check of her hands, her neck, her face. Not that there had to be scars where a man could see. Tracker knew too well how creative a Comanchero could get with a knife and an unwilling woman.

He moved his hand from behind his back, watching her expression as the weapon came into view. It didn't change. Just because the knife had been out of sight didn't mean it had been out of mind.

"Sorry about the knife. I forgot." Hell, now there was a calming thing to tell a terrified woman. He looked toward the house. Still no one coming. Very slowly he reached down and slid the knife back into its sheath, attempting a smile.

"It's just your luck to get scared out of your bloomers by a man who doesn't know what to do with your fears."

He didn't really think she heard him, which was probably a good thing. He was pretty sure decent men didn't refer to a woman's bloomers. Tia would have had his head if she'd heard, because lord knows, she'd tried to teach him better. Sometimes he just had a hard time remembering the rules.

Ari didn't respond to his smile or his words. She just kept staring at the knife in its sheath, still screaming in rasping pants of soundless terror.

Time to try something else. Grasping the knife between his forefinger and thumb, Tracker made a big production of removing it. She stopped breathing altogether. Holding his hand as far away from his side as he could, he reached back and set it on a ledge behind him.

"It's okay, ma'am. No one's going to hurt you." Least of all him. How could anyone hurt a woman like that? Tracker had had the same thought when he'd first seen Desi huddled in Caine's coat over a year ago, wearing her fear like a second skin. Now, looking at Ari, he experienced it all over again. She was so delicately formed, she made him think of fine china. The kind a man was afraid to touch, but felt compelled to because the sheer fragility of it demanded cherishing. Protecting. Because what it represented was what kept every man hoping.

He stepped to the left, away from the knife.

Ari's focus switched from the blade to his face. Tracker debated trying another smile, but as wild as he must look to her, all dark and scarred, he opted for remaining expressionless. At least she'd stopped screaming.

As she panted for breath, he had a chance to study her more closely. Each angle of her face was cut with precision, the fine grain of her skin reflecting the sun like cream, the blue of her eyes shining with the brightness of a summer sky. Her lips were plump and soft and as silky looking as a rose petal. He remembered a poem he'd read once where the author compared his love to a red, red rose. Ari was like that. A beautiful flower that flourished no matter how much shit had been thrown at her. He might never know how much, but the Moraleses had started her healing, and being at Hell's Eight would finish it. There was no judgment there, just acceptance. A lot of lost souls came to Hell's Eight and found peace. Ari would, too. She had a sister and a niece to love her. A family waiting to claim her. All Tracker had to do was get her there.

Looking into her terrified eyes, he remembered that silent scream that couldn't find a voice, imprisoning her in a memory from which he couldn't save her. Tracker wanted to promise her that he'd hunt down the men who'd done this to her, and make them pay. But Caine had already made that promise and Hell's Eight had already fulfilled it. That left her with a stranger's word on something she likely wouldn't believe. Not that Tracker didn't think she wouldn't appreciate knowing it someday. Just not today.

"Ma'am." Where the hell was Vincente and his wife? "I don't have the knife anymore. And my gun belt is clear over there by your feet."

She blinked. For a heartbeat Tracker thought he saw sanity in Ari's eyes. She licked her lips. Her gaze locked with his and then went to the gun belt.

He read her intent before she dived, but he wasn't fast enough to catch her before she got her hands around the pistol. If his reflexes had been a hair slower, he wouldn't have gotten there in time to stop her from blowing his brains out. He caught her hand, gun belt and all, letting their momentum roll them over, taking as much of the force of the fall on his shoulder as he could.

"Let go. Those guns have a hair trigger."

She sank her teeth into the back of his hand. He swore and held on. One wrong move and she'd kill them both.

"Dammit! Let go!" What she lacked in muscle she made up for in wiggle. It was all he could do to keep her finger off the trigger. He pressed her down into the dirt, using more and more of his weight until she went limp beneath him.

"Ma'am?"

Ari didn't respond. Tracker carefully removed the pistol and gun belt from her grip. She didn't fight. He stood. She continued to lie in the dirt at his feet.

He'd thought it odd that she didn't have scars from her ordeal. She did. He'd only been able to see what was uncovered. And all it had taken to bring them out was one fool, half-naked Indian reaching for his knife. Hell.

You're ugly enough to scare a bad woman decent.

Once again his father had been proved right. The older Tracker got, the more he began to accept that the insults his dad had tossed out in Tracker's youth were actually truths he'd been too stubborn to accept. The proof lay prostrate on the ground at his feet.

It wasn't right that Ari lay in the dirt like trash thrown aside. Looking at her there, her skirt hiked around her thighs, her beautiful blond hair a tangle around her shoulders, he grimaced. It was easier than it should be to imagine her time with the *Comancheros,* to envision the hell she'd been through. They'd probably walked away from her, leaving her just like that when their lust was spent. Left her to rot in the devastation of her soul, this woman who had been created to be cherished.

Tracker wasn't any different from the *Comancheros.* Faced with Ari's reaction, faced with his own demons, he wanted to walk away, too. Instead, he found himself kneeling, sliding his hand beneath her head, lifting her to his chest.

"It's going to be all right, Ari. I promise."

Her hair smelled like sweet flowers and heaven, her skin like vanilla and spice. Innocence and passion, a hint of who she might have been if she hadn't been stolen, raped, sold. Looking toward the house, making sure no one watched, Tracker rested his forehead against hers.

"A lot of people have been looking for you a long time, little one."

No one harder than him, for reasons he didn't understand, except that he was driven. He took a napkin from where it had fallen and wiped at the smudge of dirt on her cheek. It felt right to be the one caring for her. Goddammit, he was losing his mind. This was dangerous. She was dangerous. It had to stop. Now.

"Goddammit, Vincente, I know you can hear me. Get out here."

In Tracker's experience, women in a swoon didn't stay out long, and he didn't want to trigger another bout of hysteria when she woke in his arms, en route to the house. So he sat there and held her, and pretended that he could make it all right, while he gave her a minute or two to come back to herself. After all she'd been through, she deserved that minute. And it was the only thing he could give her.

The screen door slammed. Vincente and a plump woman hurried out of the house. As soon as they reached Tracker's side, Vincente was apologizing and the woman was fussing. Tracker handed Ari over to Josefina and glared at her husband. "Why?"

"I did not think she would have such a reaction. She has been doing so well lately."

"She's not your daughter."

Vincente shook his head. "Our daughter died in childbirth. Our hearts were so empty, and then we found this one and it was another chance."

A second chance to love. Not many got them. "So you loved her so much you sent her out here to be scared out of her wits?"

"No. I know who you are, Ranger." Vincente took the napkin, wetted it and handed it to his wife. "There was no danger to her."

"Just to her sanity."

"Yes, but we hoped…" The old man sighed. "She is such a good daughter, a good mother. It is only when the bad times haunt her that this happens."

Tracker's breath caught. "Mother?"

"She was pregnant when we found her."

"Son of a bitch."

"It has not been easy."

"She loves the child?"

"With all her heart."

How the hell could Ari love a child who had to remind her of the hell she'd survived?

Josefina looked up as Ari moaned. "She's waking. You should leave."

"I can't."

"You must."

Tracker looked at Ari. He'd promised to bring her home, no matter how he found her, sane or crazy. "Not without her."

3

They settled on a compromise. Tracker retreated to the barn, and the Moraleses took Ari to the house. He watched as she stumbled between them up the path, clearly disoriented, yet trusting the older couple in a way that suggested they'd done this many times before. As they made their way to the back door, Josefina kept her body between Ari and Tracker. She tossed wary looks over her shoulder at him as she shielded Ari protectively. What was more interesting, though, were the glares she shot her husband. Obviously, the woman blamed Vincente for the incident, which reinforced Tracker's own sense of being set up. Shoving his hat on his head, he swore and closed the barn door. He hoped the old woman gave the old man hell and indigestion.

An hour later, Tracker sat on the bed in the small but comfortable bedroom at the front of the barn, still stewing. The old one owed him an explanation. The vague excuse he'd tossed out at the washhouse wasn't going to cut it. Tracker disliked being anyone's pawn. He disliked people who tried to manipulate him.

The Ari he'd met at the wash shed was the woman he'd been expecting to find—traumatized by her experiences, tortured by her memories, rekindling her past in everyday events. A woman broken by tragedy. He'd thought he'd prepared himself for the reaction she might have to his appearance. After all, her attackers had been men like him. Men who wore their violent history in their eyes, on their skin and in their dress. Men who killed as easily as they laughed. Men who did what they wanted and to hell with the consequences. But Tracker could have avoided seeing that woman if Vincente had handled the introduction differently. Why the hell had the old man forced the issue? Had he wanted Ari to fear Tracker?

He grabbed his pistol from his gun belt where it hung by the head of the bed. Grains of sand clung to the metal. Desi said there was a difference between him and the *Comancheros,* and maybe there was. He wasn't one to prey on the weak, but he'd done things in the name of revenge that would scare her curly hair straight and take the look of respect from her eyes. Things that kept him taking bigger and more dangerous bounties, because they took him to places where he was comfortable, places where there was no right and wrong, just a man's ability to come out on top in a fight.

Tracker yanked his saddlebags toward him. He was very good at coming out on top.

Lately, the line between an outlaw and himself had been growing vague in his mind. As the years passed, killing had become easier in some ways, yet harder in others. Tracker could still pull the trigger, but it bothered him more that whenever such a deed was done, justified or not, he couldn't stop thinking about it. Right was right and wrong was wrong; that's the way it was out here. The way it had always been. So why wasn't he comfortable settling with that anymore? Why did every bounty he took now involve a moral debate inside himself if it went sour? Why was it getting harder to live with pulling the trigger? Why was he now seeing the faces of the men he killed, reliving the battles at night when he should be sleeping? Shit. Tracker was who he was. Better than he could have been, not as good as he should have been. He was an Ochoa. Outlaw, killer, bounty hunter, Texas Ranger.

He tugged his cleaning kit out of a saddlebag. The smell of gun oil blended with the scents of hay and cow as he opened the oiled leather wrap. All familiar, all comforting. He took another breath, seeking the edge that the familiar gave him against the anger seething inside.

Laying the cleaning rod aside along with the rags, he began disassembling the gun. It was a daily ritual and as soothing as the scents around him. It was also necessary. Dirty guns misfired. Misfires on the other guy's part were a good thing. Misfires on his end of the battle were dead-before-his-time bad.

The outer barn door opened. He could tell from the sound of footsteps crossing the floor that the owner was small. He could tell from the swish of skirts that the owner of those footsteps was female. Josefina with his breakfast, no doubt.

"I'm in my room," he called out.

It was as natural as breathing to prop his rifle across his lap just in case. It was rare that a woman came to his room intent on murder, but it had happened a time or two. Such occurrences tended to make a man wary. And he'd seen the anger in Josefina's eyes. Clearly, she wasn't ready to give up her daughter, though apparently Vincente was. The why of that was a puzzle to be solved. As was how they knew Ari's name. A woman with no past would nave no name.

There was no response. Maybe Josefina didn't speak English. *"Estoy en mi quarto."*

The footsteps halted just outside his door.

The hair on the back of his neck stirred. A tingle went down his spine. "You can come in. I'm decent."

Metal rattled against china. Whoever was outside his door was nervous. He cocked the hammer on the rifle.

"Come in."

The door swung open.

"Hello." The distinct Eastern tones gave away the identity of who stood in the door. Ari. Tracker tilted the rifle downward and slowly replaced the hammer as shock ricocheted through him. He blew out a breath.

Ari stood in the doorway, a napkin-covered tray in her hand. She was the last person he expected to see. Tracker stood and leaned the rifle against the wall. He took off his hat. "Hello."

The tray rattled. Ari licked her lips. Her gaze didn't meet his, and her voice shook along with the tray. "I wanted to bring you your breakfast."

She was lying.

"Why?"

She blinked and licked her lips again. The plates again rattled on the tray. He took a step forward and removed his breakfast from her grasp.

He smiled. "My stomach might cut my throat if a second breakfast lands on the ground."

Her gaze flicked to his before retreating back to the floor. Shit, it was always a mistake to smile.

"I'm sorry."

It was a common statement, expected even, considering what had happened. He hated hearing it from her. As he placed the tray on the small pine dresser to the right of the door, he took the opportunity to study Ari from the corner of his eye. She wore a pink calico-print skirt, with a white, buttoned-down blouse. Nothing was out of place. Every button was buttoned; her shirt was evenly tucked inside the waistband. Her shoes were freshly polished. It was almost as if, through impeccable grooming, she'd tried to erase the craziness of earlier. Hell, she'd even managed to tame the intriguing wild-ness of her hair, corralling it into a neat braid, coiled up in a tight bun anchored at the base of her neck.

A few rebellious tendrils tickled her nape, bringing his eye to the long, elegant line of her throat and the daintiness of her ears. He didn't normally notice a woman's ears, but Ari's were cute, with lobes that just begged to be nibbled. His gaze naturally traveled down the side of her neck, following a tempting path to the pulse beating in the hollow of her throat. He wanted to sprinkle kisses along that path, touch that too-fast pulse with his tongue, take her in his arms and promise her again that everything would be all right. Son of a bitch, what was it about the woman that made him think in terms of suicidal acts? He wasn't some sort of knight in shining armor. He was a fucking outlaw turned lawman. No better than he had to be in any situation. He had nothing to give a woman like her.

Tracker straightened. Ari's glance cut to the rifle, to his face, then his hands. He knew how they looked to her. Sun darkened and scarred, they were as ugly as his visage. About the time the urge to tuck them out of sight got overwhelming, she looked away. Even her embarrassed blush was pretty.

"My parents told me…"

The flush on her cheeks became fiery. He waited for her to continue. She cleared her throat and smoothed her palms down her skirt. He wondered if they were sweating. She tried again.

"My parents said I had an…episode with you."

Her uneasiness was rubbing off on him. He took a step back toward the bed, giving her some room to breathe. "That's one way to put it."

She kept giving the pistol wary glances. "Did I hurt you?"

He cocked an eyebrow. "You're wiggly but not lethal."

She went still, blinked. He could almost see the wheels turning in her mind, see her searching for a memory. Saw the moment she gave up searching. "Oh, good."

He could let it go or bring it out in the open. He opted for the latter. "You don't remember what happened?"

She shook her head. Her gaze left his and her lip slid between her teeth. She looked very young right then. Too young and too innocent to have been through what he knew she had. "No."

"Did Vincente and Josefina fill you in?"

Her hands, which had been smoothing her skirt, now clutched it. "No. They used to try, but I'd go craz…" She shook her head, took a breath and started over. "I'm sorry. I thought I was getting better."

"This has been going on awhile?"

"Yes."

"How often?"

This time when she looked at him, it was with resentment. With a snap, she shook out her skirt. As if snapping material snapped her spine into place, she stood up straight and looked him dead in the eye. This was the Ari who haunted his dreams.

"I owe you an apology, Mr. Ochoa, not an explanation."

"Sorry. I kind of take it personal like when a pretty woman tries to shoot me."

The color left her face and she swayed. He grabbed her arm. Christ, she didn't have enough bulk to keep his fingers from meeting.

"I tried to shoot you?" she whispered.

"Whispering doesn't change the fact."

Her fingers touched his. "I won't faint."

"I'm not convinced."

"It's just a shock." She licked her lips. "Hearing what I do when I get like that."

He studied the paleness of her cheeks, the shadows darkening her blue eyes. He considered saying something outrageous just to get the blush back.

"You really don't remember what you do, do you?"

"No."

He released her arm. "That has got to be as scary as he—heck."

Her right hand moved to cover the spot he'd touched. To remove or to hold on to the sensation? Tracker shook his head, disgusted with himself for the weakness that had him hoping it was the latter.

"It can be."

"And that's your explanation?"

She shrugged and gathered handfuls of her skirt with her fingers, gathering her composure as she did so. She was obviously humiliated. "I'm sorry I behaved oddly, and I'm sorry if it scared you."

The last was said in a rush. She turned on her heel and headed out the door.

"I wasn't scared," he called after her. Ari could leave him many ways, angry, happy, but not humiliated.

Her footsteps stopped. There was a swish of skirts as she turned, and then the sound of her footsteps coming back. And damned if they didn't sound angry. She stopped in the doorway, her arms folded across her chest. He wondered if she would still stand that way if she knew how uncertain it made her appear. Maybe she wouldn't even care. Compared to crazy, uncertainty was quite a step up.

"You weren't?"

"Nope."

"Why not?"

"I could say because you were scared enough for the both of us."

Her eyelids lowered. At her left temple, a curl was working loose, he noted absently. "But you won't."

It was an order. A rather intriguing one, considering how scared she'd been before.

"No, I won't."

"Then why weren't you afraid?"

He gave her the truth. "Because I'm one mean son of a bitch."

She didn't blink at the curse or the declaration. "I see."

Did she? He doubted it. He waved her to the lone chair in the room. "So now that I've come clean, why don't you?"

"About what?"

About how she'd ended up here. About how she'd kept her name. About how in a part of the state where lawlessness was rampant and blond women were money on the hoof, she existed peacefully with only an old man for protection.

"How about starting with how long you've been here."

"A little over a year. Ever since my husband was murdered."

Pretending nonchalance he didn't feel, Tracker slid the

tray off the dresser and onto his lap. There were beans, rice, scrambled eggs sausages and tortillas on the plate. He forked a bit of each into a tortilla. "You were there?"

"Yes."

"What happened?"

She licked her lips again, leaving them moist and shiny. They were redder and more swollen than before, as if she'd been chewing on them. They would look just like that after a man's kiss. His kiss, Tracker admitted to himself. No matter that she wasn't for him, he wanted Ari like hell on fire. Just another one of life's little jokes.

Straightening her skirt around her legs, Ari took one of those deep breaths he'd learned meant she was struggling for composure. The breath pressed her small breasts up against the cotton of her bodice. It was too easy for Tracker to imagine what they'd look like naked. He wondered if her nipples would be pale or dark, or maybe as red as her lips. He liked the thought of them being red from his attentions.

He mentally shook himself. He was little more than an animal. A woman like Ari would never look twice at a man like him, even before the events of the last two years. And after? Shit. She'd run like hell.

His cock couldn't care less what his brain said, however. It responded to her in a purely primitive manner, swelling and stretching to life.

Ari motioned to the tray in his lap. "Your food is getting cold."

"You avoiding my question?"

"What if I am?"

He took a chance that pretending disinterest would make her comfortable. "Then I'll rein in my curiosity and stop asking."

For a moment he wasn't certain it would work. She crossed her ankles left over right. And then right over left. She licked her lips. Checked her bun. Sighed and then said, "I don't know what happened."

"You don't remember?"

She shook her head and looked away. "I had a blow to my skull. I can't remember anything before I opened my eyes and saw Vincente and Josefina looking down at me."

That was convenient for the Moraleses. Tracker folded the tortilla around the contents. "Not even your husband?"

He took a bite of the tortilla. She shot him a glare. "I'm not crazy!"

He chewed and swallowed. "I didn't say you were."

She frowned and bit her lip. Her teeth were very white against the ruby-red flesh. If she kept biting her lips like that they were going to be raw. "Only a crazy woman couldn't remember her husband."

It was just a whisper, but it contained so much pain. He wanted to reach out and hold her, and tell her it was a blessing she couldn't remember, a gift she should hold on to, because the truth was too horrible to be borne. Instead, he took another bite, chewed and swallowed, before saying, "Head wounds can be tricky."

"That's what the doctor said."

"At least you have your child."

Her whole expression softened. "Yes."

Tracker set the tray aside. "How old is your baby?"

"Six months. He's just beginning to crawl."

The last of Tracker's hunger left him. Six months was too old. Ari would have had to have gotten pregnant when she was with the *Comancheros*.

"What's wrong? Don't you like the food?" she asked.

"I'm just feeling a bit off my feed. It was a hot morning for plowing."

"Pappa is determined we have more garden space."

"I noticed."

Ari shifted in the chair, clearly wanting to leave, but just as clearly held in place by another desire.

"Something on your mind?"

She nodded and took one of those betraying breaths. Threading her fingers together, she clenched them until the knuckles showed white. "My parents are going to ask you to leave."

"I figured that." Nothing like having your daughter falling into a fit at the sight of the new handyman to clinch a decision.

"I don't want you to go."

It was his turn to blink. "Why?"

"I heard my parents talking. I know who you are."

Who he was seemed to be pretty important to these people. "And who's that?"

"You're a Texas Ranger. One of the meanest."

"I guess that would depend on who you talk to."

She looked disappointed, and more than a little skeptical. Her gaze lingered on the scar slicing down his cheek. "You're not mean?"

"Mean enough to get the job done."

"I need you to be very mean."

"I'll ask you again—why?"

"My father is in trouble."

"He didn't make any mention of it."

"He wouldn't. He likes to think he can handle everything, but he's old now and he can't fight the way he used to." She glanced at Tracker, fear in her eyes. "The men who would hurt him are vicious killers. They have no consciences or souls."

"How do you know?"

She shook her head as if bewildered. A curl fell loose from her bun, bouncing against her cheek. She shoved it behind her ear. "I just do."

He bet she did, even if she was talking to him as if he couldn't trigger a bad memory if he wanted to.

"I know enough to know that if things continue the way they are, those men are going to kill my father. He knows it, too. That's why he wants the garden bigger. So Mama and I can support ourselves."

"Would those men be the gringos who came to town last fall?"

"You've met them?"

Tracker shook his head. "Haven't had the pleasure yet." But he would. It was a bit too coincidental that trouble of that type came to the small town where Ari had taken shelter after the Moraleses had found her. As a matter of fact, a lot of the circumstances surrounding Ari's rescue were convenient.

She frowned. "If you do, you'd better be good with those guns."

It'd been a long time since someone had questioned Tracker's skill. "I'll keep that in mind."

She licked her lips again. His cock hardened, pressing painfully against the seam of his pants. He barely bit back a "Stop doing that."

She stood up so fast her skirts swayed. "I want to hire you."

He stood, too. Another interesting tidbit. "I'm a Texas Ranger. We're not for hire."

She put her hands on her hips, determination giving her a

confidence he hadn't seen before. "We're not in Texas, though, are we?"

Technically, the area was in dispute. "Close enough not to abandon the principles I serve, no matter how pretty the woman is who asks me."

She made a slashing motion with her hand before running it over her hair. More tendrils threatened to break loose with the next pass of her palm. "I don't want you to kill anybody."

To give his hands something to do besides reach over to let one of those curls entrap his finger, Tracker picked up his gun and began reassembling it. "What do you want me to do?"

Her arm dropped to her side. "I just want to scare those men so they leave my father alone."

It wasn't the first time Tracker had been asked to scare somebody, but it was probably the first time he believed the person asking really thought it could be done without anybody getting killed.

"Why do they bother him?"

A tinge of red on her cheeks, a hint of tears in her eyes, and she said, "Because of me."

"Why?"

The blush of embarrassment deepened and she looked away. "Men think I am…available."

"Because of your son?"

"Yes." Her expression tightened and her hands fisted. "I think they threatened him."

"Vincente?" The old man didn't strike Tracker as the type to cower at a threat.

"No." Her gaze dropped to his pistol. Her fingers clenched and unclenched as if it was all she could do to keep from grabbing it from him. "My son."

That put a whole new spin on the issue. "Did Vincente tell you that?"

"You don't believe me?"

"Yes, I believe you. The baby is the family's most vulnerable point. It makes sense for a man to threaten it to get what he wants."

"I'd go to them if I thought it would keep him safe."

She would, too. Tracker could see it in her eyes. Even if she couldn't remember, she had to be scared shitless at the thought, but he didn't doubt for a minute that she would sacrifice herself for the safety of her son. She had the same fighting spirit as her sister. Likely the same recklessness, too. He'd have to keep an eye on that.

"It won't."

"I know."

But if the gang turned up the heat enough, if she got desperate enough, she might see it as her last hope.

"Please. I don't want them to hurt my family. I owe them so much. I wasn't...well after the murder. They thought I was going to lose Miguel."

"Miguel is your son?"

"Yes." She took a step closer and placed her hand on Tracker's arm. The heat of her touch seeped slowly through the leather of his shirt. "Please." Another step brought her skirts around his legs. "Help us."

He placed his hand over hers, pressing just firmly enough so she couldn't let go. "What are you offering me if I do?"

The pulse in the hollow of her throat beat double-time. The fresh scent of soap blended with the acrid smell of fear.

She swallowed hard and lifted her chin. Tears trembled on her lashes. "Whatever you want."

He slid his palm up her arm, trailing his fingers up the side of her neck before working them through her hair, to anchor them beneath the bun. It would take so little to tug her hair free of the constraint. So little to break her. He let his thumb skim down until he found the hollow of her throat.

Take her up on her offer, the devil that sat on his shoulder urged. Tracker was tempted. Her pulse throbbed against his thumb in silent reprimand. *She offered,* the voice continued.

Yes, she had. It wouldn't be the first time he'd traded services for sex. It likely wouldn't be the last. That didn't mean he had to like it.

Her big blue eyes widened and locked on his. Tears spilled down her cheeks. Her lips trembled. "Please."

He caught a tear with the edge of his thumb, halting the downward spiral. Son of a bitch. He needed a kick in the ass. A man didn't pass up opportunities like that.

"You loved Miguel's father very much."

"Vincente and Josefina are my family."

Interesting way of skirting the statement.

"They're not mine," he retorted.

She grabbed his wrist. Her short nails stung as they dug deeply. "I'm begging you for your help."

"And you just naturally went for my base nature. Because a man like me wouldn't have a higher one."

"No!"

"That's okay, sweets. I'm willing to be as low as you want me to be."

"I don't want you to be anything! I just want you to help my family."

"Then why don't you just ask for my help?"

She pushed at his hand. "I did."

He tipped her chin up so she had to look at him. Had to know with whom she was dealing.

"You tried to hire me. You begged me, but you never asked me with any expectation that I would agree."

"Why would you?"

Christ, she'd just got done hauling out his reputation, but when it came to seeing him, she didn't see a decent human being. "Yeah. Why would I?" He let her go. She stepped back immediately, rubbing her hands up and down her arms.

"Are you going to help us?"

There was a smudge on the pristine white of her shirtsleeve where he'd held her.

"I'll help you." The jury was still out on whether he'd help the Moraleses. Something about their story struck a sour note.

He grabbed his hat off the bed.

Ari stood in the doorway, blocking his way. "What are you going to do?"

"Go to town."

Her eyes grew big again. "But you don't have any help."

Grasping her shoulders, he turned her around and nudged her ahead of him. "I'm not going to solve your problem today."

"You're not?"

"No." He grabbed Buster's tack. The bridle jangled as he dragged it off the rack and carried it over to the stall. "I'm going to get a drink."

4

Tracker was a drinking man. Ari didn't know why she was surprised. Men like him who wore that aura of death around them played hard and drank hard. At least that's what she'd heard from Josefina. It was why Ari never went to town. Because drinking men couldn't be trusted. But even though she stood there watching Tracker prepare to saddle his horse, she didn't believe it. It didn't mesh with what her instincts said were the truth. It didn't mesh with her own experience.

She touched her cheek where she could still feel the warmth of Tracker's hand. He'd been angry with her and hurt, but his touch had been anything but angry. If she didn't know better, she would have called it seductive, maybe even tender. He was a very strange and confusing man. And he was her only hope.

Tracker hefted the saddle onto his horse's back. Despite the anger and frustration she could feel coming from him, he was gentle with the animal, too. She admired the maturity that allowed him to control his emotions. She admired his physique. He was truly beautiful from behind. His broad shoulders tapered to lean hips and tight buttocks that flexed as he turned. A mature man in his prime, he was beautiful in a very masculine way. Her gaze dropped to his buttocks again. *Very* beautiful.

"Don't you have a baby to attend to?"

Dear heavens. How had he known she was looking? Heat flooded her cheeks.

Ari had two choices: apologize or brazen it out. She chose the latter. Tracker wasn't the type to admire cowardice. And there was something about him that made her want his admiration. Of course, the fact that she'd lapsed into an episode likely would always color how he saw her, but she could try. She was more than that scared woman she couldn't control. She lifted her chin. A perceptive man would figure that out. "Josefina will call me when he wakes from his nap."

Tracker's response to that was a grunt. He tied off the girth strap. His hands were large yet deft, going through the process with a certain grace that held her gaze. He handled a horse well. How would he be with a woman?

"Then why don't you find something else to do besides stare at me?"

Because staring at him made her feel alive for the first time since she'd awoken after her husband's murder. Vital. More than just a crazy woman with no past. "This suits me fine."

The truth was, she liked having his hands against her skin. That brief touch still lingered in her senses like a brand. It had been…arousing in a way she couldn't remember ever feeling before. She frowned, closed her eyes and studied the sensation, trying to follow it back into the black void that used to be her past. As she had every other time she tried to remember, she hit a wall of nothing. She sighed and opened her eyes. Her gaze collided with Tracker's.

"Anybody ever tell you that staring at a strange man will get you into trouble?"

"But I'm not staring at you."

The look he shot her was hot enough to make her toes curl. Hate her or resent her, Tracker Ochoa desired her. That was an exciting thought. She was a widow, but she was almost at the end of her mourning. And he was a very virile individual.

"I warn you, sweets, I'm not a nice man."

She tried to remember all that she'd ever heard of him, and he was right, no one had ever said he was nice. She nodded. "I understand."

He flipped the stirrup down off the saddle horn. The light of the barn slashed across his face, highlighting the set of his chin, the fullness of his lower lip, the hint of muscle she could see through the open neck of his shirt. His skin, the color of cinnamon coffee with just a touch of cream, stretched tight over his collarbone. There was a scar just to the right of his throat. Rather than detracting, it emphasized the sheer virility of the man. Beneath the brim of his hat, his eyes watched her admire him. Narrowed as they were, he should have looked scary, but beneath the hooded lids, she could see heat simmering. Desire. For her.

"Do you?"

She nodded again.

"What do you think you understand?"

There was something so…alive about flirting with Tracker. Even when it was a bluff. It made her feel so far away from that void, so far away from her troubles. It was stimulating. "That you want me."

The swear word he uttered was vile and not one she was

used to hearing. But instead of being repulsed, she was intrigued. It was the first break in Tracker's control, and she'd caused it. She couldn't help a small, proud smile.

"You're playing with fire." He gathered up the reins and hooked them over the saddle horn. "I'm a dangerous man."

She'd be more afraid if his voice wasn't so softly enticing, with dark notes that stroked along her nerves in a provocative lure. "I'm a crazy woman."

"You're a mother."

What did that have to do with anything? "You're a lawman."

"I was an outlaw before that."

Interesting. But not as scary as it should be. Excitement hummed in her veins. She should be afraid. She wasn't. She was actually a bit exhilarated. "You couldn't have been much of one if you ended up a Ranger."

"I was a damn good outlaw."

He stopped fussing with the saddle and turned his full attention on her. His mouth quirked up in a smile that, twisted by the scar, seemed to give his expression a cruel edge. Until she looked into his eyes, and then she saw the sensuality waiting to be unleashed.

A shiver went down her spine. "And now you're a damn good Ranger."

"Don't curse."

She didn't recognize the woman who retorted, "Then don't talk nonsense," but she liked her.

So did Tracker, if the softening of his lips was to be believed.

"I told you I'd help you." He gave the saddle a tug, testing the girth. "You don't need to seal the deal with your body."

All right, that was embarrassing. She took a breath as heat

seared her cheeks. But she didn't retreat and didn't back down. She'd sworn when she'd woken up to nothing that she'd face her new life with courage. Courageous people didn't run from the truth.

"I'm sorry about that."

Tracker swung up into the saddle. "It doesn't matter."

But it did. She'd insulted him. He was a lawman. He lived his life doing right, and she'd taken in his size, the vicious scar cutting his cheek, the darkness of his skin, and judged him to be amoral. "It does."

She took a step forward. He watched. She took another. His eyes narrowed. She took a third. She couldn't take the fourth. The sleeping demon coiled behind the blank wall of her memory stirred. There was something wrong with the way he sat the horse. Something familiar and horrible in his long hair, flowing from beneath the hat. Something wrong with the illusion of power when she had none. She took a breath, desperate for the memory to continue, but terrified that it would. The horse shifted, leaving Tracker backlit by the sun pouring in the doorway. The sense of danger increased. Dear God, she didn't want to know.

"Please." *Please make it go away. Please make it go away. Make it go away.*

She blinked and Tracker was there, studying her with that intentness she didn't like. As if he could see what she couldn't. As if he knew what she didn't. Suddenly, flirting with him wasn't fun anymore.

"You really don't remember anything, do you?"

"No."

"And you've asked?"

"Yes."

"Are you sure you got the right answers?"

No. "Yes." She motioned with her hand, hurrying him along. "I thought you were going to get a drink?"

"I thought you were trying to seduce me."

She blinked, the last of the darkness fleeing before the outrageousness of the statement. All she had to defend herself with was a bluff. She wasn't a confident woman. She didn't think she ever had been, but she wanted to be, and with the birth of her son, she'd decided she would be. Vincente and Josefina were wonderful, but they were old and they had lives of their own to live. She'd heard them talking at night about wanting to move back to Mexico and live with Josefina's sister and her family. They just couldn't take her with them. She was too white to be safe, and they were too old to protect her. They'd saved her life, and never made her think they begrudged her, but she was their son's responsibility, not theirs. She had to learn to make her own way and find a place where she and her own son would be safe.

"Was I?" she asked.

"Might have been my mistake."

No, the mistake had been all hers. "I'm sorry. I'm not usually so…" She waved her hand. "It's just been so long."

"Since you've been with a man?"

She blinked at the bluntness. She hadn't even thought of that. "No." She looked at him and answered with dawning comprehension, "I think it's just been a long time since I felt alive."

"Son of a bitch." He walked his horse forward the two steps it took to tower over her. "Screwing me won't keep you alive. In case you haven't noticed, you're white and I'm Indian."

He was doing it on purpose, trying to intimidate her. Using crudity to push her away. Was this the real man? Did it even matter? He was right: she was a mother. She was right: she was crazy. Whatever she did to feel alive, it couldn't involve using this man. He wore the pain of his life on his person and in his eyes. It wasn't her place to add to it.

"I'm sorry," Ari said, hearing Josefina call to her from the house. "Miguel is awake. I have to go."

Tracker backed up the horse. "So do I."

Her stomach dropped to her toes. Was he leaving? Panic must have shown in her face because he swore and the horse shifted.

"Don't worry. I'll be back. I haven't forgotten what I promised."

She felt guilty at the relief that flooded her. Helping her meant putting his life on the line. It was wrong to ask someone to do that, but she had no choice. She needed him. Without him she had no way to protect those she loved. And to save those she loved, she needed this man to risk his life. It wasn't right. It just wasn't. She pushed back the curl that fell over her eye. With an annoying stubbornness, it bounced back. She inhaled a breath.

Tracker's anger struck her like a blow.

She took a step forward. His hands tightened on the reins. If he turned away now he'd never know how she felt, because she'd never get the courage to say it and he would always think her a coward. Formless memories howled behind the wall as she took that step. He scared her and he drew her.

But she owed him. That was all that mattered.

The horse tossed his head as she placed her hand on his rider's thigh. Tracker controlled the nervous prancing with tension on the reins and the pressure of his knees. Muscle flexed against her palm. He was a very strong man with a reputation that made the worst outlaws cower. They said he was lethal with a knife, deadly with a gun and brutal with his fists. But looking up at him, all she saw was a man with the same haunted look in his eyes that she saw when she looked in the mirror. She wore a calm facade to hide her turmoil. He wore anger. But beneath both facades was pain. Common ground.

"I'm not afraid of you."

He snorted and backed the horse up. "Who are you trying to convince, me or yourself?"

She closed her fingers around the lingering warmth from his skin. *Both*. She couldn't meet his gaze. "I'm not afraid of you."

He gave a curse she couldn't understand, then muttered, "I'm going to get that drink."

She didn't have anything to say to stop him. Ari watched as Tracker walked the horse out of the barn, ducking his head to avoid hitting the lintel. Not for the first time, she missed the freedom to vent her frustrations that men had. Since her husband's death she'd often wanted to pound on something or someone. And failing that, drink away the pain of memory she couldn't recall.

Josefina called again. Before she left the barn, Ari grabbed Tracker's untouched plate of food. Because of her, he was going hungry. Why did life have to be so complicated?

When she got to the yard, she could just make out rider and horse in the distance. Blowing errant curls off her forehead, she sighed and muttered, "Have one for me, too."

Miguel was his normal cheery self. After tying his nappy, Ari blew on his plump little belly before tugging his shirt down. His toothless smile and happy giggle were as familiar as the routine. If it hadn't been for him in those bleak months following her husband's death she wasn't sure she would've survived. Until his birth, her nights had been plagued by nightmares and her days with the struggle to remember.

But the day Miguel was born, she found an anchor for all the emotion inside, a reason to live that had nothing to do with needing to remember. Miguel was her future. She followed it. Josefina had been worried about her getting up to nurse the baby. She'd felt that maybe it would be too much for Ari to handle, and had suggested they put him on a bottle. But Miguel's frequent need to feed had been a blessing, breaking the pattern of nightmares and allowing Ari to start a new, healthier pattern.

She touched Miguel's button nose now and smiled into his deep brown eyes. She loved him so much. He gave her so much. She slid her hand down his cheek, marveling at the perfection of his much darker skin, searching as she always did for some familiarity in his features, checking the shape of his eyes, the sound of his laughter for some reminder of the man she had married. As always, there was nothing.

She picked him up, not finding her usual peace in his presence. "Your daddy would've loved you very much, cutie pie."

"*Sí*, he would have been a very proud father."

Settling Miguel against her shoulder, Ari turned to Josefina. "I wish I could remember him. It would be good to be able to tell Miguel something of his father."

The woman smiled. "Vincente and I will tell him what he needs to know."

There was that possessiveness in Josefina's voice again that had been showing up more and more of late. Combined with the wording that eliminated Ari's importance, it made her uneasy.

Josefina held out her hands. "I will take the little one."

Ari turned away, not missing a flash of displeasure beneath the other woman's smile. She refused to feel guilty. Miguel was her son. "Thank you, but I thought I'd take him outside to play."

"It is dirty outside."

"I'll put a blanket down."

"You are still unsettled from this morning."

No, she wasn't. She was actually doing quite well. Better than she had in a long time. And that was because of Tracker. The man had blown into her life like a tornado. All she knew of him was from legend and their brief interaction, but she felt she'd known him forever. Felt as if she needed to know more.

Are you sure you're getting the right answers?

The Moraleses had given her a safe haven in which to heal and to have her child. She hadn't questioned anything in those early months, just accepted the past as it was painted for her by Josefina. But with the rising tension in the household during the last few weeks, she'd begun to do some thinking on her own, because something was wrong and no one was talking. Josefina had become snappish and possessive of Miguel. And as a result, Ari had begun to notice how much of her life was controlled by the Moraleses.

And now they were going to send Tracker away under the pretext that he had upset her. Why? When he was the best protection they had?

Miguel grabbed a handful of her hair and pulled. She winced as she gently pried his fingers free before holding his hand in hers and bringing his fingers to her lips.

"He is getting *muy fuerte,*" Josefina praised, stroking his little arm.

Ari smiled. "Yes, thank goodness." He was precious. The

most precious thing there was. It didn't make sense that Vincente would send away a Texas Ranger. And not just any Texas Ranger, but the legendary Tracker Ochoa, a man they said had once ridden into a blind canyon filled with outlaws lying in wait, and came out unharmed, with ten bodies draped over saddles. Men like that didn't ride into their tiny town every day. They should be thinking of ways of keeping him there, not sending him away.

"I think we need to ask Tracker to stay."

Josefina's expression snapped closed. "No. He is a bad man. He will bring trouble."

"We already have trouble."

"Vincente will handle it."

"Vincente is only one man." And not a young one.

"It will work out." Josefina patted Ari's hand. "You will see. Vincente will talk to these men. We do not need the likes of *that one*."

"*That one* is a respected Texas Ranger." Ari didn't know why she felt the need to defend Tracker, but she did.

"He has bad blood." Josefina made a sign to ward off evil. "He attracts evil to him. You can see it in his eyes."

The only things Ari had seen in Tracker's eyes were pain and loneliness. And desire.

Josefina squeezed her hand before taking Miguel from her. "Your illness affects your judgment. You must trust me in this."

Must she? The inner discontent that had been growing this last month flared. Ari wanted to reach out and grab Miguel out of the woman's arms. Lord in heaven, was she really so crazy that she would turn on her family?

Are you sure you're getting the right answers?

The skepticism in Tracker's question bled into her beliefs.

67

What did she really know about the Moraleses beyond what they told her? And if she was their daughter-in-law, why was there nothing of hers in the house? She and her husband had lived elsewhere, but couldn't someone have brought her things? If for no other reason than to stimulate her memory?

"I want to go home," she told Josefina. There was the slightest hesitation before the older woman set Miguel down on the blanket on the floor of the main room.

"You are home."

Ari licked her lips and tried again. It was so painful for the Moraleses when she brought up their son. She couldn't blame them for always changing the subject. "I know this is difficult for you, but I need to go to the home that I shared with Miguel's father. I know you think it's only going to… upset me again, but it's something I need to do. I need to touch something from Antonio's and my life together."

So it would feel real.

"You have proof of your life together in your son."

Ari had tried before and never succeeded in convincing Josefina that Miguel had nothing to do with his father in her mind. He somehow seemed more connected with her survival than her past. Of course, she hadn't tried very hard. But Tracker's arrival had done more than stir feelings of being a woman. It had also stirred her need to find some part of herself that had been lost on that bloody day when her husband had been killed.

"When I look at Miguel, I see nothing of Antonio. When I look at my baby, I see Miguel's eyes, Miguel's nose, Miguel's face. It's almost like Antonio never existed."

Josephine stumbled and bumped into the small table beside the horsehair sofa. The lamp on top rocked. Ari hurried over to catch it before oil spilled over the floor.

"Are you all right?" she asked.

Josefina straightened and smoothed her hair with a hand that shook. The shaking might have been from the small fright, but that sick feeling in Ari's stomach grew worse.

"Antonio did exist, didn't he?"

Josefina made the sign of the cross. "How dare you ask me such a thing? My son was very much a man."

Ari immediately felt guilty. "I'm sorry. I didn't mean to upset you. I keep trying to explain that he's just not real to me. I need him to be real. I need to go home to touch that part of me that I lost."

Josefina was shaking her head before Ari even finished. "No. It is not wise."

"I wasn't asking permission."

For the first time in the eleven months since Ari had been here, Josefina looked angry. "You are ungrateful."

"I just need to know."

The older woman slashed the air with her hand. "You would open old wounds for everyone. Bring back the grief that we have just buried. For nothing." She slashed the air again. "And your memory will not come back."

"You don't know that."

"I know the Lord shields you from what you cannot bear. My son is dead. Your life with him, it is also gone as if it never existed, but you have a future here. We are your family now. Vincente and I will share memories of Antonio with you. You will share them with Miguel. It is enough."

"No, it's not." Ari had never been more sure of anything in her life. She picked Miguel up off the floor and turned on her heel and headed for the door. "I need my life back."

"You do not know what you do," Josefina called.

She stopped at the door and looked back. The woman was

completely distraught and there was a wildness in her eyes. "No, I don't. That's the problem, and if you won't tell me, then I'll have to go find the answers for myself."

Josefina's small brown eyes narrowed. "I won't allow it."

For the first time since Ari had woken up in the back of the wagon to see Vincente and Josefina's faces looking down at her, a sense of determination dominated.

"You're not going to have a say."

Being outside in the sunshine didn't help chase the blackness from Ari's spirit. The sun on her skin was just one more aggravation. She was angry. She was resentful. She was frustrated. Why couldn't Josefina understand how badly she needed to know what had happened?

She walked around like a cripple because nothing made sense. Getting vague answers had been all right at first, but as her body healed, so did her mind. She couldn't go on being a mother with only eleven months of life experience. Josefina should be able to understand that. Yes, Ari had lost her husband, but she was still living. She just wasn't alive.

Are you sure you're getting the right answers?

Damn Tracker and his insinuations. This was all his fault. He had to go and voice her own recent doubts, giving them weight. What if there was more going on than Vincente was telling her? What if they were important things she needed to know for her son?

"We have to know, baby." She kissed Miguel's soft black hair as she walked down the road. "We have to know."

Miguel grabbed a handful of her blouse and dragged his mouth to it. He was such a happy child, rarely fussing. She was lucky to have him. She freed her blouse and gave him her finger instead, closing her eyes for a heartbeat to let the tension go. She needed to relax. Tension always brought on the flashing lights behind her eyes that were the first sign of a pending episode.

The sun was bright against her eyelids and warm on her skin, reminding her that it was a beautiful day. This was the prettiest part of summer, before drought turned the grass brown. Everywhere she turned there was blue sky, green grass and colorful flowers. Everywhere except around the Morales ranch. That was dry and dusty, the vegetation eaten by the cow and trampled under her feet.

There was no sign of Vincente, so no opportunity to ask him if he would take her to her old home. Wherever that was.

Supposedly, the home she had shared with Antonio was fifty miles to the east. She'd never gotten an answer from the Moraleses as to why she and Antonio had lived so far away from his parents. It certainly wouldn't have been Josefina's preference. There were lots of opportunities around Esperanza, but maybe Josefina had been too much in her and Antonio's life? Maybe Ari had needed distance between them. New wives rarely got along with their mothers-in-law. The fact that theirs was a mixed marriage could have added to the tension. Maybe Josefina hadn't been too happy to have Ari in the family.

Ari sighed. She didn't know. No one would give her answers. Vincente would just tell her to count her blessings and to be grateful. She was tired of being grateful.

The sound of a gunshot carried in the afternoon breeze. It came from the direction of town. Her heart skipped a beat.

I'm going to get a drink.

Tracker was in town. He wouldn't be so foolish as to announce that he was a Texas Ranger, of that she was sure. But his looks were Indian enough that someone might easily pick a fight. Sober, he'd be a match for anyone, she didn't doubt. The man wore his experience like a cloak of honor. But drunk he would be fair game for any troublemaker.

She bit her lip. She couldn't afford to lose him now. He was their only hope, and he really couldn't know how bad town had gotten lately. Vincente was always telling how the gringos delighted in flexing their power in senseless violence.

Keep him safe, Lord. I need him.

For more than just her son's protection. Something deep within her recognized Tracker.

Ari checked the watch pinned to her blouse. A gift from her husband, Vincente said. It was a plain watch with no engraving. A simple gift. It could have belonged to anybody. Her husband must not have been a very romantic man. She wondered if she'd been happy with him. Was that what her memory was hiding? she wondered. An unhappy marriage? Did they worry that she'd remember interference on their part, and take her son away from them? She would never do that. Family was everything, but so was the memory of that family.

She couldn't take this anymore. She couldn't just sit around watching the days bleed, one after the other, into a senseless future because she had no past.

Ari hitched Miguel up on her hip. If she wanted to change what had always been, she needed someone strong enough to take her where she needed to go. That would be Tracker. The man she hoped would be her hero. The man getting drunk right now.

She sighed. There was nothing she could do about his drinking. Town was dangerous.

She'd just turned to go home when another gunshot

sounded, followed by three more. Her heart skipped a beat. Shielding her eyes from the sun, she saw something even more terrifying: a rider was between her and the house.

She stopped dead. So did the rider. Backlit by the sun as he was, she could only make out his silhouette. There was nothing soothing about it. The rifle braced on his thigh, his long hair blowing about his face... Lights flashed behind her eyes. She pulled Miguel tight to her chest, holding his face to her in case he screamed. Any sound would be dangerous. They were like wolves in their ability to find her when she ran. Any sound was betrayal. She kissed Miguel's head. She had to keep him safe. She couldn't let them get her son. Had the rider seen her? *Please don't let him have seen see me.*

There was no safe place to hide here. No one to help her. But Tracker was in town...

The rider turned, facing her. Oh, my God, she had to run! A scream welled, but she smothered it. She couldn't fall apart. Couldn't let him get her. She had to protect Miguel. She had to escape.

Spinning on her heel, she ran, her heart thundering in her ears. Or was it the sound of his horse? Was he going to run her down? She ran faster, her skirts tangling around her legs, slowing her.

Please God, don't let him catch me. Not this time. Not this time.

She ran until she couldn't run anymore, chanting Tracker's name like a talisman with every step, pushing herself when her body demanded she quit, not stopping until a hand on her arm spun her around.

"*Que pasa, hija?*"

The lights stopped flashing. Ari blinked and looked around at the collection of buildings and people. She'd run all the way to town. A middle-aged woman stood beside her, holding her elbow. She had kind eyes. Ari had been tricked by kind eyes before.

She shook her head. "Nothing."

The woman clucked her tongue and told her in Spanish to go home. That it wasn't safe for her to be here in town. One glance around confirmed it. Even as she assessed her position, men lounging about buildings straightened and took notice. Their gazes crawled over her skin, lingered in her hair, dismissed the baby in her arms.

Fear shivered down her spine. A man with a dirty sombrero pushed back from his face stepped off the wooden walk. Another followed suit.

"Tracker." She had to find Tracker.

I'm going to get a drink.

Lifting her chin, filling every step with a confidence she didn't feel, Ari locked her gaze on the cantina, pretending she didn't see the men along the way who fell into step beside her. Licking her lips, she hugged Miguel closer. Josefina was right. She didn't know what she was doing, and now she'd endangered her baby.

"Venga aquí, muchacha," a man on the left called. Another picked up the call, while a third added encouragement. She wasn't going anywhere near him. She wasn't going near any of them. Miguel fussed. She kissed his head and kept walking, whispering Tracker's name like a prayer.

She took the steps to the cantina in a near run, her heels making staccato taps on the wood. No one stopped her from going in. No one stopped her once she was inside. The minute it took for her eyes to adjust to the dim light was the longest in her life. The stench of stale sweat, whiskey and tobacco burned her nose and lungs. She coughed. Miguel fussed again. Wooden chairs creaked as men turned to stare at her.

In almost a panic, she searched for Tracker. He was in the back right corner, a bottle of whiskey set in front of him on a rickety-looking table. In his hand, he held a full glass. His hat was pulled down over his eyes. Not by a twitch of muscle did he indicate he saw her. She needed him to see her.

Hurrying across the floor, doing her best to steer clear of everyone as she maneuvered between the tables, she was vividly conscious of how loud her heels sounded against the plank floor. Her heart pounded in her ears and her breath caught in her lungs.

Please don't let him be drunk.

If Tracker was drunk it was going to be very, very bad for her. She looked over her shoulder at the line of men forming a wall between her and the door. If he wasn't drunk it was going to be very bad for both of them. She reached his table. He didn't move.

"Tracker?"

Was it her imagination or did he draw a deep breath? He raised his head, and through the shadows cast by the oil lamps on the wall she could see his eyes. There was no comfort there. His gaze flicked left and then right, calmly taking in, in a split second, everything that terrified her.

"Yeah?"

She had to suck in two more breaths before she found her voice.

"I thought about it, and I've decided what matters."

"So?"

Betting everything on a hunch, she leaned over and slid the shot glass out of his reach. Drawing one more breath, she met his gaze and held out her hand. A plea. An invitation. "I've come to take you home."

5

To Ari's surprise, Tracker's fingers closed around hers, then threaded between them until they were palm to palm. He got to his feet with that easy grace that was so much a part of him, and brought her hand to his mouth. His lips were warm and firm, but she didn't have time to appreciate the sensation before he tugged her behind him. A glance around revealed why. The men who'd been following her through town were now lined up in the center of the cantina, watching them.

"I'm sorry." It seemed she was always saying that to him. She hugged Miguel.

"Don't worry about it, sweets." His smile wasn't much comfort. It merely added to the overall sense of danger.

A trio broke away from the pack. Tracker turned and his quiet "Stay back," blended seamlessly with the tension filling the room. Ari looked around for a weapon.

"I don't have any quarrel with you, Indian. We just want the woman."

Ari grabbed the whiskey bottle off the table.

"I'm not particularly interested in what you want," Tracker drawled.

"She's not worth dying for."

"She's mine, and what's mine stays mine."

"And who are you?"

"Tracker Ochoa."

A ripple of unease went through the crowd. A few of the men shook their heads and stepped back. Even here at the edge of Mexico, Tracker's reputation carried weight. But along with the fear, Ari could see excitement on the faces of others. Again the force of a reputation, but this time it was working against them. She held little Miguel close and kissed the top of his head. What had she done?

"Tracker?"

"Nothing to be worried about, sweets. The boys and I are just going to have a chat."

Chat? It was going to be a massacre.

"I'm sorry."

Tracker palmed his pistol but didn't draw it. Ari wanted to scream at him to pull it from the holster. She tightened her grip on the bottle. "Nothing sorry about a woman coming to get her man, is there, boys?" Tracker was saying.

The "boys" gave her looks that varied between resentment and lust.

"She your woman, *señor?*"

There was the barest of hesitations before Tracker nodded. "And the baby's my son."

"The Moraleses claimed him as their grandson."

"They were doing me a favor." He cocked the hammer back. "You all understand how some men might be tempted by my absence."

"*Sí.* She's a very pretty *puta.*"

In a blink, Tracker's pistol was in his hand. A shot rang out. The speaker grabbed his ear and yelped.

Tracker smiled that scary smile. "The next one to speak disrespectfully about my wife will be eating a bullet."

The man's friends grabbed his arms and pulled him aside. Ari counted. There were seven enemies still standing. She had one bottle. How many bullets were in Tracker's gun? With the muzzle of his pistol, Tracker pushed his hat back. "Anyone else want to keep me from my lunch?"

The crowd parted, leaving a clear path to the door.

"Sweets?"

"Yes?" Ari took a step forward, placing her hand in the middle of Tracker's back, concentrating on the feel of hard muscles beneath her fingertips. She'd never been so scared.

"We're leaving. Is Miguel ready?"

He was in her arms. How much readier could he be? "Yes."

"Let's go then."

Going meant entering that crowd. Giving the men an opportunity to swarm them. Before Tracker took his first step, she leaned her forehead against his back. She probably wasn't supposed to show weakness, but she was terrified, and she needed that momentary contact for strength.

"While you're back there, sweets, do me a favor."

"What?"

"Take that pistol out of my waistband and carry it for me, would you? I'm a bit tired."

"My hands are full."

He turned, saw the bottle and smiled. "We won't need the whiskey."

Because she would have the gun. With a shaking hand, she set the bottle on the table.

Hostility filled the expression of every man that remained. They wouldn't hesitate to kill Tracker, her baby and eventually her. Ari didn't have to remember her past to know that. The future was in every hard, greedy gaze that fastened on their corner of the room.

She slipped her hand between Tracker's back and the warm metal of the gun and pulled the weapon free. "No. We don't."

She expected a cutting remark. She didn't expect the approval in Tracker's voice as he said, "You just take care of that gun for me, and it'll all be fine."

She didn't see how anything could be fine, even if they survived this. She was always doing something crazy, because it drove her crazy that she couldn't remember anything before eleven months ago, and her mind was always in such turmoil. She didn't bother trying to explain all that to Tracker. All she said was, "Good."

They started moving forward, one step at a time into that lecherous, hostile crowd. As they came abreast of the men, she forgot to breathe, expecting all of them to reach out and grab her. Her hand tightened on the pistol and she pointed it at the one staring at her the hardest. He had close-set eyes. She didn't trust men with close-set eyes. He threw his hands up and backed off. It wasn't enough.

"You have a filthy mouth." She lowered the gun and pointed at his groin.

He backed up farther. "I meant no offense."

"I was offended."

"Keep up, sweets," Tracker calmly interjected.

She couldn't make her feet move. She was stuck in the moment of power. A hand on her arm dragged her forward. "You want them dead?"

Yes. Images of men—dark-skinned, light-skinned—flashed behind her eyes. All of them with the same lust-filled expression on their faces. All of them waiting to hurt her. She stumbled against Tracker's side. Yes, she wanted them dead. All of them. Every leering one.

"Yes."

Without missing a beat, Tracker took aim. Men dived aside, reached for their guns. Dear heavens. He was serious.

"No!"

"Make up your mind. My supper's getting cold."

It was up to her. It would be so easy to say "dead." Faces flashed in front of her mind, laughing, sneering, all male, all dark, all of them familiar, yet she didn't know a one. As each face flashed in front of her mind's eye, panic rose. And the flickering lights began. She quickly shut the door on the memory, but the panic lingered. As if he could read everything that happened behind that door, Tracker cocked an eyebrow at her. If not for the scar on his face, he would've been a very handsome man.

"Home?"

She nodded. "Yes, I came to take you home."

No, that wasn't what he'd asked her. It didn't seem to matter. His hand squeezed her arm and tugged.

"Let's go then."

No one said a word as they walked through the cantina. She had no doubt, if it were any other man leading her out of there, that bunch would have fallen on them like a pack of ravening wolves, not being satisfied until they'd torn them apart and there was nothing left. But Tracker walked through the crowd of men as if he was looking forward to have one step in his path and challenge him. Since cowering wasn't going to get her anywhere, Ari borrowed a bit of Tracker's bravado, squared her shoulders and lifted her chin, keeping the gun up, despite the ache in her wrist. It was surprisingly heavy.

As if sensing the seriousness of the moment, Miguel grabbed her blouse and buried his face in her throat. As soon as they were on the street she released her breath.

"A little too soon to be breathing a sigh of relief," Tracker said, taking the pistol from her hand and putting it back in his belt. Grabbing her arm, he hustled her over to where the horse stood patiently waiting. "Tighten your grip on that baby," he said as he lifted her. She grabbed the back of the saddle with her free hand.

Without further ado, he stepped backward into a stirrup and swung his leg over the horse, turning his body. The saddle dipped with his weight, and Ari dipped right along with it. His left arm swept back and pushed her upright as he settled into the saddle. If he hadn't left it there she would've tumbled right off when the horse spun.

Miguel laughed. Ari cried out. Tracker swore. Switching her grip to his waist, she pressed her face into his back, relishing the feel of muscle beneath his skin. She held her son tightly between them.

Tracker didn't slow the horse until they got back to the ranch. He was strong. So strong. And he made her feel so safe. For the first time in eleven months, she felt she could breathe.

The horse stopped in front the barn. Tracker grabbed her arm, offering support. "Slide down."

It was awkward, holding Miguel. Tracker swung her out a little. She squealed. Miguel giggled. Tracker swore. It was getting to be a pattern.

Vincente came hurrying up. Tracker waved him away. "Go back to the house. Make sure that gun of yours is loaded."

When Ari turned to go with Vincente, Tracker grabbed her arm. "We need to talk."

More ominous words had never been spoken. "About what?"

"About why I'm about to paddle your ass." He hauled her through the barn door.

"Your horse?"

"Deserves better than he's getting, but he'll wait."

The growl in Tracker's voice sent a shiver down her spine. It should've been one of terror, but it wasn't. That odd sense of being alive tingled through her, spreading until her fingers curved with the need to touch him.

Inside the barn door she stopped, blinking. He kept going, taking her with him. She stumbled. Miguel giggled again. Tracker gave them both a dirty look. His hair swung out and fell over her shoulder as he spun back around. Miguel grabbed a handful, his eyes widening at the novelty.

"Hell, now. You don't want to be chewing on that."

Oblivious to Tracker's frustration, Miguel dragged his new treasure to his mouth.

Tracker stared as if he'd never seen the like. "That's disgusting."

Whatever Miguel touched went into his mouth. "You haven't been around too many babies, have you?" Ari asked.

"No." He motioned with his free hand to Miguel. "Any chance he'll let go soon?"

It might've been her imagination, but there wasn't as much anger in Tracker's voice now. There was still that growl, though. Another tingle started where he gripped her arm, spread over her shoulder, moved down to her breasts. Her breath caught. Her "no" was a little hoarse.

"Figures." Not even bothering to fight Miguel's claim to his hair, Tracker pulled her into the bedroom and stopped dead. He stood there holding her arm, Miguel holding his hair, and Ari realized he didn't know what to do. The last of her fear flitted away. Whatever the Ranger's past, whatever horrible things he might have done in the course of his job, he wasn't a danger to her. But he was a temptation. Strong and handsome, he would be a temptation to any woman. Another thrill went through her.

"Make him let go," he grunted.

Excitement, she realized. Those thrills were excitement. Tracker Ochoa excited her. It was shocking. It was…nice. She tossed her hair back off her face. Her neat bun was a thing of the past. "You make him."

"Do you think I won't?"

She was pretty sure he wouldn't. Tracker didn't have the look of a man comfortable around children.

"No."

A flutter of sensation went through her, followed very quickly by a surge of heat as the side of Tracker's pinkie touched her breast. It wasn't fear. It wasn't frustration. It wasn't depression. It was excitement. And she was feeling it, when she'd given up on feeling anything good ever again.

His expression a mix of determination and hesitation, Tracker reached out with his free hand. Miguel let go of his hair, grabbed his finger and held on. Tracker blinked. Content with his prize, Miguel laid his head against Ari's shoulder. He sighed that little sigh that told her he was going to sleep shortly. Her heart stirred when Tracker didn't tug his hand free. He was a good man. She glanced at his expression and hid a smile. Albeit a frustrated one.

"In about two minutes he'll be asleep, and you can tear into me then," she told him. It was comfortable in this moment with him. The world was so far away. Her life so far away. As far away as her memories. There was just now. It was funny, when one had no past, how comfortable one could get with the present moment. And right now, she was with Tracker. A man who'd offered her understanding. A man who'd saved her life. A man who made her feel alive. Excited her. She licked her lips.

Tracker's gaze flicked to hers before dropping to her mouth. His own mouth lost its hard edge. Her breathing quickened.

"What makes you think I want to tear into you?"

The fullness of his lips. The tension in his muscles. The desire in his eyes. The increased pressure of his hand.

She tilted her head, glancing at him sideways, not quite so brazen that she could look him directly in the eye as a delicious hunger built inside. Hunger for him. For his touch. For the sheer joy in living that she felt in his presence. He made the nothingness of today feel like the possibility of tomorrow. "Just a hunch."

Little flickers of lightning sparked out from where the side of his hand rested on her collarbone. It wasn't her imagination that his touch grew heavier. It wasn't her imagination that his fingers spread down, caressing the soft upper curve of her breast. She should stop him. She told herself she would as soon as it stopped feeling good. He made her feel so good, so alive.

"You're playing with fire."

"I know." But at least she was playing.

"You don't want this." His hand slipped lower.

Didn't she? "You seem awfully sure of what I want and what I don't want."

"I have more experience than you."

"But not in what I want."

His eyes narrowed and his pinkie slipped down to graze the tip of her breast, which grew hard and tingled with sensation. It felt so right.

"I'm a widow, Mr. Ochoa, not a virgin you have to worry about scaring."

"You have no idea what I worry about."

"It shouldn't be me."

His eyelids flickered. "You think you're woman enough to handle me, sweets?"

Was she? She didn't know. And neither did he. "Are you willing to let me try?"

"No."

He was lying. She knew he was lying. He wanted her. And she wanted him. Holding his gaze, she reached up and slid her hand across his cheek. She paused, dragging her fingertips downward. He didn't have much of a beard. She frowned at the vague sense that there should be a beard. She waited for a memory, an emotion to follow the fragment of a realization. There was nothing except the vague acknowledgment of there once being a beard. Opening her hand, she slid it farther up his face. The edges of the scar abraded her palm.

He didn't look away. His eyes studied hers. Again she had that sense that he saw more than she remembered, held answers she needed. "What are you doing, Ari?" he asked at last.

"I'm not sure." She frowned, concentrating on the feelings. "I think I'm experimenting."

"With what?"

"How it feels to be alive."

"Sweets, what you're doing is more like asking to know what it would be like to die."

"Not for me." She already knew how to die. It was living

she struggled with. A fight she might have lost if not for Miguel. And now this man…. She threaded her fingers through Tracker's hair. It was softer to the touch than she expected. Like heavy dark silk. "To me, you feel like life."

"Because I make you remember?"

She shook her head. "I don't remember anything, but with you, I don't care." She touched her thumb to his lips the way he had to hers. How could she begin to explain to him the freedom that came from feeling part of the world? The joy of feeling pleasure? The sense of coming home? "You just feel… right."

His eyes narrowed and his mouth tilted up in a sensual quirk. He had beautiful eyes. A rich brown so deep, like fine chocolate. And his mouth. Such a beautiful mouth.

"Right?"

She pressed her thumb against his lips again. "Don't laugh, but I think I've been waiting for you, Tracker Ochoa."

This close, she couldn't miss his start. "Hell."

"Does that mean you still want to paddle my butt?"

That small smile grew. "Yeah, but not for the same reason."

She blinked. He wanted to spank her for pleasure? "Why don't you just start with kissing me?"

The shake of his head sent his hair spilling onto her breast. Another connection.

"You don't know what you're asking."

"I know kissing sounds better than spanking."

His lips quirked at the corner. "Sweets, you'd be safer taking the spanking."

She shrugged, not looking away. "Maybe I'm tired of being safe."

There was possession in the cupping of his hand around

hers, hunger in the press, acceptance in the withdrawal. "I like you being safe."

Nothing was colder than the moment when he took his hand away. Nothing more annoying than yet another person telling her what she felt, what she wanted. "You don't know me."

He took a step back. "But I've known a lot of women like you. Women who want excitement for the moment. Only problem with the plan is I'm not your toy. Bad enough that claiming you in town is likely to get me killed."

She took a step forward. Then a bigger one, so that her skirt wrapped around his legs. He made her feel so brazen. So sexy. "Since when are you afraid of being killed?"

Ari had a point, Tracker realized. Since when was he afraid to take what life offered? Since when did he worry about the future? Hell, since when did he think he'd have a future?

"I'm not." He motioned to Miguel, who'd fallen asleep. "Put him down."

Ari hesitated, her hand stroking the baby's head. Her tongue flicked over her lips, a pink dart of temptation. Tracker wanted that tongue in his mouth, on his skin. His cock flexed in protest when she bit her lip. Damn it, he wanted that kiss.

She squared her shoulders. It was a different woman who held his gaze, confident, passionate. It had to be an illusion. Tracker stepped back, making room for Ari's escape. She gave him a look that was completely unreadable, turned in the opposite direction than he expected and placed Miguel carefully on the bed. The boy didn't wake as Ari took the pillow and pulled it down, bracketing her son between it and the wall. When she turned back to Tracker, her chin came up.

"Prove it."

"Daring me?" he asked, not sure which answer he desired.

A "no" that would put an end to this, or a "yes" that would draw him in.

She smiled a siren's smile. One that no man could resist. "Throwing myself at you didn't work."

The hell it hadn't. "You want the kiss that badly?"

She nodded and took a step forward. "Oh, yes."

He took a step of his own, his gaze drawn to the press of her nipples against the cotton of her blouse. She wasn't faking it. She wanted him. "Why?"

"I already told you." Her next step brought her within reach.

He caught the curl that tumbled from her bun. It wound around his finger. "Because you want to feel alive?"

Her fingers curled around his wrist as if she was afraid he'd bolt. She didn't have to worry. He wasn't going anywhere. "With you."

She reiterated that, as if it was important. And maybe it was to her. No woman liked to feel she had needs just any man could fulfill.

Tracker nodded, stretching out that curl, letting it go, watching it bounce back, as if the trauma had never happened. Was that what she was doing? Bouncing back from the trauma of her past? "Because you think I'm different."

"I know you're different."

"You don't remember anything that happened before you arrived here."

If she did, she wouldn't be within a hundred yards of him.

She took the last step, sliding her hands up over his shoulders. Hot little hands that sent shivers of pure sensation down his spine. "Are you always this argumentative?"

"Probably."

Her nails pressed into the back of his neck. "Just my luck."

Or his. He brushed his fingers over her cheek, snagging the remnants of the bun at the nape of her neck. Two tugs and the braid came free, unfurling down her back. He followed the trail with his fingers, tracing the subtle indentations of her spine to the hollow of her back before retracing the path and drawing her gently forward. Giving her time to reconsider.

Damn it all to hell, the one thing she had to be sure about was kissing him. There was only so much honor a man had when faced with such temptation.

"Don't you want to kiss me, Tracker?" she asked. As if there was any doubt...

"I want to do a hell of a lot more than that." His cock was rock hard, ready to go off like a green boy. And all he'd done was run his fingers up her spine.

A shadow flitted through the clear blue of her eyes, gone in a heartbeat. He was making her nervous.

"Could we just try a kiss?" she murmured.

"We can do whatever the hell you want."

Shit, now he was swearing. A touch of his thumb to her cheek tilted her face to the side. He lowered his head, watching and waiting for that moment when her past came rushing forward, waiting for the protest that would save them both. It didn't happen. There was just the flash fire build of anticipation searing through him, stopping his breath in his lungs, his heart in his chest the split second before his mouth touched hers, and then there was no going back. No going anywhere but into the fire that threatened to burn him from the inside out.

Her mouth was sweet, soft and compliant beneath his. She kissed like a virgin with no idea what to do.

He pulled back. Her eyelids lifted slowly. The softest of smiles touched her lips. Hell, she didn't have a clue.

"I like that."

So did he. He liked being the one to teach her about pleasure.

"Good." He smoothed his thumb over her lips, pulling the lower one down until her mouth parted, moist and ready for his attentions. "Now, this time let's try it with your mouth open."

She blinked and caught her breath in shock, or anticipation. He couldn't tell, and truth be told, didn't want to know. Shock would mean he had to pull away, and he needed to know how she tasted. Needed it with everything in him. And if it was anticipation? Hell, if he began to believe she was anticipating that kiss, he'd lose control.

Replacing his thumb with his mouth, he fitted his lips to hers. Perfect. A perfect fit. In a haze of rising desire, he stroked his tongue over the plump flesh, giving her time to pull back. She had to pull back. For both their sakes.

She came forward, arching her body into his, giving the soft, whimpered gasp of pleasure he craved, dreaded, relished. She wasn't herself, wasn't for him. He clung to the knowledge, battling for sanity as her hips pressed to his, rubbing when he expected her to pull away, giving when he expected her to flee.

"Tracker." She breathed his name into his mouth like an answered prayer.

He caught her hips in his hands, stilling their restless movement. "Don't."

"Oh, yes." Her eyes opened as he ended the kiss. Try as he might, he couldn't find a lick of fear in their depths. Only an abundance of anticipation. "I knew it would be this good with you."

So had he. Son of a bitch, so had he.

"You're going to regret this." Later, when her memories returned, she was going to hate him.

Her leg slid up his. Her foot hooked behind his knee, trapping them together. "No, I won't."

He didn't argue. He was done arguing. Done fighting her, himself. He gathered her skirts in his hand as he kissed his way down her neck. She liked that, moaning and shivering every time he kissed the soft white flesh. His own memories flashed through his mind. His father's anger, his mother's face rigid in death. His first love, his first heartbreak, his first understanding of what it meant to be Indian in a white world. His first whore, his second, third. Faces blended together in a mass of indifference he'd tried to maintain.

"Oh my God, Tracker."

An indifference that was nowhere around with Ari.

"Yes, Tracker."

He lifted her up, kissing her breasts through her shirt. She moaned his name again, her thighs naturally parting. He wouldn't allow her to be indifferent with him.

A world of hurt was coming his way when this was over, but for now there was lightning-hot pleasure, breathless joy and the delusion that he mattered. To her.

Her hands tugged at his hair. "Kiss me again."

"Ah, hell." He needed his ass kicked. His mouth slammed down on hers as he pushed her up against the wall and stepped between her thighs.

"Yes." The jubilant sigh of satisfaction fanned his desire into a flickering flame. The woman kissed like hell on fire, innocence and passion riding instinct in a potent combination that shredded his control and left him on the verge of coming.

"Sweets." His cock found its home between her thighs. "We have to stop."

"No."

Her hips pulsed in counterpoint to his thrust, sliding her pussy along his cock, gasping every time the thick head caught on her clit. Son of a bitch, even the layers of clothing between them couldn't hide the heat of her desire. She wanted him, and if he unbuttoned his pants and opened the slit in her drawers, he could be inside her.

Tracker dropped his forehead to Ari's as he unbuttoned his pants. He wouldn't take her, but he needed a taste. Just a taste of that sweet heat.

"You don't want this with me," he moaned, anger and frustrated desire hoarsening his voice to a growl.

But he wanted it with her. He wanted his cock deep in her pussy. He wanted to fuck her hard and deep until the impossible happened. Until she was his.

Ari shook her head, a denial of his words or her need? He didn't care. He worked his cock free. It surged against her, falling naturally into the niche between her thighs, leaving just a thin layer of linen between him and that hot pussy. His hips surged forward, pressing the fat head into the pad of her pussy. Even through the material she was soft and giving. Eager. It would take so little to give them what they both wanted.

He looked down. He couldn't see anything but the press of her nipples against her blouse, and her skirt bunched between them. Damn, he wanted to see what he could only imagine. The swollen folds, wet with her desire, open and hungry for his mouth, his cock. He pressed against her once, twice, the urge to thrust riding him hard.

Her answer was a moan and a tightening of her legs around him. "Don't stop."

He kissed her hard and fast, allowing himself just that much of a taste. His cock throbbed and burned as he pushed against her. "We have to."

"No. I want you." Her eyes opened. Her legs spread wider. "I want you."

He snarled with the impossibility of it, the perfection of it, bending his knees to get a better angle. He moaned as his cock slipped between the folds of delicate material, finding flesh even more delicate, sliding through the proof of her desire into the well of her vagina, notching there. She held his cock in a kiss of heat for an endless moment.

"It means nothing more than this," he growled, keeping from tearing into her through sheer force of will. He'd been searching for her for so long, and now she was here, offering him everything when he could have nothing.

"Yes." She struggled against him, rocking her hips and trying to coax him deeper. "Just this."

"There can be nothing more than this."

Her head fell back against the wall, exposing the creamy line of her throat. A pulse of his hips emphasized his point. Her pussy parted, the supple muscles working over the head of his cock in inviting flexes as they struggled to accept him. The flesh of her throat was sweet and salty against his lips. He strung hard, biting kisses down her skin, nipping at the juncture of her shoulder and neck, lingering when she moaned and tilted her head, giving him better access.

"Take me."

He thrust deep, and she took him fully. "Yes. Oh yes!"

Pulling back, he thrust again and again. Her pussy accepted more and more until she held him balls deep, her strong muscles rippling along his cock, inviting more. Close. They were so close. His cock flexed. His balls tingled in prerelease. It was so good.

The barn door creaked. Familiar footsteps scuffed across the hay-strewn floor. In the periphery of his mind, Tracker knew he had only seconds to let Ari go if he wanted to preserve her reputation. His feet wouldn't obey his order. He was so close. She was so close. "Vincente's com—"

Ari didn't let him finish. With surprising strength, she held him to her, grinding down on his cock. His snarl blended with her moan of pleasure. He couldn't wrench away, couldn't face Vincente, couldn't save her reputation. Couldn't stop the orgasm from taking over as her pussy spasmed on his cock and she cried out. Son of a bitch. Tracker pressed a kiss to her lips. She was perfect. She was his.

A pistol cocked. He couldn't summon the strength to reach for his knife. If Vincente pulled the trigger, it was no more than he deserved.

"This is how you treat my hospitality?"

Ari jumped, and Tracker's cock flexed within her at the inadvertent caress. He drew her face against his chest, giving her a place to hide as he slowly separated their bodies.

With a wave of the gun, the old man indicated the door.

"Take your son and go to the house, Ari."

Ari's "no" seared Tracker's heart.

He smoothed his hand down her cheek. "Go. I'll settle this."

She grabbed her son and fled.

When the barn door closed behind her, Vincente said, "You will marry her."

Shit. "She deserves better."

The old man didn't budge, just kept that rifle trained on Tracker's gut. "Maybe, but you are her choice."

Son of a bitch. Tracker stared at the gun, stared at the resolution in Vincente's eyes, remembered the hot clasp of Ari's pussy.

He hadn't planned on this.

6

The night was peaceful. The small pond a mile east of the Morales ranch was bathed in the faint light of a half-moon. Branches swayed in the soft breeze, their reflections dancing across the glassy surface of the water in a rhythmic ballet. Somewhere in the stillness of the night, Shadow waited.

Tracker struck a sulfur on his boot and lit a smoke. It'd been a hell of a week, in which one puzzle had been solved and another developed. The solution to the first puzzle was good. Ari was found. The second was not so good. Vincente was insisting he marry her. Josefina was against it. For seven days he'd suffered burned meals and angry looks. Where Ari stood was a question mark. As soon as he'd protested the notion, she'd fallen back into politeness, as if it were a shield against rejection.

She believed herself to have been married to a Mexican. She had a child who looked more Mexican than white. To her, there was no reason for the flatness of his refusal. She didn't know the truth and he couldn't give it. A white wife for a man like him would be more trouble than she was worth in most cases, but when that woman was Ari? *Shit*. He flicked the smoke into the water. That would be a dream come true. And Vincente had known it and announced the bans despite Tracker's protests.

"You never did have any respect for a good smoke."

"Hello, Shadow."

Buster tossed his head and whickered a greeting of his own.

His brother stepped away from the tree he'd been leaning against and crossed to his side. "Took you long enough to figure out I was here."

Tracker shrugged. "Guess that means I'm buying next time we get to town."

They'd been playing this more sophisticated form of hide-and-seek since they were kids.

Shadow motioned for his fixings. Tracker handed them over. "Consider my forgiving the debt a wedding present."

"You heard?"

"Not much else anybody's talking about around here. There's all kinds of stories about how it happened, but somehow Ari Morales landed as a groom the great Tracker Ochoa."

Landed? That was an interesting way to put it. "I've been waiting for the lynch mob."

Shadow smiled. "This would be a good spot for hanging. Not many trees around these parts big enough to hang a man your size, but that one over there could probably do it."

Tracker's gaze followed Shadow's pointing finger to the tall oak. *Yeah. It probably would.* "Thanks for the sympathy."

Shadow sprinkled tobacco on the paper. "I wasn't aware you were looking for any."

Tracker wished he hadn't been so quick to toss away his

smoke. He had nothing to do with his hands. "I'm going to be the number one attraction for a shotgun wedding."

Shadow rolled the smoke, ran his tongue along the edge of the paper and twisted the ends. He put the cigarette into his mouth. "To a woman you've been half in love with ever since Desi told you about her. There have been worse reasons to marry."

"Shit."

Shadow struck a match. Light danced over his face as he applied it to the tip of the cigarette. "You denying it?"

Hell yes. There was no future for him with the woman. "Go home, Shadow."

His brother shook out the match and smiled. "When you do."

"I told you I had a bad feeling about this."

"All the more reason for me to stay."

One of the problems with having a twin brother was he often had some of your same qualities. Like stubbornness.

Tracker pushed his hat back. Frustration gnawed at his gut. "This isn't your destiny."

"It's always been you and me against everything. Might as well add destiny to the list."

"No."

The end of the smoke glowed red in the night. "Not your call."

"The hell it isn't. I don't want you here."

Shadow blew out a stream of smoke. It faded like Tracker's patience into the darkness. "And here I was counting on being your best man."

"Son of a bitch, you're a stubborn bastard."

He smiled. "I am, aren't I?"

"I wouldn't be bragging on it."

"Then I'll brag on my new sister-in-law instead. She's a looker."

Tracker snatched the smoke from Shadow's hand, took a deep drag. The smoke burned his throat and lungs. He inhaled deeper, burying beneath the discomfort the need to punch his brother for admiring Ari.

"She looks just like Desi."

"Yes, she does." But somehow a touch softer. A touch more delicate.

"Does she have her spirit?"

I've come to take you home.

Tracker nodded. "It's a bit buried, but it's there."

"Word is she's a widow."

"That's what they say."

"You believe it?"

He remembered the innocence of her kiss. A woman who had been loved would have held some instinctive memory of that, wouldn't she?

"I don't want to."

"You know she's not a virgin."

With me gone, there was just her, and there were eleven of them.

"I know." She'd known rape and betrayal. He couldn't fix that, but he could make new memories for her. He could show her tenderness.

Tracker flicked the cigarette into the water. It hit with a faint hiss. "Now might be a good time to get on that horse and ride."

"No."

"Something about this setup stinks."

"I noticed."

It was all too convenient. Vincente was just too accepting.

Josefina too possessive. Ari was too safe in a part of the country where she shouldn't be.

"What's the plan?" Shadow asked.

Tracker cocked an eyebrow at his brother. "What makes you think I have one?"

"The fact that you're sitting out here by yourself, tossing perfectly good smokes into the water. You only do that when you're planning."

Tracker grunted. "The wedding date has been set for next week."

"Any idea why the stall?"

"Nope."

"Wonder if it has anything to do with the group of *Comancheros* raiding a couple hundred miles northeast of here."

Shit. "How close are they likely to be to the route we'll go?"

"Too damn close."

They had limited options as to what route to take home. It was wide-open country between Eperanza and Hell's Eight, but there were only so many places with potable water, only so many places one could cross rivers, canyons. Whatever route they chose, it was going to be brutal. "With a baby along, we don't have any choice but to take the shortest one."

And the shortest route was likely what the *Comancheros* would be taking on their way back to Esperanza.

"Yeah, but I did discover a shortcut."

"Where?"

Shadow squatted and pulled his knife from his boot sheath. He sketched a rough map. "Here at Drunk Hole."

Drunk Hole was a major stop on the trip, being the only reliable source of water within thirty miles. He tapped the blade to the right. "This blind canyon here?"

"Yeah."

"It's not actually blind. We'll have to climb a bit, but there's a narrow pass near the top."

Tracker wasn't surprised Shadow had found an alternate route. His brother was fanatical about not being committed to anything, even the distance from point A to point B. Sometimes Tracker thought even his commitment to Hell's Eight chafed. "Can we make it with the baby?"

"It'll be rough." Shadow stabbed his blade into the ground. "Is Ari as game as Desi?"

He'd carry her the whole damn way if he had to. "She'll make it."

Shadow shook his head. "It's going to be a hell of a trip."

"She can't stay here."

"You sure?"

Tracker met Shadow's gaze dead on. "You hear anything in town about a band of gringos raising hell?"

"The only grumblings in town are about a certain Indian raising hell in the cantina."

Tracker couldn't find his smile. "Then I'm sure."

"Shit."

Tracker studied the map, ran timetables in his head. If the *Comancheros* were two hundred miles northeast, it would take them anywhere from five to seven days to get to Esperanza. Drunk Hole was three days out for both of them. The only way to get past the *Comancheros* with the baby and a woman was to get past Drunk Hole first. He touched the indentation left by the knife. "Can you get to Virgin's Crossing and back by tomorrow night?"

"Sure."

"They still have that telegraph line to San Antonio?"

"As long as no one's taken down the lines. You want me to send a telegram to Hells' Eight?"

"Yes."

"You know sending the telegram is going to alert everyone to where we are?"

He knew. "I don't see where I have any choice. It's going to be a race to get through Drunk Hole before the *Comancheros* get there. And even if we do get through, there's no guarantee they won't pick up our trail. And if Vincente got in contact with Ari's family, they could be waiting for us on the other side, anyway."

"Shit, they know she's been found?"

"Yes." Tracker still had a lot of unanswered questions, but of this he was sure. Things were not as they appeared where Ari and her "family" were concerned. And the men who hunted Ari would be desperate to keep her from getting to the Hell's Eight stronghold.

"Things just keep getting better and better."

"Told you to go."

Shadow chuckled. "Where would be the fun in that?"

It was their motto. Their thumb-their-noses-at-death, Ochoas-against-the-world battle cry. It didn't resonate as deeply tonight. The sense of destiny and doom increased.

Tracker forced a smile. "None at all."

"How are you going to get Ari to agree to leave here?"

"I'm not giving her a choice."

Shadow looked askance at him. "We're going to need her cooperation."

"We're not going to get it."

Shadow pushed himself to his feet. "There's no way in hell a kidnapping will work."

"We're going to have to make it work, because there's no

102

way in hell I'm telling a woman that I don't think she was ever married, that the people she loves like family are holding her for sale. That the rosy past that was created for her is all a myth. That in reality, her real-life family was killed. That she spent a year with *Comancheros* being raped and abused, enduring things that no woman should ever have to—"

Shadow cut him off. "Enough."

Yeah. It was enough.

Shadow bent, pulled his knife from the dirt and flipped it into the air once. Twice. "So, we're going to steal her?"

"Tomorrow night."

"Are you worried that kidnapping her is going to bring back memories?" Shadow flipped the knife a third time.

Hell yes, he worried about that. Tracker reached and caught the knife midflip. "I don't see that we have any option."

Shadow took the knife back. "She's going to hate you, brother."

"I know." He just hoped to hell he could keep her hating him long enough for them to get to Hell's Eight. Her memory would come back. It had to. But when it did, he wanted her safe and with her sister. It helped to have family around when your world fell apart. Desi would know how to help Ari. Desi knew about betrayal.

"There's a chance we're seeing demons where there are none," Shadow offered.

Tracker hadn't survived this long by ignoring his instincts, and his instincts were screaming. "That's not a chance I'm willing to take. Even if we leave tomorrow night and ride hard, chances of beating the *Comancheros* to Drunk Hole are slim to none."

"We've faced worse."

"Yes. But this time we can't afford to lose."

"Send the telegram."

Shadow slipped his knife into its boot sheath with a small snap. "Then we won't lose."

The ranch was quiet, the house dark. Ari's window was open to the warm night. They were going to have to have a talk about safety.

Easing up to the windowsill, Tracker paused. It was going to be too easy. He pressed his back against the wall and listened for any sound coming from her room. He heard nothing. Which meant nothing. Anyone could be in there. Anyone could be waiting. An owl hooted near the corner of the house—Shadow asking if the coast was clear. He didn't have time to waste on scouting. He palmed his knife. It felt cool in his hand, familiar.

The horses were ready and waiting. The cradleboard Tracker had fashioned to carry the baby was tied to Buster's saddle. What supplies he could find were packed. All he needed to do was grab Ari and Miguel and ride like hell. So why was he standing outside the window doing nothing?

He didn't like the answer when it came to him. He didn't hold any illusions that, when this was over, he was going to be the one Ari smiled on. But he was determined that she would be able to smile, period.

He slid his leg over the windowsill. The leather of his pants made a soft whisper of sound. Just inside the window he paused. It only took a second to assess the room. Ari lay on her side on the white sheets, the thick braid of her hair draped across the pillow behind her. Miguel slept beside her, pillows on either side of him keeping him put. Neither stirred as Tracker crossed the wood floor. He stopped beside the bed, making sure his faint shadow didn't fall over Ari. She looked so innocent, so untouched by life, it was hard to believe she'd survived what she had.

He picked up Miguel first. The boy was heavier than he looked and felt surprisingly sturdy. As Tracker tucked him against his chest, he didn't make a sound, just rolled his head onto Tracker's shoulder and, with total trust, went back to sleep. Tracker cupped his hand around the boy's head. His hair was straight and soft, sticking out in absurd tufts. There was nothing about the child to make him smile, but even now he felt the urge. A wave of protectiveness took Tracker by surprise. Someone so small, facing so much, would need guardians in his life. Strong men to guide him. It couldn't be him, but Hell's Eight would stand for the boy. Would keep him safe until he was old enough to claim his inheritance and extract vengeance on those who hunted his family.

A call came from the window. Shadow was waiting. Tracker passed Miguel to his brother. The baby went with only a slight whimper of protest. The plan was that Shadow would strap the boy into the cradleboard and have him ready to go by the time Tracker got Ari out to the horses. Tracker had a feeling that strapping a six-month-old infant into a cradleboard he wasn't used to being in was not going to be that simple. Still, he'd rather be doing that than this. He crossed back to the bed, tugging four strips of material out of his pocket. One he balled up in his left hand.

Leaning over the bed, he placed his hand on Ari's mouth. She came awake, her scream breaking against his palm. The memories weren't as buried as he'd hoped.

"Hush, it's just me."

Ari stopped clawing at his hand. Tracker took advantage of her confusion and slipped the gag into her mouth. When she grabbed at his hands, he slid the second strip across her mouth and rapidly tied it behind her head. She screamed behind the gag. The sound was muffled, but still audible. He glanced toward the door. Vincente and Josefina were older. Hopefully their hearing wasn't great.

"Be quiet."

She was anything but. Her foot caught him on the inside of the knee. He twisted to block the next kick. Her knee grazed his balls. The pain wasn't severe, but bad enough to convince him to stop playing around. He grabbed her shoulders and flipped her onto her stomach. The mattress dipped and the supporting ropes creaked as he straddled her hips, using his weight to keep her in place. She reached back, fingers curved like claws. She was a fighter. Not that it would do her any good. He caught her hand and pressed it into the small of her back. It didn't take any effort at all to snag her other wrist and repeat the process. Her screams were muffled by the pillow as he tied her wrists together. For all her spirit, she didn't have much muscle. The *Comancheros* would have had no trouble forcing her to their will. Sliding down her thighs, Tracker used his knees to keep her legs together. While she flopped about like a landed fish, he tied her ankles.

He turned her over. Her eyes screamed betrayal. He didn't flinch. "We've got to move and we've got to move now."

She shook her head, desperately trying to see where Miguel had been lying. Tracker cupped her head in his hands and turned her face to his. "He's already at the horses."

She shook her head again, struggling against the bonds, bucking on the bed. The ropes under the mattress creaked. The last thing he needed was Vincente in here. Tracker put his hand to her throat. "If you don't keep quiet I'll be forced to quiet you."

Angry, reckless, her eyes dared him to.

If she were a man, he'd simply knock her out. But she was a woman and he didn't hit women. She didn't need to know that, however. Sometimes perception was stronger than fact. "Do I make you?"

She slowly settled back against the mattress, but her muscles were tense. In a heartbeat she'd be fighting again.

"Do you want me to leave you behind?"

That got through. Her eyes narrowed with hate. He touched his fingers to her cheek.

"Hold on to that thought."

Leaving her on the bed, he went through drawers, grabbing a couple pairs of pantaloons, a dress and petticoats. He tossed them on the bed. A shawl hung on a nail by the door. Her shoes rested beneath. Sweeping them up, he brought them to the bed and dropped them on the pile. A pillowcase worked as a bag. He tossed it out the window before going back to the bed to pick up Ari.

He slid his hands under her body. She wouldn't meet his gaze. He could feel the moisture of her tears against his arm. He wanted to tell her he was sorry. He wanted to tell her the truth. He didn't. The truth would hurt too much.

The sound of a pistol cocking broke the silence.

Shit. Tracker released Ari and straightened. He slowly turned.

Vincente stood just inside the door, dressed in a nightshirt, a pistol pointed at Tracker's midsection.

"I have been waiting for you," the old man whispered.

Not the words you wanted to hear from a seventy-year-old with arthritic fingers currently crooked around the trigger of a gun pointed at your gut. "You have?"

"Sí."

At least the man was whispering and not shooting. "Mind if I ask what made you think I'd come calling tonight?"

"Lower your voice. We do not want to wake Josefina."

"You're the one with the gun."

"*Sí,* I am."

"So how did you know?"

"You are a man of habit. Always you put your saddle away at the end of the day. Today you left it at the ready. When men of habit break them, it is for a reason."

Tracker feigned nonchalance, feeling Ari's eyes on his back like twin daggers. "I could just be running from a shotgun wedding."

Vincente shook his head. "You came many miles to find Ari. You would not leave without her."

"You're right." He turned slowly back toward the bed. "That being the case, I'll just be going."

He made only a quarter turn before the old man hissed out, "Do not."

Shit again. "Make up your mind, Vincente. Time's wasting."

"Not so much time that I cannot say what needs to be said."

"I think the fact you're letting me kidnap your daughter-in-law says it all."

"It is right that she leave this way."

Tracker shook his head. He couldn't care less what the old man's reasons were. And Ari didn't need to hear them, because for sure they were the type to tear her world apart. She needed her illusions, in order to keep her sanity.

"I'm not your priest, old man. I don't want to hear your confession."

"But Ari must hear." Vincente nodded to the bed. "She

must not think that we did not love her. That we are terrible people."

Shit. Vincente wanted forgiveness. Tracker tried another tactic. "You keep talking and your wife will wake up."

Vincente shook his head. "She has taken her special tea. It makes her sleep when her mind will not. She will not wake if we are quiet."

Tracker didn't feel an ounce of sympathy. "It's a hell of a thing, a guilty conscience."

"Yes." Vincente sighed and rubbed his hand down his face. "Our son did not die."

The bed ropes creaked at Ari's shock about a truth she didn't need to hear.

"Shut the hell up."

Vincente held the weapon higher. "I am the one with the gun. I will decide who talks."

"She doesn't need to hear this."

"She does. Her memory returns in the night. She says things, remembers things she does not recall in the morning. I do not want her thinking badly of us when the forgetting stops."

Tracker didn't see how she could think any differently. "Let it go."

"She is a good woman. She deserves the truth."

He said that as if it justified everything. "Yes, she is," Tracker agreed. "And I need to get her out of here now."

Vincente didn't appear to hear. He stepped to the side so he could see Ari. Tracker had the overwhelming urge to step between them again, to shield her.

"Antonio was always such a good boy, raised to do right, but maybe a bit spoiled because he was the only one." Vincente looked for understanding. "It was easier to make him happy than to see his tears. He became used to such things. When he got older, he still wanted everything given to him."

It was a common enough story. Ranching was a hard life with little profit. Many young men went out in the world for easier pickings. Some stayed on the right of the law, others went to the left. Vincente's son had obviously chosen the second route.

If only the old man would lower that barrel a fraction more... "You done?" Tracker asked.

Vincente shook his head. The pistol held steady. "My wife could not accept what Antonio became. Every day she prayed for his return to the path we had laid out for him. But he got further and further away and my wife's heart broke more and more." An apologetic look filled Vincente's eyes as he pleaded for understanding. "Josefina cannot see Antonio for who he is. She still sees him as a little boy who just needs guidance."

There was no shielding Ari now. The only thing Tracker could offer her was the full truth. "So when he brought you Ari, you agreed to hold her for him."

It was a statement, not a question.

"I was not here when she was brought, but had you seen her, you would have understood why I would not have said no, had I been."

Tracker had seen Desi. It was entirely too easy to imagine how Ari had looked. "I understand."

Something bumped his thigh. Ari's foot. He reached down. She twisted away. He caught it, needing to hold her as Vincente delivered blow after blow with his confession. She needed comfort. Tracker was all she had.

"Antonio is a *Comancheros*," Tracker said.

Ari went very still. Tracker looked over his shoulder. Her gaze was locked desperately on Vincente, as if through sheer force of will she could change the words coming from his mouth. She shook her head.

Vincente hung his. "To my shame, yes."

"That's why your ranch can remain undisturbed and undefended."

"Yes. Last fall, he came here with Ari, talking big, not caring that she was injured and pregnant."

Behind them Ari moaned. Tracker swore under his breath. Vincente kept going, as if he couldn't see the devastation his words wrought.

"He said he just needed a place to keep her until he could find this man who would pay to have her."

Ari's family attorney. The man who'd ordered the death of them all. The man who hunted Ari and Desi, because whoever owned them owned their inheritance.

"Your wife had to know it was wrong."

"She is not reasonable when it comes to Antonio." Vincente looked every one of his years as he shook his head. "We did wrong by Ari. It had to be made right."

Tracker squeezed Ari's foot. It was all the comfort he could give. "So you were the one who sent me the message."

The old man nodded. "*Sí*. I got to know her. She is a good woman. She deserves a life bigger than the lies we told her. Bigger than what my son would have."

"You told her the lies about her past so she could be happy."

He nodded again. "We grew to love her."

"And Miguel?"

"I love him, too."

"But he means more to your wife." Tracker hazarded the guess as he glanced toward the window. Much longer and

Shadow would come check out the delay. One look at the gun and he'd shoot. Tracker didn't want Vincente dead.

"My wife sees in him another chance to raise a child."

"And you don't?"

"I'm an old man in failing health. For my son I have done things that do not make me proud, but I will not do this. I will not give to him an innocent woman and baby."

"No, you won't." Tracker palmed the knife tucked up his sleeve. If it meant he had to kill Vincente to insure that, he would.

"He has chosen his path. I have chosen mine." He motioned with the gun. "You must take her and leave."

Tracker looked over at Ari. She was lying still in the bed, staring at the ceiling, tears leaking from her eyes.

How much of what she'd heard did she understand? How much did she remember?

"There were no gringos in town, were there?"

"I only created them to keep Ari out of town, so there would be no questions."

"While you waited."

Vincente frowned. "Yes. You took longer than I expected."

"I was delayed." Getting Tucker's pregnant wife to safety. Fighting off Comanches. Dropping off stray women at Hell's Eight.

"You should know that Antonio knows she is worth money to a gringo."

"Perfect."

"They will be coming for her soon."

"What will you say when they get here and she's gone?"

Vincente smiled sadly. "I will tell them I am an old man and no match for the great Tracker Ochoa."

He backed into the hall and grabbed a bag and tossed it

onto the bed. It clanked and rattled. "Food for the baby and his mama."

"Thank you." Tracker picked up the bag and hefted it. There was probably enough for a couple days. "Why are you doing this?"

"I'm sick. If *Dios* wills it, I will live long enough to get my wife to her family in Mexico. But either way, when I die I'll not have this stain on my soul."

Men had done less for bigger reasons. "Fair enough."

Vincente let the muzzle drop. "You can leave the way you came."

Through the window, like a thief in the night. Tracker took the bag and set it on the ground outside the window.

He went back to the bed and picked up Ari. She didn't fight, didn't struggle. And when he looked down, she was staring at Vincente, all the agony in her soul reflected in her eyes.

"I'm sorry, *hija*."

She turned her head away.

It was hard to hate the old man. A parent's love for his child was absolute. Tracker remembered that rush of emotion he'd felt when he'd held Miguel. The utter need to protect and shelter. Love was a son of a bitch in all its forms. "*Vaya con Dios,* Vincente."

"*Gracias. Y tú tambien.*" Vincente stared at Ari, his heart in his eyes. Ari didn't turn her head. Didn't acknowledge his existence. Vincente would have to find his forgiveness elsewhere.

The old man turned his attention back to Tracker. "Promise me you'll make an honest woman of *mi hija*."

That he couldn't promise. "I'll do what's best."

"Take her to a place where she can have peace, a family, her dreams."

He was taking her to Hell's Eight. "I will."

Vincente left the room, gun dangling at his side, shoulders hunched. A broken man coming to the end of his life, with his sins riding his back.

Tracker swore under his breath and headed for the window. No sense pushing his luck by trying for the front door. As he eased Ari to the floor, he gave thanks he wasn't going to live long enough to be old. Long before he was faced with the prospect of staring down death with nothing but his failures to contemplate, his luck would run out and he'd die somewhere alone, likely with a bullet in his back. But before that day came, he had one last mission to accomplish.

He sat Ari on the windowsill and brushed the curls from her forehead. She stared at him with the uncomprehending shock he saw in the faces of soldiers who'd seen one battle too many.

He remembered the sweetness of her kiss, the heat of her passion, the purity of her smile that day in the barn, their one time together, as her desire rose to meet his. She had a future. She just needed the opportunity to believe in it.

He removed the gag from her mouth. "It's time to go home, sweets."

7

Ari clutched the knowledge harder than she clutched the saddle horn. She needed something real to cling to as her mind spun with Vincente's revelations. She'd never been married. There'd been no murder. There'd been no disaster from which she needed to recover. She was just a crazy woman Vincente was holding for his son, so his son could make a profit down the road. And she'd made it so easy for them. Believing what she was told. Wanting it to be that simple.

Why? Why had she wanted it to be that simple? What was her mind hiding from her? What could be so awful that she'd be content with a fiction that didn't even make sense when she held it up to the light of day? She should have questioned it.

She looked at her son. She should have questioned a lot of things.

It's time to take you home.

So, where *was* home? What was waiting for her when she got there? Was any of it good? A pounding began behind her

eyes, the way it always did when she thought of going back…
where? Where was home?

She put the thought into words. "Where's home?"

Neither Tracker nor the other man, whom Tracker had introduced as Shadow, his brother, gave any indication they'd heard her, though she knew they had. The two heard every little thing, even what she didn't want them to. Which could only mean she'd asked a question they didn't want to answer. Sure enough, when she looked back over her shoulder at Tracker, she caught him exchanging with Shadow one of those glances that passed for communication between the two.

Tracker pulled his horse off to the right and dismounted beside a small stream. He untied Miguel's cradleboard from the saddle and, after checking for snakes, propped it against a rock. The stream was barely more than a trickle in places. It would be dried up in a month. Riding then would be torture. Hot, dusty and thirsty. She frowned. How did she know that?

Shadow rode past her. The only acknowledgment he gave her was a brief nod. He was a very rude man and very good at ignoring her. He dismounted and led his horse over to the water.

"I asked a question," she said as Tracker stood. She couldn't see his eyes for the barrier of his hat brim, so she snatched his hat off his head. Neither man said a word. They just watched her—Shadow with the neutral expression that said nothing, and Tracker with that cautious concern.

"Don't worry. I'm not going to have an episode." She didn't think even she could handle that.

Tracker jerked his chin upward, indicating his hat, which she still held. "You done or were you planning on hitting me with that?"

It did look as if she was getting ready to swing. Lowering her arm, she shrugged. "I couldn't see your eyes."

The explanation sounded lame. Tracker didn't even blink at the absurd explanation. He merely reached up and took the hat from her fingers.

"I'm rather fond of the shape it's in already."

She'd been crushing the brim. "I'm sorry."

Her hands felt empty without the hat. She needed something to hold on to. She settled for the saddle horn instead.

"I—" Ari couldn't finish the sentence. How did one put into words the emptiness inside? The longing for something solid in a world that was as insubstantial as dandelion fluff? How could she tell a man she barely knew that she needed to see his eyes, because when he looked at her she believed she was something more than nothing? Something more than crazy? She couldn't.

"You trying to tell me you're feeling a bit lost right now?"

Lost didn't begin to cover it. She had nothing. *Nothing.* "A little."

Tracker held up his hands. They were darkened by the sun, with scars slashing the backs in a random pattern, but they were strong hands. Tendon flexed over bone as he motioned her toward him, and she slid off the horse into them, her feet dangling in the air.

There was no panic when his hands closed around her waist, just a sense of rightness. Ari closed her eyes, absorbing that feeling. Instead of setting her away, Tracker held her against him. More strength and, God help her, comfort. The wall she'd built around her emotions cracked. A tear leaked down her cheek.

Don't hold me. Don't be nice to me. Don't. Don't.

"What can I do?"

Nothing. There was nothing he or anyone could do.

The wall cracked further. Of their own volition, her arms slid around his neck and her legs curled around his, anchoring her to him. "Don't lie to me."

His deep drawl rumbled in her ear. "It's not a habit I planned on picking up."

She leaned her head against his chest. His heart beat in a slow, steady rhythm against her cheek. He smelled of leather, sweat and horse. She should be repulsed. She just wanted to get closer. To crawl inside his skin and dare the memories to come. When Tracker held her, fear disappeared. "Thank you."

She flattened her palms against the cool leather of his shirt. Beneath, she could feel the hardness of muscle. He was such a solid man. "How do I know?" she added.

"What?"

"How do I know you've never lied to me?"

He let her slide down his body, easing her away only when the buttons on her shirt caught on his belt buckle. He stepped back. She immediately felt bereft. She caught the bottom corner of his vest, halting his retreat. "Don't."

"Don't what?"

Don't walk away.

She shook her head and let him go, giving him a small smile. "Nothing."

He studied her, and then, almost as if expecting her to run, he reached out. Why would he expect her to run from him? The back of his fingers touched her cheek. She closed her eyes and let the familiar sensation flow through her. When she opened her eyes, he was waiting. His gaze held hers with the same surety with which he'd held her body a few minutes before. "I won't leave you. And I won't lie to you."

"Promise?" She so needed a promise.

"I promise."

"And it is said that the Hell's Eight never break a promise."

"No, and neither do I."

He wanted her to see him as more than a Ranger doing his job, she suddenly understood. He wanted her to see him as a man.

He'd never been anything else to her.

She forced a smile that she hoped didn't look as wobbly as it felt. "That's even better."

His fingers slid across her neck. A shiver went down her spine and his big palm cradled her head. His thumb wiped the tear from her cheek. "What's wrong, sweets?"

"You're going to take me home."

His thumb wiped away another tear. "That should make you happy."

"I have no idea what to expect."

"A very warm welcome."

"How will I even know when I've arrived?"

"You'll know it when you see it."

"What makes you so sure?"

"You'll have to trust me, Ari."

She preferred "sweets" to "Ari." Ari sounded formal, distant even, on his lips. Everyone called her that. Only Tracker called her "sweets."

"I guess so."

Tracker dropped his hand from her cheek and settled his hat on his head. The brim was a bit bent where she'd grabbed it. She liked the idea that she'd left her mark on him, but hated the way the brim shaded his eyes, hiding his thoughts from her. Touching her cheek where he had, she realized he was right. She had no choice but to trust him.

The same way you had no choice but to trust the Moraleses.

She pushed the knowledge aside. Tracker was as different from them as night was from day.

"I've got breakfast ready," Shadow called from where he crouched in front of Miguel. He had a knotted red bandanna in his hand. Miguel was watching it with wide-eyed fascination. Whatever else he was, Shadow was good with her son.

Tracker waved her forward. "You'll feel better once you have something in your stomach."

"I don't think so."

He cocked an eyebrow and smiled—a smile that made her want to stand on tiptoe and kiss him. His eyes narrowed. The right corner of his lip quirked up a little, just enough to feed the longing inside her.

"What happened to trusting me?"

Her smile was confident, but inside, she felt tremulous. How did he do this to her? Draw her attention away from her troubles, to the pleasure between them? The sensation of his hand on her cheek was fading. She wanted to replace it with something even better. "It was a passing fancy."

His gaze never left her mouth. "Uh-huh."

She cut a glance at Shadow. He was watching her. So was Miguel. It would be scandalous to accept the invitation Tracker was extending. But she wanted to. The best she could do was turn her back to their audience and blow him a quick kiss. And even that was shocking. Not only to her, but to Tracker.

His eyes widened and then narrowed, the heavy-lidded expression so sexual that her knees went weak. He had beautiful, expressive eyes. And right now they were nearly black with the memories she knew she had invoked.

"You're awfully brave when we have an audience."

She remembered their time in the barn, the searing pleasure that had obscured everything but the joy they'd felt. Cocking her head to the side, keeping her voice low, she teased, "I don't know. I think I was pretty bold the last time, in the barn."

"That you were."

The sensual softening of his lips emboldened her. She liked feeling that way. Liked who she was with him. Free. Natural. The self it felt she should be, but couldn't remember. "Maybe when you get me alone again, I can try for something bolder."

"Damn, sweets, I'm not sure I could take it."

"Me, neither."

Behind her she could hear her son start the whining that preceded a wail. Her breasts swelled and tingled. She didn't have a change of clothes if her milk let down. "I have to take care of Miguel."

"Yup."

She couldn't make her feet move.

Tracker's hands on her shoulders turned her around. "I told you, I'm not going anywhere."

"I know." But she couldn't help feeling that there was something beyond her awareness looming like a thundercloud over this happiness, just waiting to unleash its fury on this new beginning.

Shadow was unwrapping Miguel from the cradleboard. The curse word he uttered wasn't pretty.

"Mr. Ochoa!" she snapped.

Shadow all but thrust Miguel at her. "Damn, what are you feeding that kid?"

With her next indrawn breath, she understood. Letting him dangle at arm's length, she gasped, "What did *you* feed him?"

Shadow didn't meet her gaze. "What makes you think I fed him anything?"

Tracker came up and stopped dead before taking a step back. "Good God!"

Shadow took two steps back and one to the right. "All I did was give him some of my burrito. To keep him quiet while I was waiting for you two to mosey on out."

"You gave beans to a six-month-old baby?"

"He liked them."

"Sure as shit doesn't smell like they're liking him back," Tracker muttered, waving his hand in front of his nose.

Miguel's face crumpled. His chin wobbled. A tear trickled down his cheek. To Ari's shock, Tracker took him away, saying, "Give him to me."

"Do you know how to change a baby?"

He walked over to the saddlebags. "Can't be as complicated as setting a charge of dynamite." He rummaged through the bags until he found a clean nappy, soap and a cloth. Miguel just stared at the big man who held him. As Tracker's hair fell forward, he grabbed a handful and brought it to his mouth.

"You'd think none of them had ever eaten a bean before," Tracker said, rubbing the little boy's back.

Miguel grunted, another tear spilling from his eyes.

"Don't you go believing them. Their shit stinks just like everyone else's."

Shadow burst out laughing.

"Oh, my God! Tracker!" Ari cried.

He gave her a hard look. "Do you want him to believe there's something wrong with him?"

She didn't. "No, but—"

He cut her off. "Then stop acting like the world's come to an end because he had a bowel movement."

He was actually angry. On behalf of Miguel.

"He's too young to know."

"The hell he is." With an efficiency that raised questions, he set about changing the dirty diaper. "As soon as you all started carrying on, he started crying."

Miguel, rid of the dirty diaper and with a fistful of Tracker's hair in his mouth, cooed happily.

"I'm sure."

"There's nothing wrong with him."

"I never thought there was."

"He's a good baby, and raised right, he'll be a good man." Tracker was looking at her like this was something she didn't know.

"I fully intend to raise him right," she retorted.

Tracker nodded. "Good. Because he's going to be Hell's Eight."

What Miguel was going to be was her decision. Ari folded her hands across her full breasts and winced. She needed to nurse her son. "That's not a given."

Shadow spoke from behind her. "Do not be so quick to deny him a place at Hell's Eight. For a boy like him, who is neither white nor anything else, being one of the Eight will count."

How had they gone from discussing Miguel's diaper to his future? "For what?"

"As a place in which to put his pride when the world would take it away."

A chill raced over her skin. She rubbed her arms. "He's just a baby."

She knew Miguel would face prejudice later in life. She'd seen a bit of it when they'd had visitors at the ranch. But he was still an infant, and the time when he'd have to face the world as an adult was many years away.

"Who will one day be a man," Tracker said quietly. "To grow up straight, he'll need a place where he's accepted."

"A place where no one will spit on him for being a boy like any other," Shadow added.

"Yes." Tracker lifted Miguel up. The boy flashed his toothless grin and kicked his feet. Tracker didn't smile back. Miguel stopped kicking and his expression grew solemn as he stared at the man holding him. "But no one will spit on you and live, little one. This I promise you."

Shadow nodded while Miguel stared intently at Tracker, as if seeing him for the first time.

Looking from one brother to the next, Ari knew the feeling. It hit her that they weren't speculating. They'd faced hatred. They'd been spat on as boys. They'd had their pride taken away. They knew the pain her son could face. She couldn't picture either Tracker or Shadow as vulnerable boys. They were too strong, too confident, but she could see Miguel as one. And she could see how easy it would be for someone to break his smiling, happy nature with senseless cruelty. All because his skin wasn't the right color. She tightened her grip on her arms. She'd kill the first person who tried.

Looking over at Tracker she asked, "What makes you so sure he'll find acceptance at Hell's Eight?"

As Tracker handed Miguel to her, the wind blew his hair back from his face, leaving nothing to soften the determination in his expression. "Because I'm there."

Yes, that would do it. Tracker was a fair man with a strong sense of right and wrong. Because of his own heritage, he could offer Miguel understanding and direction. And maybe love? She didn't know if Tracker could love her son, but if he did, there would be no shirking or holding back. He'd be a father in all ways.

It was something to consider. And in the meantime, he'd made Miguel a promise that was as solid as the man himself. Shadow was right. She shouldn't be so quick to deny Miguel a place at Hell's Eight.

"Thank you."

Miguel fussed, turning his face into her shoulder. He was hungry.

"You're welcome." Tracker motioned with his hand. "Why don't you feed him while I clean this up?"

In a minute, she wasn't going to have much choice. She sat on the rock and unbuttoned her blouse. Both men turned aside, giving her privacy.

"Where'd you learn to change a diaper?" Ari asked Tracker.

"Worried I've got a passel of kids somewhere?"

What was the point in denying the truth? "Yes."

There was a pause, as if her honesty surprised him. Shadow snorted, whether in laughter or annoyance, she couldn't tell. The seconds seemed to drag painfully before Tracker said, "I don't."

"Have a passel, or any?" Some things a woman had to know, whether it was any of her business or not.

"I don't have any."

It was her turn to smile. Leaning down, she kissed the top of Miguel's head. "Good."

"Miguel all settled?" Tracker asked, glancing to where the boy played on the blanket she'd laid out.

"For now."

"Good, then it's our turn to eat." Grabbing a tortilla from the stack, he filled it with beans and cheese, then handed it to her. "Holler when you're ready for another."

A glance at the plate revealed there wasn't that much food to go around. Especially when two of the people eating were men. Ari smiled. "One will be enough for me."

Tracker paused in filling his own tortilla. "If I can't lie to you, you can't lie to me."

"But you need your—"

Shadow grunted and reached for the spoon. "Tia would have our heads if a woman in our presence went hungry."

"Tia?"

"The woman who raised us after our family was massacred." He took a bite of his own tortilla, chewing fast.

Tracker hesitated only long enough to order her to eat, before taking a bite of his.

"Are we in a hurry?"

The two men exchanged a look that clearly said they were. "We need to get to Hell's Eight."

"What aren't you telling me?"

It was Tracker who answered. "Antonio and his compadres are on their way to Esperanza. Our paths could cross at Drunk Hole."

The blood left her face in a wash of cold. She wanted to snatch Miguel from the ground and jump on the horse and gallop. "What are we going to do?" Not for an instant did she believe Tracker didn't have a plan.

"We're going to ride like hell for the next day and a half," he told her.

"And what happens then?"

"We hope like hell we get through before the *Comancheros.*"

Two days of hard riding. How did one accomplish that with a baby? She looked at the cradleboard. Indian babies did it all the time, so it had to be possible, but Miguel wasn't used to being confined. What if he cried at the wrong time? What if…?

Tracker touched her arm, drawing her gaze. "I told you I'd keep you both safe."

She had no doubt he'd keep her as safe as he could. But there was only so much two men could do against many. And against *Comancheros*… Just the name struck unreasoning terror in her heart. It always had. She couldn't remember meeting Antonio or any other *Comancheros,* but stories about the atrocities they'd committed abounded. They were horrible men, terrifying in their lack of conscience, vicious in their treatment of those who crossed their path. Tracker had known they were coming, and he'd still held to his promise.

His hand slid over her shoulder to curve around her neck. She wished he'd pull her close. He didn't, but his thumb tipped her chin up. "Don't worry."

She licked her lips. "That's why you kidnapped me, isn't it? That's why you couldn't wait for the wedding. You ran out of time."

"Yes."

"You could have told me."

He shook his head, his long hair sliding over his shoulders. She curled her fingers, remembering how it had felt in her hands. "Telling would mean explaining. And there were things you didn't need to hear."

"Like the truth about Josefina and Vincente?"

His thumb brushed her lips. "Yeah. I would have spared you that."

"I wouldn't have believed you, even if you'd tried."

His fingers moved gently back and forth on the back of her neck. "I know that, too."

She hated the pity in his voice, hated being pitiful. At the same time, she wanted to crawl into his arms and let him shelter her from the world. He was a nice man, but right now she needed him to be the tough hombre who could take on ten men in a bar and make them all back down.

She held in a moan. *Comancheros.*

"Thank you."

"I didn't go back on my promise to marry you."

She shook her head. That's what he was worried about? "It was just circumstances that forced your hand. I understand."

He shook his head in turn. "Among my father's people, a public statement of marriage is the same as fact."

It took her a second to remember what he'd said in the cantina.

"You said that to save me."

"I knew what I was doing."

"Did you?"

"Yes. Don't worry. I'll get you safely to Hell's Eight."

"And when we get there? What then? Do you really consider us married? Do we stay married? Do we divorce?" *Do I run from the chaos of my life?*

Nothing Tracker felt showed on his face. "That will depend on you."

"I don't understand."

He reached into his vest pocket and pulled out a folded piece of paper. After the briefest hesitation, he handed it to her. She

128

turned it over. Worn from handling, frayed at the edges and torn in a couple places, it didn't look like much.

"What's this?"

He shrugged. "The answer to your questions."

She read Desi's letter over and over during the next nine hours. Memorizing every word over every brutal mile, until she wasn't sure what was fact, what was fiction, what was real and what was a nightmare. She read it until she couldn't focus anymore. Ari put the letter in her pocket and concentrated on staying on the horse while the miles passed. She rode until she couldn't even think, and still Tracker didn't call a halt.

She understood why; she just wasn't sure she was strong enough to make it through.

"Just a little longer, sweets."

Tracker had been feeding her that line for the last two hours. And she'd been feeding him the same line back. "All right."

Needing something to do besides dwell on her misery, she studied the brothers. If not for the scar on Tracker's face, it really would be hard to tell them apart. Both men had the same mannerisms, the same bold, handsome features cut into those compelling lines. The same hooded eyes that made her think of hot nights and soft sheets. She glanced down. The same strong thighs. They were twins.

She touched the pocket where she'd tucked the letter. And so was she.

A glance at Miguel revealed that he was still content in his cradleboard, tied to Tracker's saddle. She offered up a silent prayer of thanks that he was oblivious to the tension pressing down upon her. The letter crinkled under her touch. She had a twin.

She tried the pronouncement again. No sense of recognition

lifted the darkness of her past. No sense of loss weighed down her awareness of the present.

Her horse stumbled. Grabbing the horn, she righted herself. She wished she'd thought to ask Tracker more questions. Were they exact twins, like Tracker and Shadow? Did they share the same tastes, the same likes and dislikes?

Do you remember the game we used to play at the summer house?

No, she didn't. No matter how she tried, Ari didn't remember a thing. It was so scary to read about her relationship on paper, to have someone love her so much. Someone she couldn't even remember. She reached for the letter. Someone who told her that the rest of their family was dead, but that she was waiting. Telling Ari that they searched for her, would not give up. That she'd planted daisies. What kind of person planted daisies, for heaven's sake?

The paper crumpled in her grip. Not for the first time, she wondered if the reason her memory was gone was because what lurked behind that black curtain was too horrible to be borne.

"You hold that much tighter and there won't be anything left to read," Shadow said, moving his horse closer.

Her muscles tensed. She didn't like having him so near. No matter that he was Tracker's brother, there was something about the man that made her want to run. It wasn't that Shadow was any more wild than Tracker. Both men were as untamed as this land. For her, Tracker was safe, but Shadow reminded her of something else, someone else. Especially when he tilted his head as he was right now, so the shadows hugged his face.

She steered her horse away. "Thank you."

Shadow followed. "He meant what he said earlier."

"Who?"

"Tracker."

She held her ground. "What did he say?"

"Don't play dumb."

All right, she wouldn't. "I was trying to be polite and spare your feelings."

"From what?"

"From the insult of having to be told what's between Tracker and me is none of your business."

To her surprise, that earned her a quirk of lips so similar to Tracker's that her wariness faded.

"So there is some spunk in you."

Apparently. "Excuse me?"

He went on as if she hadn't raised her brows. "You're going to need it."

"Because your brother thinks I'm married to him?"

Shadow shook his head. "Because he's Indian."

"He doesn't seem to have been raised Indian."

"Doesn't matter. The problem lies in the color of his skin."

"It's the same as yours."

"Yup, but I'm not carrying on with a white woman."

"We are not 'carrying on'." She didn't know what they were doing, but it was more than that.

"In his eyes, you're married."

"As easy as it is to get married, I bet it's twice as easy to get divorced."

Shadow's gaze narrowed and anger rolled off him like a summer storm, hard, fast and furious. "You don't know shit about my brother."

"And you don't know shit about me." A press of her knees set her horse in a faster pace. Though she pulled ahead, she could feel him watching her. Why had she let so much distance get between them and Tracker?

Shadow's big black came abreast. Her heart skipped a beat when he reached down and caught her horse's bridle, pulling her up short. "My brother's willing to die for you."

She jerked on the reins; Shadow didn't let go. "I didn't ask it of him."

Shadow glared at her. The glance he cast ahead said clearly that he didn't want Tracker to hear their exchange. She braced herself.

"But if *Comancheros* came upon us right now, you'd be diving behind him and be damn grateful for the opportunity."

Yes, she would. Anyone would. "Just say what you want to say."

"He deserves better than to be used."

"I'm not using him."

"The hell you're not. You're clinging to him like a drowning victim thrown a lifeline." Shadow caught her arm and leaned closer until his face was just inches from hers. His voice, low and rough, scraped over her nerves. "If you hurt him, I'll come after you."

Light shattered behind her eyes. Shadow's face blurred out of focus until all that was left was that voice, those eyes. Cruel eyes. Hate-filled eyes. Eyes that burned with lust. Blue eyes, brown eyes, green. The colors changed, but never the emotion within. The stench of mud filled her nostrils. The sound of laughter, cruel and mocking, echoed around her. She was trapped. From afar she heard a male voice call out. It blended into the cacophony in her mind.

"Shit. Tracker, get back here!"

Tracker. Yes, I need Tracker. He won't let them hurt me anymore. I'm safe with Tracker. She screamed his name, but no one ever heard her scream. No one ever came. She needed to go away to that quiet place where nothing could touch her. She could hide there. No one could hurt her there. No one could make her feel there.

"What the hell did you do?"

"Who the hell says I had to do anything?"

The conversation went on around her, beyond the invisible walls of her safe place, unable to touch her.

"Goddammit, Shadow. You know how fragile she is."

Yes, she thought as she floated behind her walls. She felt very fragile right now. Like china balanced on the edge of a table, in that split second before it took that tumble to the floor that rendered it worthless forever. Her lungs hurt. Her eyes burned. She stared at the sun, narrowing her eyes until it was just a speck.

The speck grew larger and larger, white obliterating dark. Past destroying present. The laughter grew louder. There were hands everywhere. Restraining her, hurting her. The demons had come for her. She couldn't struggle. She couldn't get away. She could never get away. No matter how many times she ran, they found her, just as they'd promised. She would never be safe. Never be clean. She'd always be theirs.

A hand penetrated her sanctuary. She couldn't let them take her. Not again. The scream started in her soul, raged through her being, erupted from her mouth.

"Nooo!"

8

Tracker grabbed for Ari while shooting a glare at Shadow. "What the hell did you do?"

He missed. Ari's bay tossed its head and wheeled around, responding as best it could to his jerks on the reins.

Shadow shook his head, waiting for his opportunity to grab the horse. "I told her if she hurt you I'd come after her."

"Son of a bitch. What the hell were you thinking?" Tracker made another grab for Ari. Her horse crow-hopped to the left. Ari went to the right. For a perilous moment Tracker thought she was going to fall, but at the last minute she found her balance and hauled herself back up, where she lay slumped over the saddle horn while she caught her breath.

"I was watching your back."

Tracker urged Buster closer. "I don't need you to protect me."

"I don't need protection, either, but it doesn't seem to stop you." Shadow moved around to the front of Ari's horse.

The bay tossed his head and hunched his back slightly. The muscles in his hindquarters bunched.

"Shit, her horse is going to buck."

Shadow grabbed for the reins. "Easy..."

Tracker grabbed for Ari. "Easy..."

Neither the horse nor the woman listened. Miguel squalled as his cradleboard bounced against the bay's shoulder. *Shit.* Tracker had forgotten about the baby being on that side of his mount.

"Hold on, I've got to turn around."

"Better speed it up."

Tracker wheeled Buster about as Ari's horse reared. It wasn't pretty, but he managed to snag his arm around her waist. Ducking her flailing arms, he pulled her onto his lap. She immediately went for his eyes, her breath coming in short pants, her expression wild. Tracker blocked her next attempt, letting her go for the split second it took to wrap his arm across her chest, pinning her against him. His knee knocked the cradleboard this time, and Miguel howled. Ari clawed at his arm.

Son of a bitch. He had to get them under control.

He tried reason. "Ari! It's Tracker. I've got you. You're safe." There was no letup in her fight. "I've come to take you home, remember?"

The baby's cries were reaching a fevered pitch. Ari's nails were raking so hard he'd be skinned clean to the bone if they were on his flesh rather than the sleeve of his buckskin shirt. If there were any *Comancheros* within two miles, Tracker and his party would all be goners.

"Give me Miguel," Shadow called.

Tracker pulled his horse up and started untying the cradleboard. His brother came around, fighting his own battles with Ari's horse, which rolled its eyes wildly and fought any attempt he made to get closer to the screaming baby and wild woman. Tracker couldn't blame it. He'd rather be anywhere else himself.

He grabbed the strap of the cradleboard as Buster spun again, responding to the kick Ari landed against his side. In a coordinated manner that had saved their lives many times, Shadow tossed Tracker the reins to Ari's horse, while he passed over the cradleboard. The exchange was clean.

The deal with Ari wasn't. Every minute he wasted trying to calm her was one minute they weren't on the trail. One minute that went to the *Comancheros'* favor. Buster snorted and crow-hopped as Tracker corrected yet another wrong signal from Ari. That at least answered one question: they couldn't ride like this. Two spooked horses, a screaming baby and a hysterical woman were guaranteed disaster. "We're going to have to stop."

"No shit." Shadow fought with the bay. It reared and backed up, tossing its head as wildly as Ari was tossing hers, nearly dragging him from the saddle as he hooked the cradle-board over his saddle horn. "Vincente needs to train his stock better."

"Vincente needed to do a lot of things better."

"No shit."

"There's a stream over there. At least it'll provide some cover."

If they didn't get Ari and Miguel calmed down, it wouldn't matter. A man could cover his body with brush or sand, tuck himself behind a rock or bush, but there was no hiding a scream. A scream gouged a man's nerves like a pick. Screams carried.

Tracker's fury raged. Shadow had no right. None at all. He caught his brother's eye. "You ever do something like this again and we're through."

Shadow jerked as if he'd taken a blow. "Goddammit—"

Tracker cut him off. "I mean it. You come at me if you have a bone to pick. Don't you ever come at her again."

There had been enough threats in Ari's life. She didn't need any more. Especially from his brother, a man who should be protecting her.

Shadow nodded, his mouth set in a thin line. He'd be apologizing later, and maybe Tracker would be accepting it. But right now it was all he could do to hold back his rage, keep Ari from tumbling to the ground, and keep Buster from pitching a fit to rival hers.

"Don't you start, Buster."

For a moment the horse settled. Tracker took advantage of the fact to adjust his grip on Ari. She took advantage of the moment to go completely limp. He wasn't prepared for the move, and she slid out of his grip. Trying to get her back was like trying to hold greased lightning. She made it halfway to the ground before he managed to pin her against his thigh.

"At least they didn't beat the fight out of you, sweets," he grunted.

Her response was to bite his thigh through the heavy leather of his pants. This time when she kicked out her feet connected with Buster's leg. The gelding gave that little hop that warned he'd had enough. They were all going to end up on the ground if something didn't change quickly.

There was only one thing Tracker had found made an impact on Ari when she was in this state. He pulled her back up, put his mouth to her ear and said in the most guttural voice he could muster, "If you don't hold still, I'll kill the baby."

She didn't question, she didn't quibble, she didn't deny; she just went absolutely still. Whether she remembered her time with the *Comancheros* or not, some of the lessons they'd taught her had stuck.

Buster gave another hop. Tracker snapped the reins taut. "Damn it, Buster, cut it out."

Buster stood stock-still. Ari didn't even seem to breathe.

Tracker looked at the sky. The sun was beginning to set. He'd been hoping to make more time before they stopped for the night, but they couldn't go any farther the way they were, with the baby screaming and Ari in shock. He looked around. The small copse of trees to the left provided a bit of cover.

"Head for the streambed," he told Shadow, jerking his chin in that direction.

Shadow nodded and rode over. "It's dry for now."

Shit. The horses needed water. So did they. Their canteens were about dry.

Keeping a tight grip and a close eye on Ari, Tracker slowly walked Buster to the copse. Shadow swung down from his big roan and unhooked the cradleboard from the saddle horn. Miguel, seeing a warm body in front of him, let out a hopeful whimper. When he saw it was Shadow and not his mother, he let out a scream that scared a jay out of the bush. The bird took off with a squawk.

"Your momma will be with you in a minute."

Propping Miguel's cradleboard against a log, Shadow looked at Ari, regret etched into his expression. "If it hasn't dried up yet, there should be a stream about a mile over. I'll water the horses."

"Do that," Tracker replied. Water was the most critical thing. The next section of trail was notoriously dry. In safer areas, they might have camped by the nearby stream, but not here. Here it was safer to keep their distance.

Shadow mounted, picked up the bay's reins and hesitated.

"What?"

"I didn't know she'd react like that, Tracker. I expected her to spit in my face and tell me to go to hell."

"Son of a bitch, didn't watching what Desi went through teach you anything?"

His twin shook his head. "I wasn't there for her bad times."

Tracker bit back a retort as he realized Shadow hadn't been. "Well, pay attention now. Ari's mind might be protecting her by hogtying her memory, but somewhere inside, she still knows what happened. And an Indian threatening her is pretty much guaranteed to trigger her instinct to run, especially one in a black hat, with a bad attitude."

"Yeah. I see that."

Tracker sighed. He would eventually forgive his brother. He didn't have any choice. He was the other half to his coin. And he knew him too well. Shadow might lay it on the line for those he thought needed talking to, but he wasn't cruel to women. He probably *had* expected Ari to spit in his face.

Miguel released a high-pitched protest that would carry for miles. Tracker awkwardly dismounted, hanging on to Ari, holding her against his chest, and handed Buster's reins to Shadow. "Go find the water. Hopefully, I'll have things under control here by the time you get back."

"Good luck." With a wry twist of his lips, he kicked his horse into a canter. The other horses followed, all too willing to get away from the chaos.

Tracker empathized.

"It's more like I'm going to need a miracle," he muttered to himself, since Shadow was too far away to hear.

Ari's next wiggle caught Tracker by surprise. She broke away and was off and running as soon as her feet hit the ground. He made a grab for her, but she ducked and darted to the right. She ran as if the demons of hell were after her, and she was trapped in a past where there was no child, no hope. Running as if she'd never had the chance before and couldn't believe she had it now. If it had been up to him he'd let her run until she found safety. But it wasn't up to Tracker. They were in the middle of Indian country, of Comanchero hunting grounds. There was no safety here.

Miguel's screams became more frantic. *Shit.* Tracker needed more hands. One pair to soothe the baby and one pair to catch Ari. A glance showed that she was still running—another way Ari and Desi were alike. They could both run like deer. Ari disappeared over the lip of the dry streambed, vanishing from sight. Tracker turned the cradleboard so the sun wasn't in Miguel's face and chucked him under the chin.

"Hang tight there, fella, while I bring your momma back."

Miguel was unimpressed with the promise. His next cry warbled off to a dry hiccup of doubt.

Satisfied the baby was safe, Tracker leaped up to follow Ari. It was his turn to flash back to the past, when Desi had run from Caine. Caine had ridden her down. Now Tracker was chasing Ari, watching her feet fly across the ground as he did. Admiring her long blond hair as it streamed out behind her, catching the fading sun and reflecting it back in brilliant shades of yellow. She was beautiful, she was fast, and her freedom was at an end. There were some things in life that were a constant. No matter how scared Ari was, she couldn't outrun him.

When Tracker closed in, Ari looked over her shoulder. The terror in her face wasn't nearly as devastating as the acceptance in her eyes. She knew it was over. Knew there was no hope.

Goddammit, he never wanted to see that look in her eyes again.

Hating himself, hating the circumstances that made him the one to reenact her past, Tracker launched himself at her, grabbed her and hit the ground, taking her down. It was a maneuver he'd done a hundred times, with men. He'd never tried it with a woman. Though he thought he'd accounted for the weight and height difference, Ari seemed to fly into his arms as he snatched her against him and turned to take the brunt of the fall on his back. The impact knocked the wind out of him. He held her tightly as they rolled.

"It's all right. It's all right." The words never left his mouth, trapped with his breath in his lings. When they stopped rolling he was on the bottom, staring at the sun with Ari's hair covering his face, filling his mouth. He spat it free just as her elbow jabbed into his ribs. He found his breath and his voice in the same instant.

"Jesus Christ, woman, would you just fucking hold still."

Naturally, Ari didn't obey.

Tracker rolled them over again, bracing himself on his elbows and knees above her. Her hair was tumbled about her face. The second he moved his hand up to push it out of the way, she snapped at his flesh, going for blood.

"They couldn't break you, could they, Ari? Couldn't make you stop fighting?" He caught her chin, the way they must have, preventing her from sinking those small white teeth into their miserable hides. But unlike them, he didn't want to hurt her, he just wanted to set her free. Dropping a kiss on her forehead, he whispered, "You fight all you want, sweets. And when you're done, I'll be here waiting to hold you safe."

She stilled.

"It's Tracker, baby. You're with me and it's all good."

She blinked and a bit of the vagueness left her gaze.

"We've got to get back to Miguel, Ari. Don't you want to hold your baby?"

Comprehension replaced fear. Ari closed her eyes, and her pale, dry lips shaped Miguel's name. However he'd come to be conceived, there was no doubt Ari loved her son. Tracker hoped she could keep on loving him once the memories came back.

"What happened?"

Tracker so badly wanted to touch her mouth with his finger, to feel her breath on his skin. To know she was alive and here with him. The episodes were getting stronger. To the point that he could easily see her becoming trapped in one forever. And that scared the bejezus out of him. "You had an episode."

"I'm sorr—"

He put his fingers to her lips. "Don't."

"But—"

He eased his fingers away. "No more apologies. They happen. We deal with them when they come along, but they aren't something you can help, so you will stop apologizing for them."

Her eyes searched his, looking for…he didn't know what. "I will?"

"Yes."

"All right."

"You ready to get up?"

She nodded, fighting to steady her breathing.

"Good." Moving to the side, he squatted back on his heels. In the distance Miguel still cried. Poor little mite. "Because I think Miguel wants his mother."

Holding a hand out to Ari, Tracker helped her to sit up. She pushed her hair back from her face. "Is Miguel all right?"

"He was when I left him."

She stopped breathing altogether. "Left him?"

"I was a bit distracted." Tracker drew a pistol from his holster. After a quick check of the chambers and a test of the hammer, he handed it to her.

Ari took it gingerly. "What am I supposed to do with this?"

"Do you know how to fire a pistol?"

"Of course."

"Good. If anybody but Shadow or me comes up to you, you shoot first and let them explain later."

"Where are you going?"

"To check on Miguel."

"I'm going with you."

"No."

"Why not?"

"Because I can handle only one disaster at a time."

"That's not what everyone else says."

"Everyone lies." He motioned to the pistol in her hand. He'd feel a lot better if she'd stop handling it like it was a piece of fish gone bad. "Are you a good shot?"

"Not the best, but I've been practicing."

"Then at least show me you know how to hold it." She did. He breathed a little easier, but not much. The gun was big in her hand. That was going to be a problem.

A few weak hiccupping cries came from the camp site.

"You've only got six bullets. Don't waste them firing wildly. You keep that gun hidden in your skirts, finger on the trigger. Keep it cocked. Play all innocent and let them come real near. Don't give any warning. And when they get so close you can't miss, you fire. First shot to the midsection. If that doesn't kill them, you put the next between their eyes."

Horror, shock, determination—all three warred for dominance in her expression.

"If you get scared, you remember whoever it is will be coming for Miguel next."

Determination took the fore. "I won't get scared."

"Everyone gets scared."

"Not me." She tucked the pistol into the folds of her skirt as he'd instructed, and squared her shoulders. "I can't afford to get scared anymore." She looked up, catching him unaware. "Can I?"

He didn't have a choice but to give her the truth. "No. Whatever you're afraid of, you've got to face it down for Miguel's sake." He cocked his head, listening. Miguel's cries weren't getting any weaker. The boy had his mother's stubbornness. "And your own," he added, getting to his feet.

"I don't matter."

No way was he letting that stand. "A lot of people have spent a lot of grueling hours in the saddle proving otherwise."

Her chin came up. "They have, haven't they?"

"Yes, so do what I tell you and stay alive."

He held out his palm. When she didn't immediately place hers in it, he crooked his fingers. He thought she muttered something about "bossy" before giving him her hand. He pulled her to her feet, steadying her a second while she found her balance. "The gun's heavy, so don't wear out your arm pointing it into empty space. Remember that surprise is your best weapon."

Miguel stopped crying. A creeping unease raised the hairs on the back of Tracker's neck.

Shit.

"Stay here."

"No." Ari grabbed his arm. "He's my son."

"And I'm going to get him, but as mean of a son of a bitch as I am, I can't do what needs to be done if I have to worry about you, too. You interfere and Miguel will die."

Her face went white, but she let Tracker go. "Do you think there's trouble?"

Anything was possible out here. "I'm about to find out."

9

Not a bird sang for the five minutes it took Tracker to creep up on the campsite. Not a breeze stirred. Not a damn thing moved except himself, in a slow, careful crawl across the ground. It was possible Shadow had come back. It was just as possible he hadn't. Until he knew who or what had made Miguel stop crying so abruptly, Tracker wasn't taking any chances. Thirty feet from his goal, he ran out of cover. Kneeling carefully, he brought his rifle up. A man squatted in front of the baby. Too close to the boy for a head shot, and so close a bullet might pass through, making a chest shot risky. Tracker lowered the muzzle, aiming for the stranger's knee.

"Move," he whispered. He held off firing, as something about the man struck a chord. There was nothing distinctive about his clothing, but the way he held his head...

"I think you misplaced something, *amigo*."

Tracker lowered his gun. "What the hell are you doing here, Zacharias?"

"At the moment, quieting this little one so we don't have

that band of *Comancheros* north of here breathing down our necks any sooner than we have to." He looked over his shoulder at Tracker. "Who is the mother?"

"Ari."

Zacharias whistled under his breath. "You found her?"

Tracker nodded. Before he was halfway to Zach, the man came to the obvious conclusion.

"And she had a baby?"

Zach wasn't Isabella's personal bodyguard because he lacked discretion. "Cute kid. Looks Indian," he added.

Tracker nodded again. He could finally see what Zach was doing. He was distracting Miguel with a silver cross strung on a rawhide thong.

"What's his name?"

"Miguel."

Zach twisted the string. Every time sunlight flashed off the bright metal cross, Miguel kicked his feet and waved his hands. "Actually," Zach said, eyeing first Miguel and then Tracker, "he looks enough like you that he could pass for yours."

"He is."

That got him a look. "Now you can perform miracles? Because I'm guessing this boy was conceived while you and I were hunting the Packard gang."

"He's mine by claim, not blood."

"Went Indian on her, eh?"

That was one way of explaining that all-encompassing need to protect Ari that'd consumed him when the men had cornered her in that sleazy bar. The other option would have been murder. He could easily have killed each and every one. And even Zach was fast getting on his nerves. "You looking to get your ass kicked?"

"Not particularly, but you've always been a man who goes

after what he wants, and if you decided you wanted Ari and an opportunity came up…" He shrugged. "It stands to reason you'd take advantage of a God-given chance to have it all."

Zacharias always did see too much.

"A white woman like her isn't going to recognize an Indian marriage." That didn't mean she couldn't be infatuated with him.

"Well, neither would a possessive son of a bitch like you." He chucked Miguel's chin. "It's not permanent enough."

"She needs me."

Zach pursed his lips and nodded. "So you have the advantage."

"Yes." If he wanted a woman who was only with him through fear.

"Are you going to utilize it?"

Tracker shook his head. "There's no point. When her memory returns, the only thing looking at me will do is send her screaming."

"You *are* an ugly son of a bitch."

"I can still probably find the time to kick your ass."

Zach chuckled. Miguel chuckled with him, happy with the attention.

"You think she will scream because you look Indian?"

"Yeah."

Chucking Miguel under the chin again, Zach sighed. "That's going to be a problem, because this little one couldn't look any more Indian. Is she going to turn away from him, too?"

Tracker couldn't imagine it, but Ari had been through hell and back, tortured in spirit, mind and body. She coped by not remembering, but the violence of her episodes made him think those memories might be coming back. And once they did, Miguel would be a living, breathing reminder of every cruelty she'd endured. It would take one hell of a forgiving heart to get past that. How could anyone ask the victim of rape and torture to rise above it? How could anyone blame her if she didn't?

"Speaking of the mother, where is she?"

Tracker swore. "Sitting in the draw with a gun ready to shoot whoever pokes their head over the top."

Zach motioned him on. "Then by all means, you fetch. I'll stay here with Miguel."

"Afraid of getting your pretty face mussed?"

"*Sí*, that is it. For my brains, I have no concerns."

Tracker had forgotten how amusing Zach could be. It was easier to remember how deadly.

"Be sure to announce yourself, eh?"

He did more than announce himself. He made enough noise while approaching the draw to wake the dead. And when he got to the lip, for good measure, he called down. "Ari?"

She didn't answer. His heart skipped a beat for the second time in ten minutes. Shit, he was getting too old for this. There were only so many places a woman could hide. The white of her shirt gave her away. She'd tucked herself beneath a scraggly bush, behind some sagebrush, coiled up like a rattler hiding from the sun. By squinting, he could see the gun barrel pointed at the draw. She was clearly ready to strike.

Half walking, half sliding down the washout, he asked, "Are you all right?"

"Yes."

He'd feel more comfortable about that response if she didn't have such a white-knuckled grip on that gun. "Want to hand me that before someone gets hurt?"

"What? Oh?" She tossed the gun in the dirt in front of her. Tracker winced, imagining the sand in the barrel.

"Worried it might go off?"

"Yup." And now he was worried it couldn't.

"Me, too."

"Where's Miguel?" With both hands she started tugging at the branches above her head.

"With a friend." He picked up the gun and inspected it. "Problems?"

There didn't seem to be any sand in the barrel.

"Nope." Ari worked her way free of the web of branches she'd crawled beneath. She broke off several in succession, letting them dangle from her hair. "Where did you find a friend in the middle of nowhere?"

Tracker held out his hand, palm up. "Sometimes, sweets, you find friends in the strangest places."

When he did so, she placed hers in it. He drew her to her feet.

"Where's Shadow?"

"He'll be along soon. He went to find water."

"Who is this friend?"

"Zacharias is one of the Montoyas' top men. When hell opens its gates, he's the one who wanders in to stir up trouble."

The twigs looked ridiculous hanging from her hair. Tracker's fingers twitched to untangle the heavy mass. If they weren't standing in the middle of Comanchero country he'd have given in to the urge.

"Who are the Montoyas? Should I be impressed?"

"Sam MacGregor is Hell's Eight. He married Isabella Montoya. The Montoya spread is quite big." Tracker took a twig from her hand. A couple strands of hair that were stuck on it wrapped around his finger. He did love that wild hair of hers. It said more than anything else that here was a woman a man could cajole, but never tame. "And yeah, you should be impressed."

Another stick was removed and placed in his hand. "Then I'm impressed."

The next stick looked like it was going to take a while. "He'll go to hell and back for one of ours. Otherwise I wouldn't have left him there."

She headed in the direction of the campsite. "Thank you."

She was in a surprisingly agreeable mood. Falling into step beside her, he said, "Shadow told me what he said to you."

She kept walking, not looking at him. "He did?"

"Yes, he did."

"I'm surprised."

"I may not agree with all what Shadow decides is important, but he's my brother, and we don't lie to each other."

She skipped a step to keep up with Tracker's longer stride. "He loves you very much."

"That doesn't make it all right."

"It makes it understandable, though. No one wants a family member to take up with a crazy woman."

"You're not crazy, and the last time someone told me what to do, I was in knee pants." Tracker shortened his stride. He could probably get the stick out if he made a couple strategic cuts.

"Stop staring."

He took her elbow and helped her up the hillside. "You have a stick in your hair."

"Tell me something I don't know."

He could do that. "Your sister loves you, too."

There was a break in her stride. "Does she?"

"Yes. She does. She's had us scouring the country for a year for you without really knowing if you were alive or dead."

They were almost back at the campsite.

"I don't remember her."

"You will eventually."

"Maybe." She really didn't believe her memory would come back.

When they got back to the site, Zach had Miguel out of the cradleboard and was bouncing him on his knee. The baby was giggling and drooling, clutching the cross in his hand. Zach stood as soon as he saw Ari.

"*Hola,* Mrs. Ochoa."

Ari cut Tracker a glance. "You convinced him of that nonsense?"

"He's gullible."

Zach laughed. "You are as beautiful as *tu hermana*."

"You know…" She stumbled over the name. "Desi, then?"

Zach shrugged. "Not so well as I know Sally Mae, Señor Tucker's wife. Or Isabella MacGregor, La Montoya. She is a fighter, La Montoya. Her I have been with since she was an *hija*."

"Sally Mae is a pacifist," Tracker interjected.

Zach snorted. "Only until you fall sick. Then she is all orders, and if you try to get out of bed…" He rolled his eyes. "Then she is mean as a pinned badger."

"So stay in bed."

"By myself?" Zach shook his head and swung Miguel in his arms. "This is not done."

Tracker had also forgotten how charming Zach could be. When Ari smiled, he took her arm and steered her away from

Zach, toward a small rock, the only approximation of a chair there was. "Why don't you sit here and see about getting Miguel some lunch."

Zach passed him the baby, a knowing smile on his lips. He was too damn handsome for his own good. Bastard. "Thank you."

"De nada."

"Is Sally Mae really mean?" Ari asked, settling Miguel against her.

"Sally Mae is as sweet as honey. Zach is just a lousy patient."

Zach snorted. "A man can stay in bed only so long."

Ari might buy that dismissal of concern, but Tracker knew the extent of Zach's injuries. "Seems to me you should still be in it."

"When Shadow sent a message he was coming down here, I could not resist following."

"So basically, no one follows your orders," Ari observed to Tracker as she draped a blanket over her shoulder.

He took a position between Zach and her, blocking the other man's view. "Apparently not."

Zach rolled his right shoulder. Tracker spotted the stiffness in the joint and the way Zach favored the right side of his body.

"Those ribs still stove up?"

He shrugged. "Not so much I couldn't come to help."

"What made you think I needed help?"

Zach's horse whickered a greeting to something in the dusk. A horse whinnied back. Ari held very still and looked at Tracker. He mouthed, "Shadow." She relaxed, but not much.

Zach shrugged. "There was something about the way you

left that told me, this one, she is the one. Shadow sensed the same."

"Who's talking about me?" Shadow entered the campsite, leading the string of horses.

"I am."

"How the hell are you, Zach?" Shadow cast Tracker a glance. "That Buster of yours has to shake hands with everything that moves. Edible or otherwise."

Tracker took the reins and chuckled. "He does have a social side." Tracker started unpacking the saddlebags.

Miguel fussed. Ari shifted him to the other breast. Tracker led the horse aside. Shadow and Zach followed.

"You spoil that animal," Shadow said.

Tracker shrugged. "He runs when I need him to."

His brother jerked his thumb in Ari's direction. "And her, is she going to run like the wind?"

"You take what life gives you, Shadow. You know that. For however long it gives you."

"You think life's giving you her?"

"For now." Buster bumped him with his head. Tracker scratched the gelding behind his ears. "She needs me."

"And you need her."

Yes. "If anything happens to me, Shadow, you stand in my stead with her."

"You married her?"

"In our father's way."

"That means you're packing up and leaving soon, too?"

Their father's abandonment had hit Shadow harder than Tracker. Probably because Shadow had clung longer to the belief that they ever had a chance of pleasing the miserable son of a bitch.

"Not if I have a say."

"Shit. You might not have a say."

"She doesn't know her past, she doesn't know her future. She lives tossed between the chaos of the episodes and the present. Until she can face what happened, I've promised to hold her safe."

"When she does remember, there's no guarantee she'll stomach your touch."

"Tell me something I don't know."

"Do you have a plan for that?"

"I'm working on it."

Shadow's expression didn't hold out much hope for his nonexistent plan. "I hope it's a good one."

Zach interrupted. "There's something we need to discuss."

"Shoot."

"Yesterday I spotted a band of *Comancheros* riding hard this way."

"Probably Antonio and his crew."

"You know this man?"

"I've heard of him."

"Last night, I overheard them talking." Zach said that as if it were nothing.

"Jesus. You crept close enough to a Comanchero camp to hear them talk?"

"We needed to know their plans."

Zach had an utter disregard for safety. In many ways he reminded Tracker of Sam. Same devil-take-the-hindmost air. Same willingness to risk it all.

"And?"

"The one that hunts her. He is making a special trip."

Shadow straightened. "Well, that's good news."

"He's actually coming out here?" Tracker asked.

"It was said that if the *Comancheros* can bring Ari, Desi or the baby to San Antonio before the eighteenth, there is an extra thirty thousand in it for them."

So the bastard would be within reach. San Antonio was a ten-hour ride from Hell's Eight. Hell's Eight had friends in San Antonio. "Dollars?"

"Sí. Dolares."

Word of a bounty that high would have every lowlife saddle bum in the state looking for Desi and Ari.

"Anything else?" Damn, he hoped there wasn't anything else.

"Yes."

Tracker braced himself.

"I sent a signal to Hell's Eight to ride to the east corner."

He should have known Zach would know about Hell's Eight sentries strategically positioned around their land, and the smoke-signal system they used to communicate across their territory. Being high-spirited Isabella's bodyguard was enough of a challenge that Zacharias was committed to finding new ways of securing Montoya lands from outside threats.

"I also left a note at drop-off four as to where they should be waiting for us."

Hell's Eight also had locations around their land where they could leave information for each other.

"You know about the blind canyon?"

"He's the one who showed it to me," Shadow interjected.

"It was how we escaped the *Comancheros* last time."

Tracker had wondered how he and his men had cheated certain death.

"You are a very clever man, Zach."

He smiled a smile that didn't lighten his expression. *"Sí,* this is true."

"So, where are the *Comancheros* now?"

"Still north of here."

"How did that happen?"

Zach smiled and shrugged. "They were delayed at Jake's Point."

"How long do we have?"

"We'll be cutting it close. Anger makes a man ride harder."

"So does greed," Tracker added drily.

"True."

"Sneaking is going to be tough. One cry from Miguel…"

Zach knelt and sketched the area. "I have a plan. When we get to Borracho, here, I will take the horses and ride around. They will see the tracks. They will follow."

"And while you're doing that?"

"You will climb the canyon wall."

"If they catch you, Zach, it won't be pretty."

He shrugged. "Then I won't be caught."

"There is a difficulty with the plan," Shadow interrupted.

"What?"

"If they're at Jake's Point, we can't wait to avoid the heat of the day. We'll have to climb as soon as we get there."

It would be brutal for a man to make a climb that steep with the summer sun beating down. For a woman and child, it would be almost impossible.

"From what I saw, I am not sure Ari will make it," Zach said cautiously.

"She'll make it," Tracker countered. If he had to carry her himself.

"Even if he has to carry her," Shadow added.

Tracker stood. His twin stood right along with him. "What is your problem?" Tracker demanded.

"You care too much about her."

"What business is that of yours?"

"I'm the one who will have to watch you hurt."

"I've hurt before."

Shadow shook his head. "Not like this. You've never given your heart."

Zach stood in turn and rubbed out the map with his boot. "The heart goes where the heart goes, Shadow. It is a man's lot to follow."

"Who the hell told you that?"

"*Mi padre.*"

"And he was an authority?"

"He taught me everything I know."

Tracker wasn't surprised when Shadow didn't scoff. Zach was loyal to the core. A down-and-dirty fighter who always came out on top. He commanded loyalty the way others commanded smiles. He was a good man. Sam's best. And he was risking his life again for Hell's Eight.

"Then I guess I won't be arguing." Shadow rolled a cigarette and placed it, unlit, in his mouth. They couldn't risk the scent to smoke carrying in the night breeze.

"When you get back to Hell's Eight, you can light that."

"I'm looking forward to it."

"I want a hot meal." Tracker sighed. "I'm getting damn tired of trail food."

Shadow grabbed a pouch out of a saddlebag. "We've got jerky and cornbread."

Tracker glanced over at Ari. Miguel was done feeding, but was still fussing.

"Could her milk be drying up?"

"Jesus, she's not a cow, Shadow."

"Not surprising, the way we've been dragging her all over creation."

"If he is hungry, it will be a problem keeping him quiet tomorrow," Zach said, all joking gone.

"Yeah." Could a body even gag a baby?

"You will have to give him something to eat to take his mind off his stomach."

Tracker set aside a biscuit.

Shadow nodded. "That will do. I'll bring it to her."

He took the food over to Ari. She stiffened slightly as he sat down, but didn't tell him to go to hell. And when he broke off a smidgen of biscuit and put it on Miguel's tongue, Tracker saw her relax.

Zach clapped him on his shoulder. "They will work it out, my friend."

"She'll probably be gone before there's a resolution."

"Maybe, but remember, not all things that start bad end that way."

"You keep believing that." But he wasn't taking a chance on Shadow's and Ari's truce falling apart tonight. Tracker went to sit beside Ari.

Shadow stood. "Zach and I will take watch."

He was giving them privacy. Tracker nodded. "Thank you."

By the time Shadow reached Zach, the biscuit softened on Miguel's tongue, and the boy stopped trying to spit it out, his eyes bugged.

Tracker laughed. "He's Hell's Eight for sure."

She looked at him, surprised. "What makes you think that?"

"Because there isn't a man on Hell's Eight who isn't in love with biscuits."

The boy's arms waved as he finished the biscuit. Tracker broke a piece off his and put it on Miguel's tongue.

"He's a good boy."

"Yeah. He is." A boy who might have been his son, had life been different.

Ari watched Miguel chew. Was she making sure he didn't choke or avoiding Tracker's gaze? "I'm thinking of changing his name."

In that case, likely the latter. "Why would you do that?"

"Josefina named him after who I thought was his father. Antonio Miguel. Knowing what I know now, I don't want him to carry that taint."

"It's how he's raised that's going to matter."

"I know." She looked up. "But what if I don't do it right?"

"I imagine every parent has that worry."

"But I don't have any memories to draw from."

That had to be terrifying. "You're doing fine."

She was scared and wanting reassurance. The longing to be held was in her eyes. Tracker would give her anything she wanted, but the first move had to come from her. He'd burned all the bridges he could spare.

"Tracker." She rested Miguel on the blanket. He lay quietly, blinking sleepily.

"Yeah?"

"Could you hold me for just a minute?"

He opened his arms. She moved in. Things were right as soon as her cheek rested against his chest. "What's up?"

"I saw Zach talking to you earlier. None of you looked happy."

"And that's got you worried?"

"Yes."

"We were discussing tomorrow's plan."

"What do you need me to do?"

"Eat and rest."

"Translated, that means it's going to be strenuous."

"Yes. We'll be climbing."

"I'm sorry I got you into this."

"You didn't get me into anything." He rubbed his hand up her back. "But you led me a merry chase."

"And now you've found me."

"Yup." He wanted to kiss the top of her head, the curve of her ear, the fullness of her mouth. He wanted to kiss her until the worry left her expression and passion filled it. He wanted to kiss her until she was too weak and too satisfied to ever consider walking away.

There was a long pause while Ari rested against him. Probably to everyone else she appeared to be resting, but he could feel the tension building inside her. He waited for her to get to the point.

"Is she really waiting for me?"

He knew who she was talking about. "Desi sets a place for you at the table every day."

"That could just be for show."

Tracker figured Desi would forgive him for this particular revelation. "Every night, Caine says she cries that your chair goes empty."

Ari had no comment on that. "What is she like?"

"She's like you. Full of spit and fire. She makes Caine laugh, when we'd all thought he'd forgotten how."

Ari played with the fringe on his shirt. "Is Caine good to her?"

"You wouldn't think Caine would be a romantic man, but

he spoils that woman, and he'd fillet anyone that brought a tear to her eyes."

"He loves her."

"With everything in him, and that's a lot." The little Tracker could see of her expression looked skeptical. "You've got to understand, Ari, that none of the Hell's Eight have had an easy life. If it hadn't been for Tia, we would have lost any sense of conscience before we hit twenty."

"Tia?"

"The real head of Hell's Eight. The one who keeps us human. Since the massacre, we've been living more for revenge. That eats at a man. Makes him hard inside. When a man finds something that takes that loneliness away, he holds on to it. No matter what."

"That's not love."

"It's Hell's Eight love. Absolute, with no looking back."

"And Caine, Sam and Tucker have found that something?"

"Yes."

"What about you? Do you love that way?"

"I've never had the pleasure of being in love before. But I can tell you this, I'm as all-or-nothing as the rest of Hell's Eight."

"You can't love me."

Out of that whole speech, she'd picked up on the one thing he hadn't meant to reveal. "I'll keep that in mind."

"It doesn't make sense. We hardly know each other."

"I know."

"I'm not even a whole person."

That was going too far. "A person is more than their memories, but with or without yours, you still have your sense of humor, your courage, your temper—"

"I don't have a temper."

"The hell you don't."

She amended the claim. "I try not to have a temper."

"That I'll allow."

She sat back and put her hands on her hips. "Who are you to tell me what I can and cannot do?"

"Who are you to tell me the same?"

"I didn't tell you to do anything."

"You told me I couldn't love you."

She shifted in his grip. "Well, you can't."

"As I said, I'll keep it in mind."

"You're not very obedient."

"Probably because, in bed, I give the orders."

That drew a small gasp, but she didn't move away. He could work with that.

"I'm thinking about sitting you across my lap and taking advantage of this rock as a back rest. How does that sound?"

"Perfect!"

He chuckled. "Your back hurting that bad?"

"You have no idea."

"Come here then, sweets, and let me make it all better."

He held out his arms. She went back into his embrace and he pulled her onto his lap as though she belonged there.

The trust she showed with that simple gesture humbled him. She was a smart woman, a sweet woman and a trusting one. A woman who led with her heart. A woman who made a man's home a haven. A woman who needed a man's protection to flourish.

"What are you thinking?"

"I'm thinking if your daddy was here he'd be feeding my balls to the dogs."

"You think?"

"Yup."

"My daddy was a forgiving man, but he would have had something to say about my sitting on your lap in public."

Had she remembered her father? "Shadow and Zacharias don't count as public."

"They don't?"

Nothing in her expression indicated she realized what she'd said. Instinct said it would be a bad move to point out the slip. Besides, she felt good in his lap. And as brutal as tomorrow was going to be, he needed a little peace now. "Nah, they'll keep my secrets."

Ari's hand crept up his shoulder to touch his neck just above the collar of his shirt. "Good."

A few minutes passed, then she said, "How bad is it going to be tomorrow, Tracker?"

"Bad. You're going to want to cry and give up."

"But I won't."

He shook his head and kissed the top of hers. "No. You won't."

"Why?"

"Because once we get to the top of that canyon, we'll be on Hell's Eight land."

"So I've just got to get over that hill."

"One step at time. That's all it'll take."

"Thousands of one steps."

"But you only have to take them one at a time."

"It does sound more manageable when put that way."

"Good."

Minutes passed during which he thought she'd fallen asleep, but then she whispered, "Tracker?"

Weariness was taking hold of him, too. In a few moments he'd have to go see what arrangements Shadow and Zach had made for keeping watch, but right now he could hold her as night fell, and pretend they were back on Hell's Eight, sitting in a rocking chair on the big porch. In his fantasy, there was no threat of a past to come screaming forward to hack up any possibility of a future. Just two people enjoying each other's company. "Yes?"

Tilting her head back, she studied his face with blue eyes that were luminous in the dusk. "I heard what you said earlier. About never having loved anyone before."

Everything inside him went tight. It had been a long time since anyone dared mock him. His reaction was never good.

"Do you think you love me, Tracker?"

Think? He knew it. "What I feel is of no concern to you."

"What if I want it to concern me?"

"Then I'd say for the first time since I've met you, I think you're crazy."

Her hand crept around his side. The other slid around his neck. He looked down. Her blue eyes were soft in the light. Completely enchanting. His own private little witch woman weaving her spell… His cock went hard in a rush. Stupid thing didn't even care that they had no privacy. It just wanted to be in her, part of her. Home.

"We might die tomorrow."

It wasn't a shock to hear her say it. He knew she was frightened.

"I told you we'll make it."

"I understand, but I want a memory."

"Of what?"

Her fingers slid delicately up and down his neck. A tingle shot down his spine. "Of you, kissing me with love."

Could she feel the pending return of the memories? Did she fear what it would mean? "I've already kissed you."

"That was with passion."

He didn't want to go there. If he let the emotion inside him out, he'd never be able to walk away. Or let her walk away.

Her fingers closed into a fist.

"You're asking too much."

"You said once that you'd give me anything."

Yes, he had. And hell, what did it matter? He wanted that memory, too. He started unbuttoning her blouse.

"What are you doing?"

"I'm going to kiss you with love, but I want to see these pretty little breasts while I'm doing it."

"Zach and Shadow…"

"Will respect our privacy, and even if they don't, all they'll see is me holding you."

He slid his hand inside her blouse and under her camisole, and cupped her breast in his palm. Her shiver was a balm to his conscience. "I like that," he murmured.

"What?"

"Your nipple poking into my palm, demanding attention."

"A woman doesn't make demands."

He laughed and kissed her nose. "You don't have to make demands. Whatever you want in bed, I'll give to you."

Resting her head against his shoulder, she pursed her lips in a silent order.

He pressed his thumb against her mouth. He couldn't remember having such natural innocence. He couldn't match it, but he could value it. Cherish it. No matter what had happened to Ari before, this was the real woman. The woman who led with her heart and didn't hold back. He spread tiny kisses from her temple to her mouth, gentling her with tenderness, because for all her big talk, she was nervous. Nervous of tomorrow, of him. Nervous of what she was asking, because she had to know there was no going back after this. Not for him. But just in case she didn't, he rubbed his mouth over hers, kissing the corners, touching them with his tongue, nibbling, enticing them to open with light, feathery little touches.

"If we do this, there's no going back." He had to say it.

Her fingers locked behind his neck. She touched her tongue to his lower lip. It was his turn to shiver. "All I have behind me are lies."

He held her gaze. "If I kiss you the way you're asking, take from you what you're offering, no matter what the future brings, no matter what you remember, I won't let you go."

"Good."

Shit.

She pulled him down, and he went, taking her mouth with a smooth thrust. Hungry for the taste of her, finding the same hunger in her. Kissing her for the first time, maybe the last time, with no barriers between them. Just two people in this moment. Kissing her until he couldn't breathe, and then because he couldn't stop. Kissing her as she'd asked. Kissing her as if he loved her.

10

Brutal didn't begin to describe the next day's journey. The ride was hard. The sun hot. Miguel, trapped in his cradle-board, was as hot as the rest of them, and refused to be soothed. It was a nonstop job to keep him from screaming too loudly. Even the silver cross Zacharias dangled in front of his face failed to work its magic. By the time they reached Drunk Hole, everyone's nerves were on edge.

It was easy to see the more frequented path they might have traveled. It snaked among the brush and rocks, worn deep from all the wildlife that relied on the water source. The path to the blind canyon was not so clear. At a bend in the trail, Shadow motioned for them to get down from the horses.

"We'll walk from here so we don't leave any more of a trail than necessary."

From there they traveled single file. Ari carried Miguel on her back and wore a pair of Zach's boots stuffed with socks. They hoped, from the size of the shoe and the depth of the impression, it wouldn't be so obvious to anyone picking up the trail that she was female. Ari looked back at the wobbly tracks she made and shook her head. "Maybe they'll think I'm drunk."

Zach smiled. "Wouldn't be the first time."

She executed a drunken stumble. Only Zach smiled. A closer look revealed it as being so fake it wasn't worth bothering. The men exchanged glances and Zach gathered the reins of all the horses and led them away. He would circle around to lay a false trail.

Shadow and Tracker constantly scanned the high walls of the narrow canyon. They walked in deeper. The walls loomed higher. A flock of crows flew up in front of them, calling a warning. Ari jumped.

The height of the walls and the narrowness of the path gave the impression that they were walking into a yawning mouth that only had to close to swallow them up forever. "This is creepy," Ari mumbled.

The only blessing was the high walls kept the blistering sun off her skin. The slightly cooler temperature was welcome in the oppressive heat.

Tracker lifted his rifle into position against his shoulder. Shadow, too, had his rifle ready to fire.

"What is it?" she whispered.

"We're coming to the end of the canyon."

The part where their brutal little trip was supposed to get worse. The part where they would be exposed. The part where it could all fall apart. Ari shifted the straps of Miguel's cradleboard on her shoulders. She wasn't sure she could do this. Already her shoulders were bruised and her thighs ached. Already Miguel's weight seemed to have doubled.

You can make it. One step at a time.

That's all she needed to remember. One step at time. She'd

promised Tracker. She'd promised Miguel. She'd promised herself. One step at a time.

She wiped the sweat from her brow with her shoulder. More immediately formed. Miguel whimpered. Behind her, she heard Shadow move forward. Miguel's whimper changed to a coo. There were sides to Tracker's twin that surprised her. She could see him shooting up saloons. She could see him killing a man, but she never would've guessed he was an excellent nursemaid. But he was. An example being the way he kept wiping Miguel's face with precious water from his canteen so the little boy wouldn't overheat.

She turned, wincing as the ropes pressed into her shoulders.

"Thank you."

Shadow didn't smile. She wondered if he even could, or if the muscles in his face had atrophied into that solemn expression.

"It's the least I could do for my nephew."

She opened her mouth to deny the claim.

Do not be so quick to deny him a place.

Whatever problems Shadow had with her, they were with her and not with her son. According to all the rumors and tall tales that surrounded the men of Hell's Eight, Shadow was a ruthless enemy and an honorable man. She might not remember the past, but the last eleven months had proved to her that a strong, honorable, ruthless man was good to have around. Miguel would need someone like that in his life. Feeling awkward, unsure and definitely not welcome, she smiled at Shadow. "Thank you for that, too."

He glanced behind him. She couldn't help but look, too, though there was nothing to see except rocks, canyon walls and the scrub that clung to both.

"What I said before…I'm sorry."

"When you threatened me?"

"Yeah."

"You meant it, though, didn't you?"

"I love my brother."

She sighed. "Because I care for him, too, I'm going to pretend that was not a threat, but concern in a different guise."

Her next glance over her shoulder was worth the pain. Shadow actually looked surprised.

"You weren't threatening me?" she asked.

"I was just explaining…"

He really wasn't good at apologies. "It's all right. I think, in the same position, I'd do the same," she told him.

His surprise turned to shock. Ahead, she saw Tracker cast a wary glance back, and it suddenly struck her that her place between the two brothers was entirely too symbolic. Family was too important. She couldn't be the bone of contention that broke them apart. Speaking just loudly enough for Tracker to hear, she said, "Thank you, Shadow. I appreciate all you've done for me."

It was kind of good to get a last word in. It was even better to see the pleasure on Tracker's face. Such a small sacrifice on her part to forgive a man who would give his life to protect her son. And her, too, simply because it was the right thing to do. She'd been as guilty as all the others—using the brothers' skills to her advantage without seeing the men behind those skills. Oh, she saw Tracker. The beauty of his spirit behind his eyes. But Shadow she'd judged on his appearance. He looked wild and mean, so she'd decided he was.

When she looked back, Shadow was studying her as if she were some strange sort of bug he'd never seen before, and he wasn't sure if she was going to be beneficial or deadly. She allowed herself a small smile. Let him wonder about that.

She stumbled over her boot and put out her hand. The wall was right there. Wonderful. The canyon was getting narrower. Her skin crawled as the walls seemed to loom higher. Anyone could be hiding up there. And if someone was, the four of them were sitting ducks.

Please, Lord, don't let Comancheros be up on those walls.

A soft whistle came from ahead. Tracker stopped and walked back to her. The dim, flat light of the canyon was kinder to his face than the sun, softening the harsh planes, diminishing the appearance of the scar, bringing attention to the sensual fullness of his mouth and the beauty of his bedroom eyes. She wanted to snatch the hat off his head and run her fingers through his hair, wrap it around her shoulders and bind them together.

"Why are we stopping?"

"A few feet ahead we'll be in the open and we start climbing. Are you ready?"

No. She wasn't ready. She hadn't had a chance to make love to him in a bed. She hadn't had the courage to tell him she loved him, too. That she saw him as more than a man who could save her. Tell him that, though she didn't remember her past, the moment she saw him she'd recognized him in an elemental way. That she couldn't imagine her future without him in it.

"Yes."

"Good. Let's get you ready."

Tracker pulled that nasty-looking knife from his belt. "Take off your skirt."

"I beg your pardon?" She looked from him to Shadow. "I'm not getting undressed."

Shadow eased the cradleboard from her back. For a moment there was no weight, no pain, no feeling. For a moment there was peace. It was a very brief moment. From behind came the distant caw of angry crows.

"Sounds like we've got company," Shadow said.

Comancheros. They were coming for her. Lights started flashing before her eyes. A roar filled her ears. She stumbled as the ground seemed to tilt. *Oh no!* She recognized the signs. She couldn't have an episode now. She couldn't.

One step at a time.

Tracker's low drawl rumbled over the roar. Yes. She could do this, one step at a time. She reached out desperately, needing an anchor. For a moment she found nothing but air, but then the hard, callused warmth of Tracker's hand closed around hers. The lights faded. She took a breath. Another flash of light. Another breath.

"Tracker."

His hand squeezed hers. "Right here."

Someone else's hand awkwardly touched her shoulder. A scream stuck in her throat.

"Put your head between your knees."

Shadow. It was Shadow touching her. And he wanted her to do what? She didn't think she could do that even as a child.

"I think she's supposed to be sitting first," Tracker offered.

"Shit."

She was hustled to a rock and sat down so hard she gasped. She would've complained except the small pain broke the hold of the lights. And she could breathe.

Until her head was shoved between her knees.

"Let me up."

"In a minute," Shadow said.

"Now." Before she puked.

"I'll just do this while you're recuperating," Tracker said, tossing her skirt up over her knee.

"Hey!" *This* was that wicked knife hacking through her petticoats. "What are you doing?"

"You can't climb in that skirt or those boots."

"But I can't be—" the knife sliced through her petticoats from crotch to hem "—naked."

Shadow chuckled. "This you can trust me on. Tracker would never have you naked in front of anyone else. He's a possessive son of a bitch."

That was little comfort as the air blew over her inner thighs.

Tracker cut the pieces of petticoat he'd removed into strips, and started wrapping them around her legs. By the time he got to her knees she understood what he was doing. He was making pants for her. When he cut off a foot of fabric from the bottom of her skirt, though, she started having concerns. "I hope you packed the other skirt."

"I need this to wrap your feet and hands, otherwise they will be cut to shreds."

She was nearly naked in front of two men, with the sun burning skin that had never felt its touch before. "Well, as long as I'm being scandalous for a good reason."

Tracker stopped tying a knot at the side of her knee and cupped her calf with his hand. Heat seeped through the material to her skin and then to the nerve endings beneath. His dark eyes took on a smile that spread to the corners of his mouth. And even sitting there in the open, she felt a trickle of arousal.

"No one will look at you cockeyed."

She tested the wraps. Surprisingly, though it felt weird, she could move her legs. "Says you."

"Yes. Says me. Your husband. The man with a reputation for being touchy."

His hand left her leg to cup the side of her face. His thumb settled against her lips. "And I intend to be very touchy about you."

"Good." She breathed the word against his thumb, leaning her cheek into his palm.

Tracker stroked her cheek with a finger. Taking his hat off with his other hand, he plopped it on her head. "You're getting red."

It immediately fell over her brow. "I can't see a thing with this on."

Tracker took the last strip of her petticoat and tied the hat around her head.

"I must look a sight," she murmured.

He kissed her lips, the soft way he had last night. The way she knew meant "I love you."

"I'm not concerned with how you look. I'm concerned with how you arrive at the top."

"And how will that be?"

"Alive."

She tested the wrapping again. She could bend her knees, to a point. She held out her hand. Tucker took it immediately. She stood, turned around and looked up. All the way up.

"What's wrong?" He was too intuitive.

She rubbed her palm down her thigh and tried not to think about how exposed she was. "I'm going up the canyon wall."

"One step at a time."

She was beginning to hate that phrase.

"You're going to need your strength. It's going to be a…" Shadow stopped, obviously reconsidering his choice of words. "Devil of a climb."

Ari was touched. It was the first time the man had moderated his language around her.

The canyon face was a dull brown, interrupted with splotches of green and gray rock. It seemed to go on forever. "How far do we have to climb?"

Shadow pointed to a notch three-quarters of the way up. "There."

They were wasting time and it was a long way up. She squeezed Tracker's hand. "Would this be a bad time to mention I think I might be afraid of heights?"

"You are?"

"I really can't remember, but I think it might be a good idea to become afraid. Trying to climb that is crazy."

"It's our way home, sweets. And I promised to bring you home."

He took out a length of rope and tied it around his waist. "What is that for?"

"I'm not taking any chances on you falling."

She drew a breath and took a step in her new fancy "pants". "Well, then I guess there's no sense putting it off."

"That's good, because we've got company coming."

"Son of a bitch. There goes the plan." Tracker grabbed his supplies off the ground before tying the other end of the rope around her waist. "How many do you think, Shadow?"

"Sounds like only about ten horses. Half probably followed Zach. Better odds, at least." But they'd all be heavily armed. *Comancheros.*

They definitely needed to go. Without waiting for prompting from Tracker, Ari grabbed up Miguel's cradleboard. When she tried to slide it onto her shoulders, her arms could barely move. They were too stiff from the bite of the rope. The climb would be unbearable.

Shadow took it from her. "From this point, I'll carry him."

She got a sick feeling in her stomach. "I can do it."

"You can't climb with the extra weight." Shadow looked at Tracker. Tracker looked back. The men looked at her.

"What?" The sick feeling in her stomach was never wrong.

"We can't be sure they won't be shooting at you."

Her knees threatened to buckle. "I thought they wanted me. That's why they were holding me hostage."

"You've got a son now. If you and your sister are dead, he inherits."

"Money?"

Tracker's expression was grim. "A lot of it."

"I'm an heiress?"

"Yes."

So that's who she was. A woman with money. A woman used to the finer things. A woman used to having things done for her rather than doing them herself. A woman who had had everything. She looked at her hands, with their split nails and calluses. A woman who had lost it all. A woman who stood to lose it all again. A cold, empty feeling spread through her gut.

"You keep him then," she told Shadow as the feeling spread, numbing her fear, her hope, an inner pain she couldn't remember. Grabbing a ledge, she started climbing. Tracker moved around her, climbing with an ease she envied, taking the lead. Stones fell on her hands and hair.

"I'd rather go first," she told him.

"Sorry, sweets." The apology didn't sound sincere. He handed her a knife.

She reached for it warily. "What's this for?"

"First in line clears the path of snakes."

She jerked her hand back. "I changed my mind."

Tracker might be a handsome man, and he might be charming, but she wanted to smack the smile off his face. "I thought you would."

A chuckle came from right behind her. She glared at Shadow. Damn him, he was smiling, too. "I want a gun."

"No."

"Don't say no. I have my reasons."

"You're not clattering up that rock wall with a gun in your hand."

"You're carrying one."

Tracker's hand on her butt urged her forward. "But I'm not likely to shoot off my foot."

"I'll bite," Shadow interjected. "What's your reason?"

She tentatively put her hand on the rock above; thinking of snakes made her think of spiders and scorpions. " I'm going to shoot the first man who looks at my bloomers."

Unbelievably, Tracker laughed. Overtaking her, he wrapped his hand under her braid, tilted her head back and kissed her lips. "There'll be no worry about that."

"Not if you give me a gun."

"You don't need a gun." He gave her another kiss and a swat on her ass.

"Why not?"

"Because if there's any shooting that needs to be done, I'll be doing it." His hand skimmed down her body, grazing her butt as she crawled upward. "And I'm the better shot."

"Well, I don't want you looking up my bloomers, either."

Shadow laughed. "Now there is something every man wants to hear."

"Oh, shut up." She liked it better when Shadow had been quiet.

"He's only speaking the truth, sweets," Tracker stated.

"Has anybody ever told you that you're both very contrary men?"

"I don't think it's ever been put quite that way before."

"Then let me be the first."

"Duly noted." He looked back down the blind canyon. "Now, sweets…"

"What?"

"Get that cute ass moving."

Looking down, she could see why. Riders followed the same path they had, weaving among the trees and rocks, distance making them look like small ants. Ants that were rapidly getting closer. The *Comancheros* were heavily armed. The flashes of light off their weapons were almost blinding.

She started climbing as if the hounds of hell were after her, which they were. Snakes, scorpions and spiders weren't anywhere near as scary as *Comancheros*.

Halfway up, the shooting started. Bullets pinged off rocks, splattered into the dirt. She looked down. The *Comancheros* had dismounted when the canyon became too narrow for their horses, and were nearing the base of the of the cliff wall on foot. Some of them started to climb.

Tracker came up beside her, while Shadow lagged behind. Shielding her, she understood, putting their bodies between the bullets and her son. Just as they reached the ledge that Shadow had shown her, he slid his arms out of the cradleboard and shoved it at her. "Take him."

He took a position behind a rock, pulled his rifle off his

back and took aim. There was a gunshot, then a scream. When she looked down again, the *Comancheros* were diving for cover.

Their shouts echoed up the canyon, echoed in her blood. Horrible. Threatening. Familiar. The bright light splintered behind her eyes. So familiar. The shouts were so familiar. Tracker grabbed her arm and hauled her up against him.

"Not now," he growled. "Move!"

Yes. She needed to move. But she couldn't. Her fingers were locked on the stones and her feet stuck in the sand on the ledge on which they stood.

Tracker dragged her behind the rocks and spun her around. His hand anchored at the base of her braid. His mouth slammed down on hers. Hard. Hot. Pain followed by tenderness, so much tenderness. She anchored herself in the softness of the emotion, letting the lights beat harmlessly in the background.

"Not now," he growled against her lips. "You can't afford to fall apart now." Tracker kissed her again, his big body sheltering her and Miguel. "You need to climb, for yourself, for your son."

For them. "One step at a time," she gasped.

"Exactly." His gaze narrowed on her face. He looked every inch the warrior, his expression hard, the scar on his cheek white with tension. A man not to be trifled with. A man to be believed in. "Don't look down. No matter what you hear, just keep looking up."

"And keep climbing."

"You've got it. It's your job to get Miguel out of here."

She touched her fingers to Tracker's hair, holding it in her fist as Miguel did, wishing she had his blind faith that everything was going to be all right.

"And yours is to come back to me."

"Mine is to keep you alive."

She shook her head, knowing there was no time left. She had to leave. "You owe me a night in your bed."

"Since when?"

"Since now." She pressed her fingertips against his lips. Her fingers were shaking. She didn't care. This couldn't be the last time she saw him. It couldn't. "Promise me you'll make it."

"Ari…"

She pressed harder, cutting off the truth he always gave her. "A full night. You and me together in a bed with nothing but love between us. Promise me that."

For a second, he didn't move or say anything. For a second she couldn't breathe. Then he pressed a kiss against her fingertips.

"Deal."

It wasn't a promise, but she'd take it.

"Now, get Miguel out of here."

Clever of him to put it like that. For herself, she might not try so hard, but for Miguel? For Miguel she'd do anything. She scaled the canyon wall as fast as she could, heading toward the notch Shadow had pointed out, taking chances on footholds and handholds, scrambling to keep her balance on the loose rock and narrow ledges. Tracker was right behind her all the way, his big body shielding her from the few bullets sporadically hitting around them, as Shadow laid down intense cover fire.

Her foot slipped. Her knee slammed into a rock. Pain shot through her leg. Against Tracker's warning, she looked down. Oh my God, they were coming up fast. More bullets pinged off the rocks around them. Tracker grabbed her shoulder and shoved her to the right, into a channel carved between the rocks. It offered protection.

A rapid rattle started immediately. She froze. A knife blade flashed over her head. Blood splattered her face. A snake's head dropped beside her. The rattle continued as Tracker grabbed the snake's body and tossed it down.

"Climb."

Nodding, she swallowed her gorge and did as she was told. As fast as she could. Keeping her gaze on that notch in the canyon wall that signified safety. As fast as she climbed, she wasn't as fast as the men behind. Between Miguel's screams, she could hear their shouts getting louder. The *Comancheros* were going to catch them. She was too slow. Her poor baby. All the memories she had revolved around him. She tugged on the rope, getting Tracker's attention.

"Cut me loose."

He ignored her and kept climbing.

"I'm slowing you down."

"Climb."

She slid her arms out of the cradleboard straps, turned around and leaned back against the wall. Tracker's body came over hers. Miguel's screams filled her ears. "Cut the rope and save my son," she whispered in response to the concern in his eyes.

"All or nothing, sweets. It doesn't matter what might happen. This is what it is. You and me. And they're not getting our baby."

He was right. What had she been thinking? Together. They had to stay together.

"I'm sorry."

He stood back and handed her the cradleboard. Her arms screamed when she slid them back into the straps. She climbed as quickly as she could, ignoring the pain in her shoulders and legs, knowing Tracker protected her back, her baby. She wouldn't let them have Miguel. They couldn't have her baby.

She was concentrating so hard on climbing that she didn't even realize when she reached the notch. She reached up and there was nothing there. Her foot slammed down hard enough to snap her teeth together. Shadow surged past and pulled her up. She screamed. Miguel screamed right along with her. She tore the cradleboard off her back, ignoring the pain in her shoulders, and checked him over.

"Oh, my God. Oh, my God." *Don't let him be hit. Please, Lord, don't let him be hit.*

Tracker was right behind her. "Son of a bitch, was he hit?"

She shook her head. "I don't know." She tore at the knots that held the baby to the cradleboard. Again there was a flash of a blade in front of her eyes, and Miguel was free. She snatched him up and held him to her, pressing his face to her chest. His screams subsided. Too soon he was snatched out of her arms.

"Let me see."

She didn't have a choice. Tracker inspected him, then anchored him against his chest.

"It's time to go." He grabbed her arm and started running. The path was narrow and treacherous. So narrow she wasn't sure if they could get through it in places. Awkward also, because Tracker held her hand, dragging her along faster than she might have run on her own. The lights started flashing behind her eyes again.

One step at a time. One step at a time. Just one step.

As soon as they were away from the ledge, Tracker pulled

his knife from his boot and cut the rope binding them together. He handed Miguel to her. She could only stand there and stare at him, feeling her world fall away. "What are you doing?"

After another hard kiss, he said, "Run, baby."

Climb, run. He was always making her go away from him. She grabbed his hand. "You come with me."

"I can't let Shadow have all the fun."

The lights flickered faster. He was leaving her. "I'll wait."

His fingers squeezed hers. Past the forced smile on his lips she could see the sadness in his eyes. "I'm glad we had that kiss."

"I want more."

"Me, too." A volley of shots, then a whistle rose above the cacophony. "I've got to go. You've got to run." He pointed. "That way to your sister."

The only thing he didn't say was "have a good life," but it was there in his voice. He didn't expect to survive.

"You come back to me, Tracker Ochoa. I'll be waiting."

The lights flickered faster, consuming her vision. In the back of her mind, she heard other voices yelling, screaming. She couldn't lose another person who loved her. She couldn't face another person leaving her behind.

"You hold on, Ari. Be strong for your son." Tracker's thumb brushed her lip. "Make me proud."

"Wait!" She searched for an excuse to keep him with her. "How will I know they're Hell's Eight?"

He touched the pocket of her blouse. Paper rustled. "Ask them for their letters." His eyelids flickered. He handed her a pistol. "The chambers are full. You've got—"

"Six shots," she finished for him.

He gave her a hard look. "Don't waste them. Pace yourself."

The first Comanchero came over the edge. Tracker snatched the gun from her hand and put a bullet between his eyes.

Shoving the gun back into her hand, he yelled, "I have to get to Shadow. Run."

She did, stumbling over rocks and ledges. Listening with everything in her for another shot. A war cry echoed behind her. A volley of bullets pinged off rock. Another war cry came from down below, answering the first. Shadow? Did that mean the first was Tracker? She looked back. There was nothing to see. Just the bend in the narrow passage, hiding from sight the chaos behind.

Miguel screamed. She wanted to scream along with him, but she didn't have the breath. Her ankle twisted. She didn't stop. The war cries echoed in her head, growing louder and louder, joining the flashes of lightning. She stumbled over a rock and fell to her knees. Miguel's screams tore at her. She had to get up. Had to find the strength to go on.

Men loomed in front of her. She jerked the pistol up. Her thumb slipped off the hammer, so she tried again, unsure whether this was real or not. Not even caring. She had to protect Miguel.

The gun was snatched from her hand. A voice as smooth as molasses drawled, "You don't want to be doing that, ma'am."

He had no idea how much she did.

She gasped out, "Hell's Eight?"

"Caine Allen at your service."

"Tracker. Shadow. Need help." Her whole body shook. The light obliterated her vision. There were only shadows left to see. "So many. So many."

So many she couldn't see. So many shadows haunting her mind.

"We were just heading on through when we ran into you."

Hands grabbed and lifted her. She was passed from one set to another as men pushed into the opening. A sea of men flowed past her. All lethal, all deadly, all armed to the teeth. The last one paused and tipped his hat before waving her in the direction from which they had come. "They're waiting for you."

They? "Who are they?"

No one answered.

She walked in the direction indicated, her feet like lead weights, fighting the oblivion that beckoned. Four more steps and she was in sunlight. She saw horses. Four men. Three women. Two of the women came rushing forward. The third hung back, a small, slender silhouette restrained by a man's hand on her arm.

Desi! Oh God. Don't leave me, Desi!

The lights flashed. Pain exploded behind Ari's eyes. She fell to her knees, holding Miguel. The gunshots reverberated all around. Miguel continued to scream. Behind her, Tracker fought for his life.

The slender woman took a step forward. Ari couldn't look away. Sunlight shone off the blonde of her hair, reflected from the blue of her eyes. Her hair hung in a thick braid down her back. The severe style exposed the perfection of her skin and the fullness of her mouth. She was slender and short, and she was crying as if her heart was breaking.

"Desi?"

"Oh, my God, Ari."

The pain was unbearable. Ari couldn't hold on. Memories

she couldn't stop surged forward, riding emotions she didn't want to feel. Agony. Shame. So much shame. So much harder to bear than the pain. Betrayal.

The ground beneath her shifted. She tumbled forward into the darkness. She didn't fight, didn't resist. There was peace in the darkness. It didn't demand answers, didn't ask questions.

"Why?" she whispered, as Desi's face swirled in and out of the darkness. "Why did you leave me with them?"

11

He didn't need this. Tracker stood on the front porch of the small house Desi had built for Ari. No one had argued when she had insisted. Everyone wanted the miracle of the reunion. Everyone wanted Desi happy. The overhang shielded him from the sun. He wished it would shield him from Desi. The woman was on a mission and no one could equal her single-mindedness. She'd cornered him as soon as he'd ridden into the barn, waited impatiently while he got Buster settled, and then hauled him here. Now, she stood in front of him, arms folded across her chest, toe tapping, ready to explode. The big redbone hound that followed her everywhere plopped at her side.

"Can I talk yet?" she demanded.

"What's stopping you?"

"You! You threatened me!"

"I said I'd kill for a bit of peace."

"And I gave it to you."

"So now I have to listen to you?"

"You're being very rude."

Yes, he was, because he didn't want to hear Desi tell him that Ari didn't want to see him anymore. As unrealistic as it was, he wanted to hold on to the sweet memories a few more hours, before they drowned under the bitterness of hatred. Which only proved he could be as big a fool as anyone.

"What took you so long to get here?" Desi demanded. "We've been back for two days!"

"I had to get my horse."

"We have lots of horses."

He took off his hat and wiped his brow on his sleeve. On top of everything else, he was hot. Zach had had to abandon the extra horses to escape. There was no way Tracker was going to leave Buster with the *Comancheros*. "Buster is *my* horse."

She waved her hand. "Fine. I understand. That whole what's-mine-stays-mine Hell's Eight thing."

He nodded and agreed drily, "Yeah, that. So what are you champing at the bit to tell me?"

"It's about Ari."

"Don't worry." He settled his hat back on his head. "I'll steer clear of her."

"No!"

He paused, his hand on the brim of his hat. "No?"

"You can't do that."

"Zach said her memory came back."

"Yes. At the canyon, in the middle of all that chaos, she remembered."

He slowly lowered his arm. "What more is there to talk about?"

"Getting her well!"

Son of a bitch. Everything inside Tracker went cold. "Ari's sick?"

"She won't talk to me, Tracker," Desi whispered. "She won't talk to anyone."

"Why not?"

"I don't know. The only thing she said when she saw me was to ask me why I had left her with them."

The agony in Desi's eyes tore at Tracker's heart.

"I didn't leave her, Tracker. I wouldn't. I chose her, but it was a trick." Tears filled her eyes. "They said they would let her go. I just had to choose…"

There was nothing to do but pull her into his arms. When it came to Desi, he didn't have much defense. She was too much like Ari. He patted her back awkwardly. "I told you before, it was just a game to them. They never intended to let either of you go."

"But Ari thinks I left her."

"No, in her heart she doesn't."

"Are you sure?"

He wasn't sure of anything, except he knew if it were him and Shadow, he'd never be able to believe such a thing for more than the minute it took to get his head clear. "Yes."

Desi sniffed and rubbed her face in his shirt. "She won't talk to anyone. She won't even let Miguel in."

"She sent him away?"

"Well, no. She was so exhausted we thought it best to keep him while she slept."

That sounded reasonable. "So what's the problem?"

"I don't know." It was almost a wail. Desi never wailed. She might demand, she might order, but she never wailed. For such a dainty thing, she had a backbone of iron. "Ari asks about him every day, but she never asks *for* him."

Tracker took off his hat again and ran his fingers through

his hair. Christ, had no one talked to Ari? Simply sat down and talked to her? "What have you been doing?"

Desi shrugged and stepped back, wiping her face on her sleeve. "Respecting her wishes. What else can I do?"

Talk to her. Listen to her. Ask her questions. Desi and Ari shared the same past, the same horrible experiences. But dammit, letting her hole up in the house that had been built to make her happy? No one talking to her? No one even knowing what was going on with her, just assuming that leaving her was the right thing? That sounded like a lot of chickening out to him.

He ran his hand over the back of his neck, the small store of patience he had trickling steadily away. "What do you want from me?"

He was tired, sweaty and feeling every one of his thirty-one years. He'd spent two days chasing down his horse, a night stealing him back and another two days getting here. He hadn't rushed to return home, because the inevitability of Ari getting her memory back had put a drag in his step. His time with her had been a taste of the forbidden, a taste of the magic that others took for granted. A taste of love.

Her face red and splotchy from crying, Desi still managed to look beautiful as she pointed to the door. "I want you to go *in* there and make her *better*."

And next they'd be asking him to make the sun rise in the west. "You too chicken?"

Her head snapped up. "Yes, but that's not the point."

"You've got a point?"

Desi folded her arms across her chest. "Don't get sarcastic with me, Mr. Ochoa, or I'll sic Boone on you."

Tracker looked at the big redbone hound at Desi's feet. The dog cocked a wrinkled brow at Tracker, moaned and flopped onto his side. "Hell, I think that dog has gotten even lazier."

"Don't swear, and he's just conserving his strength."

"For what? Dinner?"

Desi bristled predictably. Her devotion to the dog was as complete as his was to her. "If I tell him to, he'll attack."

Tracker didn't doubt he would. Boone had proved his loyalty to Desi the day she'd been kidnapped. He'd attacked her attackers, received a knife wound and been left for dead. But he hadn't died. Limping and bleeding, severely injured, with no direction from anyone, he'd started to trail his mistress, his baying a battle cry that had echoed through the hills, calling the Hell's Eight to Desi's aid. Without him, no one would have known where she was until it was too late. The act of courage and devotion had forever earned him a place at Hell's Eight. And when he'd sired puppies, there hadn't been a family within a hundred miles that hadn't clamored for one of his offspring. Boone was a legend. The why of it just baffled a person when they looked at him.

"If you tell him to attack, I'll have to defend myself."

She gasped. "You'd hurt Boone?"

Tracker thought she was going to throw herself over the dog's body. The hound opened one eye and looked at Tracker. Tracker shook his head. Boone moaned, and damned if it didn't sound like reproach. Shit, the two of them were too much.

"And have Caine kick my ass? I don't think so."

"He would, too."

"But not because he loves Boone."

"He does."

Desi had a way of overlooking things that didn't serve her purpose.

"He loves him because he loves you, which is also why he'd be kicking my ass."

Desi smiled that gamin grin that was so infectious. "See? He loves him."

Tracker pinched the bridge of his nose between his thumb and forefinger. "Is there a point to this discussion?"

"Yes."

He waited. She bit her lip. Never a good sign.

"Just tell me. I'm too damn tired to pull the information from you."

"Someone has to confront Ari."

He had a horrible feeling what was coming. "So?"

"We discussed it."

"Who is we?"

"Tia, Sally Mae, Bella and I."

They were all in on this? Shit. The horrible feeling changed to a sinking one. "And?"

"We've decided it's a job best left for her husband, so we're all keeping away and letting you handle it—"

"I'm not really her husband. Not in her eyes."

"You can't renege now."

"You have no idea what you're asking."

"She's my sister, Tracker. I know her better than you."

Not in this, she didn't. "It's impossible."

"If it was, you wouldn't have married her."

"I was saving her a—her butt."

Desi folded her arms across her chest. "Are you trying to tell me you don't care about her?"

"I'm trying to tell you it doesn't matter what I feel. In case it's escaped your notice, I look a he—heck of a lot like the men who abused her."

Desi bit her lip. "Caine looks an awful lot like the men who held me hostage."

"I hardly think it's the same."

"It has to be."

"Why? Because you want it to be?"

"Yes." Desi raked the wild mass of her hair off her face. The curls sprang right back, willy-nilly, to where they wanted to be. "Yes."

"Things don't work that way, Desi. You know it."

"All I know is that I was just as scared and just as humiliated as Ari. I was terrified of every man I saw and all I wanted to do was run away and hide. Preferably in a place that had a bathtub, so I could sit there and scrub the filth and shame from me. But along came Caine. He scooped me up and plopped me down in his life." She smiled wryly. "You know him. He just has a way of moving forward and taking everyone with him. He treated me like a wife. He had expectations of me as a wife, in and out of the bedroom. In some ways it was a godsend to have such a clear path laid out for me. I didn't have to think. I just had to be the woman he saw me as. And when it was all said and done, it worked, because all along he'd been seeing me."

"I'm not Caine. And Ari isn't you."

Her expression became even more stubborn. "But the circumstances are the same."

He couldn't do it. He couldn't walk in there and play husband to a woman who would cringe at the thought of his touch. Who would scream when he rolled over in bed and put his arm around her and pulled her close. "I'm her worst nightmare."

"You're the only one who can do it. You're the only one who can take away the horror and make it right."

"And how in hell am I supposed to do that? Terrify her into being a proper wife?"

"I don't know. I just know that she trusts you, and her healing started with you."

"And now my part is done."

Boone got to his feet, sensing his mistress's tension. A low growl rumbled from his throat. As she dropped her hand to his head, the dog looked at Desi and then at Tracker. His face sagged, the wrinkles tumbling into a mournful expression, and he whined anxiously.

"Are you telling me you don't care for her, Tracker?"

How did he answer that one? Whether he cared for her or not had no bearing on anything.

"Well?"

"She's going to hate me."

"But she'll get well."

At what cost?

Desi pressed her point. "Don't you want that?"

Hell, yes. He wanted that more than anything. *Shit.* "Anyone ever tell you you're a dirty fighter?"

"Just Caine."

"Let me add my name to the list."

"Will you do it?"

He slapped his hat against his thigh. Dust flew up. Desi waved her hand in front of her face and coughed.

He was going to hell for worse things. At least something good would come out of this. He put his hand on the doorknob.

Desi licked her lips. "Tracker?"

"It's too late to be nervous, Desi. You put Ari in my hands and there she's going to stay. No interference."

"What are you going to do?"

"I'm going to take a bath. Have someone send over hot water."

"A bath?"

"Yes." Among other things.

"And after that?"

He turned the knob, feeling that crash of doom descending. "I'm going to have dinner."

Heat and stale air surrounded him as soon as he stepped into the house.

"Go away."

Ari's voice sounded just as stale as the air. Tracker trailed the sound to the bedroom at the back of the house. In the dim light, he could see her seated in a hard-backed chair by the bed. She was fully dressed. Her hair was loose around her shoulders in a wanton tumble that made his fingers itch to sink into the silken mass. He loved her hair, loved the way it curled around his fingers in welcome. Loved the image of life it gave. Even now, when she sat as still as a statue, with her hands folded in her lap and her skirts in neat folds over her thighs, not even looking at him. But even in the dim light, he could see the pulse pounding in her throat.

"Don't I even get a welcome home?"

The only indication she gave that she knew it was him was a small start. It beat the hell out of her running screaming from the room.

"Hello, Tracker."

"Hello, yourself."

She looked at him. "Have you seen Miguel?"

"Have you?"

She shook her head and turned her face away. "They don't bring him around me."

Interesting choice of words. "So you decided your best option was to sit with the curtains drawn, passing the time counting dust motes?"

She didn't have an answer for that. He could see why Desi had passed the job of dealing with Ari to him. It was eerie, talking to this woman who was so distant, so polite, so not there. "You did me proud, sweets."

"Thank you." She picked at her skirt. "They took your pistol."

"Caine will give it back."

"I met him."

Tracker took another step into the room. "Did you meet Desi, too?"

Her mouth thinned. "Yes."

"Good." He didn't ask about the others, remembering Desi's explanation that they were giving Ari room.

He was supposed to be playing the husband. He might as well play it all the way.

Tossing his hat onto the corner of the four-poster, he sat on the end of the bed. He started tugging on his boots. "Desi looks just like you, doesn't she?"

"She's older than me."

"Uh-huh." He pretended to have a difficulty with the boot. "Come help me with this."

"No." Still that same flat voice. Still that lack of emotion. He was getting an idea of what Desi meant when she said Ari wouldn't talk.

He put a bit of mean in his voice. "I wasn't asking." Ari didn't move. He wondered how far she intended to take this resistance. How far he would have to go. "Now."

The pulse in her throat beat faster. He waited. Her hands clenched in her lap. Anger or fear? She stood, straightened her skirt and then walked over. There was no heat in her expression, though. So, not anger. Fear. He stuck out his leg. She stood unmoving, a ghost of her former vibrant self.

He twirled his finger in a circle. "Just face away, straddle my leg and tug the boot off from the heel."

"I know what to do."

"Then how come you're not doing it?"

"Do you want me naked or clothed?"

That was a declaration of war, throwing her past between them. A woman bent over to take off a man's boot would be vulnerable in all kinds of ways to abuse. A man could make her feel ashamed in all kinds of ways. Tracker remembered what Desi had said about Caine's expectations giving her guidance. He just didn't have a clue as to what a decent woman would expect, let alone what Ari was thinking.

"What do you think I'll like better?"

She started unbuttoning her blouse. Tracker didn't say a word. He recognized a dare when one was thrown in his face. All there was to do was wait to see how far she meant to take this, and determine from there where he needed to go with it. The blouse slid off her shoulders. She had pretty shoulders. Nicely squared, slender with very elegant lines. The skirt was next. With the nonchalance of a whore, she let it drop. She stood there in her petticoats, watching him watch her. He didn't try to hide his erection. It was a knee-jerk reaction to a pretty woman, but he didn't feel desire. This was just...sad.

The petticoats were next. They slid to the floor with the same lack of ceremony as the skirt. Tracker expected hesitation when Ari got to the bloomers. But they came off along with the camisole in the way of a woman who'd undressed for men many times. And he supposed she had. With no modesty and no care. His cock throbbed and his heart ached as she revealed her body. He'd dreamed of it many times, but never like this. He wanted to call a halt, but sometimes when it came to pain, a body just had to ride it out. And Ari had a lot of pain.

He stuck out his foot. "You ready yet?"

There was a flicker of uncertainty in her eyes. Good. Let her think about what he wanted from her, because it sure as shit wasn't this. She turned, straddled his foot, giving him a clear view of her ass. It was even more of a work of art naked. A surprisingly full curve accentuated by creamy white skin. The crease between those sweet buttocks tempted him to trace it with his finger. When she bent over he got a peek at her pussy, lightly covered by blond hair. One thing was for sure, this wasn't arousing her. Thank God.

He jiggled his foot. "Well?"

She grabbed the heel and tugged. Nothing happened.

"You'll have to do better than that. I don't wear boots often, so when I do they tend to cling."

She put more force behind it. He could just catch a glimpse of the jiggle of her breasts. His cock didn't care about the higher purpose, it just responded to the magic of those beauties in motion. The boot came off. She stood. A touch of red colored her breasts and cheeks. He held up his other foot. Without a word, she straddled that leg and repeated the procedure. When she was done, she picked up his boots and put them by the door. He wondered what man had taught her that. She came back and stood before him, still naked, the only indication of any feeling whatsoever being that slight blush, which could be put down to exertion.

"Thank you."

Her gaze dropped to his groin. There was no hiding his erection. She licked her lips. Two steps forward and she was on her knees, and her hands were at the laces of his pants.

Son of a bitch. She was pushing him. But which way was he supposed to jump? He waited. She lifted his cock free of the leather. A knock at the door saved his ass. Stroking his hand over her hair, he said, "Hold that thought."

Retying his pants, he tugged his shirt over his hips, hiding his erection. He left the bedroom and went to the front door and opened it. Outside two men stood, carrying a large brass tub between them. "Hey, Caden, Ace."

"Good to see you didn't get your ass shot off," Caden grunted.

"For a horse." Ace shook his head.

"*My* horse," Tracker corrected, standing back and letting them through.

"Where do you want it?"

There weren't many options in the small house. The sitting room and kitchen were one room. The bedroom was too small. Besides, Ari was there, naked. "Over to the right there."

"Tia said to tell you she's got water heating, but if you plan on doing this too often, you need to get your own firewood in."

"I'll be sure to thank her." Tia always grumbled about the work of the ranch, but the truth was, she thrived on the challenge of organizing the growing spread.

"Ed said not to worry about it." Caden laughed, a shock of brown hair falling over his forehead, giving him that look of trouble that women seemed to love. "Course, he only said that to get Tia going."

"Those two still fighting?"

"Yup. Tia's still playing hard to get."

"And Ed's still enjoying the chase?"

For six years Ed had been trying to get Tia to marry him.

"Some things never change." Ace grunted as he set down his side of the tub.

Metal rattled against wood as Caden set down his end, then straightened. His blue eyes were serious. Not an unusual thing for Caden, but usually they were angry, too. He turned and left the house.

Ace was Caden's total opposite—blond-haired with a muscled leanness, and gray eyes that could go stone cold at the drop of a hat. A body could never tell when Ace was serious. Usually it came as a surprise. Rarely was it a pleasant one. Ace being serious meant someone was going to die. "Word is that Eastern dude is coming in on Friday's stage."

That gave them a good six days to plan.

"Good."

"Caden and I are going to ride out in a bit and make sure he gets to San Antonio safely. Don't want him to have any mishaps before you and Caine have a chat with him."

"Does he know we know he's coming?"

"Not a clue. Caine and Sam have the last of those *Comancheros* hog-tied about ten miles out of town. They've turned out to be the real cooperative sort, Sam says. Sending all the right messages to their friend at all the right times."

"Tucker's not with them?"

Ace shook his head. "Word leaked to Sally Mae about that part of the plan. You know she doesn't hold with violence."

Yet she was married to one of the most notorious men in the territory. That never failed to amaze Tracker. Somehow, the two of them made it work. Quaker and outlaw, white woman and Indian. Watching them together was like watching one of those fancy ballets. There was a beauty in their understanding of each other, a sensual rhythmic depth to their interactions, and an art to their negotiations. They did a lot of negotiating;

Sally Mae's notions didn't fit in well with the reality of this country.

Tracker thought of Ari, kneeling naked in the bedroom, terrified, fighting he didn't even know what, in ways he didn't understand. They couldn't go on like that. They had to find a rhythm that worked for them. Without it, Ari wouldn't heal.

"And you know Tucker is bound by his promise," Caden said, coming back in with a couple buckets of water.

As Tracker was to Ari. *I'll keep you safe.*

"Yeah." Tracker forced an easy smile he didn't feel. "For a man of his nature, you wouldn't think it would come easy to turn the other cheek."

Caden shook his head. "But he's doing it, and with a smile, every day."

Ace went out and fetched a couple more buckets of cold water from just outside the door, then said, "That Sally Mae is one hell of an inspiration."

"True." Caden dumped his buckets into the tub. "Got a backbone of steel and a heart of mush. A man will do a lot for a woman like that, and I've got to say, it's good to see Tucker smile. For awhile I thought he'd forgotten how."

"He's definitely easier to live with now. A lot less busted-up jaws around the place."

Ace emptied his buckets into the tub. "We'll be back with the hot water in a minute."

"Do me a favor and leave them by the door."

Ace and Caden looked at the bedroom door and then at Tracker. Ace was the one who gave voice to the question in their eyes. "You doing right by her?"

"What the hell are you going to do if I say no?"

Ace smiled a totally infectious, completely deceptive smile

and collected his buckets. "I'd likely have to take you out back and skin you alive."

Anyone not knowing Ace would think he was joking.

Caden picked up the other two buckets. "And then I'd have to kick your ass."

"You haven't been able to manage it yet."

"Might just be I haven't had the proper inspiration."

That, Tracker could believe. Caden was slow to anger and not much on fighting without purpose. But when he found one, the battle was to the death, no matter what he had to go through to achieve the goal. He wasn't the forgiving sort.

"Uh-huh." Tracker motioned them out. "Have no fear, I'm treating her with all the respect she demands."

Which was apparently none. What the hell had happened to the woman who had demanded he kiss her with love?

"Good. We'll see you later then."

Ace stopped at the door. "Almost forgot. Tia wants to know if you'll be eating at the house tonight."

Tracker glanced at the bedroom. "Tell her I'll let her know in a bit."

"Will do."

The door closed quietly behind them. There was nothing to do but go back to the bedroom.

She was where he'd left her, kneeling on the floor, head bowed, still naked, still emotionless. He'd rather see her in the middle of an episode.

Tracker sat down in front of her on the bed. Ari immediately reached for the front of his pants. Hell, he was as bad as everyone else. Taking without asking. He caught her hands in his, brought them to his lips and kissed the backs.

"Sweets?" She didn't move. "Talk to me."

She shook her head and tugged her hands away. He let

them go, seeing what she would do. She reached for his cock again and cupped him through his pants. His cock, uncaring of moral issues, perked up. Again, he stopped her.

"Are you thinking of controlling me with sex?"

That brought her gaze up.

"I'll take that look of surprise as a no."

He left her hand where it was, letting the pleasure trickle through him as he fought for words. The pleasure won. He grabbed her wrist, ending the game.

A shudder went through her and he understood something. Desi was wrong. The way to go forward with Ari was not the way Caine had gone with Desi. Tracker didn't know what was the right way, but that wasn't it. He looked at Ari's fingers, so pale compared to his. So elegant. She was a lady. And his for a time. The scars around her wrists were an abomination, but not a surprise. He knew she'd been bound, but looking at them hurt him, anyway. Way down deep inside, in a place he'd thought scarred over.

He rubbed his thumb across the back of her hand. He wasn't a man of words, but he needed to find the right ones to tell her what he felt inside. Shit, he should have talked to Sam first. Sam could charm the birds from the trees. Tracker took a breath. It didn't make it easier. He'd rather be staked out on a cactus than do this. There was nothing to do but blurt it out. She'd probably laugh at him anyway.

"Do you know, sweets, until you touched me, I never knew what it was like to have a woman touch me with caring?"

She didn't look up. He pushed on.

"I've had them touch me out of greed, out of passion, out of manipulation, but until you, being touched like that was just a cruel fairy tale someone fed me as a kid."

Still no response. He took another breath and went for broke. "I liked it."

That got a start. He tipped up her chin. She wasn't laughing. Tears filled her eyes. For her? For him? For them? Hell, what did it matter? It was all fucked up. He trailed his fingers to her cheek, trying to give her softness. "So much, I don't want to go back to being used."

Her lips worked. No words came out.

Sliding his hand back until he cupped her head, he rubbed his thumb over her mouth. "There's always been pleasure between us. Nothing's happened in the last two days that makes me want anything else."

Vague thumps announced the arrival of the hot water. Leaning forward, he replaced his thumb with his lips. He gave her a gentle kiss before reaching over to pull the coverlet off the foot of the bed and drape it around her. "That's all I want between us, sweets. Softness."

Her eyes searched his, but nothing in her expression gave away her thoughts.

"I've got five days of trail clinging to me. I'm going to take a bath."

She sat there, lips sealed, eyes screaming. Cupping her cheek in his hand, he again touched his thumb to her lips. "While I'm doing that, you can do whatever you want."

12

The hot water felt good against his aching muscles. The steam from the bath blended with the humidity of the air. Traces of clove from when he'd washed up before stepping into the tub rode the steam, covering the staleness of the air. Tia's doing. She knew how the scent made him think of hope. He'd told her that once. Right after the first time he'd gotten his heart broken, he believed. The talk she'd given him was bracing—that things happen for a reason, that when happiness came his way, he should enjoy it, because no one ever knew how long it would last. She'd likely been thinking about her husband then, dead along with her baby. When she was done, Tracker hadn't had much energy left for moping, but ever since then, whenever he was upset, he found clove soap next to his bath.

The small, cherishing act made him smile. For a man thinking he was about at the end of his rope, he had a lot of people who cared for him. So maybe he'd best get off his self-pity roll and just enjoy what was, rather than worrying about what would be. Tracker slid down into the large tub, feeling guilty for the griping he'd put up when they'd had to haul it up the mountain to Hell's Eight. After a long, difficult time on the trail, it was a godsend to be able to sink into a tubful of hot, soothing water. He closed his eyes and let the heat work at the tension inside him.

He didn't know what to do with Ari. He didn't know how to get through to her. She wore that pain like armor, afraid of letting it go because what was on the other side might be worse. There just might be a black, yawning pit that would swallow her whole.

He'd felt that way after his town had been wiped out. For his parents he hadn't grieved much, because they hadn't been much. But for Caine's parents, who'd given him and Shadow the only love they'd ever known, he'd wanted to tear open the graves, call down the grim reaper and make a deal. His life for theirs. Yeah, he knew how Ari felt, but he couldn't put a gun in her hand and give her vengeance in place of love. She wasn't cut from the same cloth. She hadn't been weaned on anger and hate. Hadn't had the softness beaten out of her, though the *Comancheros* had tried. Beneath the water, he clenched his hand on his thigh. Good people like them didn't deserve to die. Good women like Desi and Ari didn't deserve to be used. And men like Tracker shouldn't be put in charge of saving them. Not when his honor was stretched thin.

Damn, no matter what Desi said, what Ari needed was an Eastern man with Eastern manners. Someone who understood what passed for good in the world she came from. Here, the muscle a man carried on his body backed up the weight of his word. Tracker had encountered enough Easterners over the years to know their power came from money and political machinations. They might smile to a person's face, but worked behind his back as soon as he left. Rarely was anything handled directly.

Tracker wasn't good at that kind of smooth talking. He didn't know how to mince around what had happened to Ari, yet leave the core of it untouched. The pain of her memories grew like an ugly, festering boil, throbbing too viciously to be ignored. Instinct said lance the boil, release the poison. He'd tried that kind of direct confrontation in the bedroom. All he'd done was make her cry. Shit. He sank under the water, wetting his hair, releasing his frustration by uttering a water-logged "Fuck."

When he came to the surface, the hairs on the back of his neck stood in warning. He wasn't alone. Reaching into the water for the knife down by his foot, he sneaked a peek through his lashes. Ari stood by the tub, the wrap clutched around her, looking down at him. Shit again. Moving slowly so as not to scare her, he traded the knife for a washcloth on the table beside the tub.

Her eyes widened at the sight of the weapon. "You had *that* in the bath?"

Draping the washcloth over his privates, he shrugged. "Habit."

He wasn't sure how much good the cloth was going to do if his cock reacted with its normal attentiveness to her presence, but at least he made the effort.

Reaching out, she touched the knife, rocking it back and forth. "I remembered." She said it as though he didn't know.

"I'm sorry."

Not meeting his eyes, she said, "Me, too."

She looked like an angel standing there. An improbably sweet angel with broken wings. Just in case she had thoughts of doing something with that knife, he removed it from beneath her fingers. When she looked up, he motioned to his nakedness.

"You have me at a disadvantage."

"Good."

There was still no discerning her mood from her expression. He cocked an eyebrow. "Care to explain that?"

She held up her hand, her thumb and forefinger a short space apart. "You're always so big, so…invulnerable. I sometimes feel insignificant."

"Sweets, I'm the one who's not worth shit."

"You always say that."

"Because compared to what you're used to, I'm not."

"I'm used to men who fucked me however they wanted, whenever they wanted, regardless of what I wanted."

He hated hearing that word on her lips. More than that, he hated that she thought she was now the kind of woman who could use it. Of course, he might not be sending that message too clearly, since he was carrying on a conversation with her while naked. He was reasonably sure Eastern men considered that vulgar.

He pointed to the white cotton towel draped over the back of a chair. "If you pass me that towel and turn your back, I'll be happy to talk about whatever you want."

"No."

He raised his eyebrows. "You're telling me no?"

"Yes."

"I'll give you a hint, sweets. You'd be more convincing if you weren't standing there wringing your hands, avoiding my gaze."

"Don't, Tracker."

Shit. She looked as if she was about to cry. "I'm sorry."

She let the wrap fall to the floor. He couldn't take his eyes away from her body—the high, pert breasts that fit so perfectly into his hand, the slender waist that flowed to those surprisingly full hips. Her skin shone so white in the dim interior, looked so soft. He curved his fingers at the memory of how her nipple had pressed into his palm.

She took a step toward the tub. It was his turn to say "don't." If she had her mind on a pity fuck, he didn't want that, either. When she looked at him and that full bottom lip slipped between her teeth, he explained.

"You don't owe me anything, Ari. What I did for you, I would have done for anyone."

She shook her head and took a small step. "Please."

"What?"

She reached the side of the tub. "Shut up."

Her fingers slid over the rim to touch his shoulder. A butterfly caress that could have meant anything. At the moment, he was too stunned at the novelty of being told to shut up to figure it out.

"What did you say?" It came out a low growl. She merely frowned at him and waved aside his question.

"I told you to shut up. I can't think with you always throwing new obstacles at me."

He stalled. "You need to think?"

She nodded.

"Why?"

She cut him a look. He raised his hands in surrender. "I'll be quiet."

A half step was all it took for her to flatten her hand against his shoulder. She'd said he couldn't talk, but she didn't say he couldn't touch. He reached across his body and curved his fingers around hers, bringing them to his lips before placing her hand back on his shoulder and holding it there.

She stared at their hands as if the words she searched for hid there. "I've always trusted you."

What did a man say to that? "Good."

"I want to trust you now."

"But you can't?"

She shook her head. "Everyone looks at me. I know what they're thinking, what they see."

"Honey, not only are you a twin, you're a legend. Not many women get returned after being stolen by the *Comancheros*."

"But they *know*."

He couldn't blunt that truth. "Yes. But what you don't understand is, they don't care."

"They look at me and they imagine—"

He cut her off. "They imagine how much they'd like to cut the balls off the men who hurt you and Desi."

She shook her head. "You don't see—"

"Cover your eyes, I'm standing up."

He needed to hold her. Her hand on his shoulder kept him where he was. "Please, don't."

"Why?"

"You scare me."

That settled him back down in the tub. "How the he—heck am I doing that?"

"You look like *them*, but you feel like my Tracker."

My Tracker.

He had to stop holding tight to those things she said that implied this was more than for now. "I'll stay seated then."

She picked up the soap and lathered it in her hands. She slowly rubbed the lather across the skin on his shoulder above the waterline. The scent of cloves filled the air even as his cock filled with desire.

"What are you doing?"

"Touching you with love."

"You don't love me."

"You may be able to make me do a lot of things, Tracker, but you can't tell me how to feel."

"You love me?"

"I think so."

"Think?" He shrugged his shoulder away. "Am I supposed to be flattered?"

She removed her hand. "I know I'm not the kind of woman a man like you—"

Shit.

He grabbed her hand and tugged her into the tub. Ari shrieked and tumbled. It was easy to catch her, easier to direct her body to slide down his. He moaned as the plump cheek of her ass cushioned his cock in a different heat. Water sloshed over the sides as she struggled for balance.

He let her wiggle about until she ended up splayed across his chest, cradled in his arms. He could feel her blush against his skin. Putting his arms around her, he held her close. As always when he did so, she seemed to relax. Her breath expelled in a small sigh as the last of the tension left her muscles.

He rested his chin on top of her head. "Comfortable?"

"Yes."

"Good, because I'm about to tear a strip off your hide."

She hummed in her throat.

"You don't seem nervous."

"I'm pretending."

"What?"

"That this is real."

Running his hand down her side, he enjoyed the slick glide of her skin under the roughness skin of his palm. The rise of her hip caught his attention. Placing his palm there, he stretched his fingers over her ass. The full flesh welcomed the pressure he applied. "Feels pretty damn real to me."

Was she not fighting because she was scared, or because she'd given up?

"But it won't last."

"What makes you so sure?"

"I heard you and Desi talking. She's forcing you to be nice to me."

It hurt his brain, just trying to think about how to deal with that. "Ari?"

"What?"

"Shut up."

"Why?"

He leaned his head back against the rim and closed his eyes. "Because I'm in a tub full of water, which constitutes the first real bath I've had in two weeks. I've got a gorgeous, sexy woman in my arms, and finally the time to just enjoy the way she feels there."

Ari sighed and nodded, understanding. "You don't want to fight."

"Sweets, I'm so tired, I don't even want to think."

Her hand crept up his chest. She pulled herself up until her head rested against his shoulder. His cock flexed, touching her hip briefly. God, he loved the way she made him feel inside, calm where he was usually restless, peaceful where he was usually looking for a fight.

"Me, neither," she murmured.

"Then can we just sit here and feel good?" he asked, his body aching with exhaustion. "Just for a while?"

Just for a while, so he could store the memory.

She leaned forward, trying to see over the tub side. "The floor…"

Damn the floor. "If I promise to cherish the water stains, can we forget about it?"

He could have sworn that was almost a chuckle she gave as she settled back in. The scent of cloves intensified, mixing with the subtle scent of her skin. "I'll think about it."

"Take a long time thinking." He rubbed his chin along her hair. "Have I mentioned I do like your sass?"

"That's because you're contrary."

He tentatively stroked her hair. "You're not feeling scared?"

She shook her head. "You want the truth?"

"Yes."

"I'm so tired, too, Tracker. Way down deep, where I just can't get rest. I'm so tired I can't feel…anything."

He kissed her head. There wasn't a good response for that, so he murmured, "All right."

"I just want to lie here with you and…float."

"So that's what we'll do."

She didn't answer, just rested against him until he thought she was asleep. And he held her, giving her the peace she wanted. There'd be time enough later to deal with the demons. Right now they were both tired.

The water was cold. Ari woke up to the knowledge that she was, too, despite the warmth against her side. A warmth that was moving steadily up and down. Tracker. She'd fallen asleep on Tracker's lap.

Water sloshed as she moved. Fallen asleep in the tub! Who would have thought it was even possible?

Tilting her head back, she looked up. Tracker was sleeping, too, his thick, black lashes lying like shadows on his cheeks. She'd never seen him asleep before and couldn't really see him now, the room was so dark. Very carefully, she hitched herself up. A hint of the child he'd been ghosted his face in repose, softening the harsh planes, providing a glimpse into his past, when he'd been vulnerable. She reached up and rested her fingertips against the edge of his cheekbone, where that little boy lingered.

I've never been touched with love.

What a sad statement. For all the awful things that had happened to her, for all the shame heaped on her soul, she'd been a cherished child. Constantly hugged and kissed. Her days had been filled with fond touches and smiles. She had that foundation to lean on, to hope for again. She knew what it felt like to be valued. She might not feel as if she had any value left outside of Tracker's arms, but she knew what it was like to be special. Whereas Tracker... She dropped her thumb to the scar on his cheek, a legacy of his lifestyle, a warning to those who would challenge him. A vicious badge of honor, it was wider than her thumb, much lighter than his dark complexion, and pressed against her skin in a reprimand.

"I have no feeling there," Tracker murmured.

Ari jumped. His hand on her back steadied her. Or was it keeping her put? She tried to remember the first loving touch she'd ever received, how it'd felt in her heart. She couldn't. There'd been so many, starting so young, and she'd taken them for granted. But what if she'd never experienced one? Lived a childhood devoid of that security? How would that feel? She couldn't imagine it, but she could imagine how it would sound to someone when people talked of it. Tracker was right—it would be like a cruel fairy tale. She opened her palm across his cheek, cradling it, caressing him gently with her fingertips.

"Can you feel that?"

"Yes." His cock rose against her behind.

Beneath her ear, his heartbeat accelerated. He wanted her.

"Good." She did it again, shifting position so that his cock pressed between her thighs, before settling delicately over him. Tracker had known enough aggression. He needed someone to bring him softness. Love.

"What are you doing, woman?"

The growl in his drawl was just for show.

She rocked her pussy on his cock. "Touching you with love."

He moaned. She liked how he didn't hide how she made him feel. It wasn't as easy for her to be so open, but she tried.

"Now, that is an idea."

Before she could ask what he meant, he stood. There was an awkward moment when their bodies separated, skin clinging until the last moment, and then she was lifted up into his arms and they were once more skin to skin.

"You feel so good," she moaned as her nipple scraped across his chest, sending a jolt of pure lightning through her body. Such a heady feeling to be carried in his arms, to be surrounded by his strength. To know for this moment nothing could touch her and she was safe to feel what she did. That Tracker, who knew everything, wouldn't turn away.

She rested her head against his shoulder and wrapped one hand around his neck. The other she busied playing with his nipple. So different from hers in looks—small and brown—

but so similar in responsiveness. She flicked it with her nail. He grunted. His cock flexed again.

"You're playing with fire, woman."

She flicked it once more. "Where are we going?"

"To bed."

A shiver went down her spine. Outside the windows it was dark. Inside the house was warm and humid. In Tracker's arms it was heaven.

"Any complaints?" he asked when she didn't respond.

Yes, that she hadn't met him first. Thought gave birth to speech. "That I didn't meet you long ago."

His answer drifted above her head. "Sweets, I'd be a damn greedy man to quibble with the when. I'm just glad I've got you and a bed."

"You don't ask for much."

Turning sideways, he carried her through the bedroom door. "Don't get disappointed much, either."

But he hoped. He had to hope. He was human.

"I'm not the prize you think I am," she whispered.

He laid her gently on the bed. She thought about protesting because the sheets were getting wet, but when she looked up, she could just make out his expression, and what she saw there held her enthralled. He was looking at her as if he had the world's greatest treasure laid out in front of him. To heck with the sheets. A woman could wait her whole life for a man to look at her like that. A woman like her, two lifetimes.

"Now that's where you're wrong. You're *my* prize."

The emphasis on "my" sent a thrill whispering across her skin. *Tracker's.* He came over her, blocking the faint moonlight from the window. And that fast fear swamped her and she was once again trapped in that dark place where there was only pain and taking and nothing good. Lights flickered behind her eyelids.

Fingers touched her cheek. "Ari?"

Tracker. It is Tracker. Shaking her head to dispel the last doubt, she rolled to her side and drew in hard, deep breaths while her heart thundered in her chest. The pillow was wet against her cheek. From her hair or her tears? She didn't know. Didn't care. "I can't do this."

She dug her nails into the pillow, wanting to scream. Goddammit, why couldn't she do this?

The mattress dipped as Tracker sat beside her. Her body rolled toward him. His arm came around her back, pulling her against him so she was wrapped like the letter C around his hips, her head resting on his thigh. In front of her his erection rose proudly. Thick and hard, the flared crown darker than the rest. All she had to do was reach out and she could touch it, convince him to overlook her flaws through the force of passion. He wanted her to touch him; she knew he did. It'd be so easy to distract him. One touch. One stroke. One kiss, and he'd forget all about her lapse, and she could still please him. She ran her tongue over her lips as his cock bounced with his movement, imagining how he'd taste. She wouldn't do it, because it'd be a lie, and she'd promised no lies. But the temptation lingered. It was just too hard to lay her flaws out on the table like curiosities at a sideshow.

Tracker tapped her cheek. "Why?"

Please don't ask me that. Please don't make me to say it.

The silent plea went unheard. "Is it because of what you remembered, or something else?"

She pinched the inside of his thigh. He didn't even grunt. "Of course it's because of what happened. What else could it be?"

"It could be because you're home now, safe, and not looking for a protector anymore."

The carefully worded statement sat so heavily in the silence, exposing so much with so little.

"Do you actually believe I was intimate with you because I was...scared?"

"It's more likely than not."

The inside of his thigh begged for a harder pinch. "You have the strangest notions."

His hand smoothed across her hair. "Not so strange from where I sit."

She pinched him, after all. He caught her hand and drew it aside with that same calm with which he did everything. "Then you need to change your seat," she muttered.

All her snapping did was make him smile. His hand continued stroking until her heart slowed its frantic pace. The quiet of the night settled back around them.

The peace lasted three minutes before he drawled, "So do you, you know."

"You just have to have the last word, don't you?"

"Who doesn't?"

"I suppose next you're going to tell me not to think about it?"

This time his hand followed her hair down over her back and spine, catching the end of one section and drawing it back up her body until it caught on her breast. He wrapped it around once, then, taking the end like a brush, he stroked it across her nipple. She watched as he did it again, the timbre of his voice sinking deep into her bones.

"On the contrary. I want you to think about it the whole time I love you. Every minute. Every second."

"What?"

He turned her on her back, caught her shoulders and lifted her higher on the mattress. This time, when he came down over her, he stayed a little to the side. Her breath hitched, but the terror only simmered.

"Better?" he asked.

"Yes. Thank you."

"Now, I want you to think of them. I want you to remember what they did to you. Close your eyes and think hard on it. Everything you can recall. I want you to."

"I don't want to think of it. Not now."

"There's no better time than right at this moment. Remember how they kissed you."

She did. Horrible, painful devourings of her mouth. Tracker's lips touched hers once, twice, the soft and tender way that he'd taught her meant *I love you*.

"You holding on to it?"

Yes, she was, but the memories had nothing to do with this. "How far do you want me to carry this?"

"As far as you want."

"You want me to bite your tongue, too?"

His smile pressed against hers. "If you feel the need."

The kisses on her mouth traveled to the right and landed on the corner. Tingles started in her arms and spread to her hands. She needed to hold on to something. She grabbed the sheets. They weren't substantial enough. She reached up and found Tracker's broad shoulders. Sleek muscle flexed under smooth skin. She closed her eyes, enjoying the feel, remembering how easily he'd held her up against the wall in the barn. How thoroughly he'd taken her. How hard she'd come. Yes. That's what she wanted. The memory of Tracker giving her pleasure.

"You thinking on what I told you?" he asked. The kisses spread to her cheek.

"No."

He caught her earlobe between his lips. She braced herself, waiting for the bite. But there was just a flick of his tongue and the tiniest pressure that created such an intense feeling, she had to turn her head away. Tracker chuckled—a deep, dark, sexy sound that promised more of the same.

"Why not?"

"Because I'd rather remember how good you feel in me."

His body jerked against hers. "Good, because there's no comparison."

No, there wasn't. Tracker was pleasure. Pure and simple.

His lips traveled from her ear down her neck, followed the taut cord there. Other men had kissed her that way. She'd felt nothing. But now, oh now, this was good. She turned her head, giving Tracker better access. Giving the pleasure more room to grow.

"I only want to love you."

His hand slid down her shoulder, skimming the back of her arm in the barest of touches. Goose bumps sprang up in the wake of the seductive lure, spreading inward to her chest as his fingers slipped beneath her palm, tickling the sensitive surface. Another shiver shook her from head to toe. Another chuckle blended into the night.

Lacing his fingers with hers, Tracker slowly drew her hand above her head and pinned it with his. He repeated the same process with the other arm until he was holding both her hands trapped above her head while he leaned above her. His hair slid over his shoulder, slipping across her left nipple in a silken caress, sending yet another bolt of sensation through her.

"Now I've got you."

His legs straddled hers, pinning her in yet another way. His cock fell against her mound—hard, hot and eager. She braced herself for the onslaught of the lights. They didn't materialize. Instead there came the memory of when he'd first been with her—the intimate struggle to take him in, the pleasure-pain as he'd gained that first inch, the bliss of taking him all.

And for the first time, she saw Vincente's lie for the gift it was. Thinking herself a once-happy woman, she'd had no fear of Tracker that day. She'd been open and accepting, and he'd made her happy. And that memory was so much more powerful than the others.

"You concentrating?"

Ari answered with a lift of her hips, which slid Tracker's cock a fraction of an inch along her pussy. It wasn't enough. "Nope."

He leaned down. She raised up. Their mouths met. Gently. Softly.

"Am I in trouble?" she whispered.

His smile was pure seduction. Pulling back, he slid his cock along her pussy again. "Oh, yeah."

"Good." She reached for him. He caught her hands and shook his head. "You keep these up here."

"Why?"

"Because this is me creating us, and I need my focus."

He needed his focus. She wrapped her fingers around his and squeezed while she blinked back tears.

"You crying?"

"It was a beautiful thought."

"Heck, woman. I'm trying to seduce you, not make poetry."

"You're doing both."

"If I let go, are you good to keep your hands there?"

She had to ask. "What if I don't?"

His hand slipped down to cup her breast. "Then I won't kiss these pretty little breasts."

She slammed her hands back into the mattress.

He smiled, the fall of his hair hiding the scar, and again she saw the boy inside the man.

"Awful compliant, all of a sudden."

"I'm hoping for a reward."

He looked up from where he was studying her breasts. "Good."

His expression grew serious as he watched his thumb play over her nipple. She had the strange feeling he was avoiding her gaze. "We both know what it's like to be made love to for all the wrong reasons."

He *was* avoiding her gaze. Because he felt vulnerable? It was hard to imagine Tracker unsure.

"This time, I want to try it for the right ones, and see how it goes."

She reached up and cupped his face in her hands, bringing his gaze to hers. By the time she got to see his expression, any trace of insecurity was gone, but she knew it had been there. She knew only one way to make it go away.

"I want you to make love to me, Tracker. The way you've always dreamed of."

His eyes went dark and hot. "No need to go that far. I'll settle for this."

"This" began with his big hand plumping her breast before squeezing it a few times, stroking gently with his fingers from base to tip once, twice, three times, never quite touching the nipple, teasing her with the possibility. Pleasure built with the rhythm he set, arcing inward from her nipple, flowing in a direct line to her pussy. Her clit swelled right along with her breast. Her pussy ached in sweet pulses, and still he didn't touch her where she needed him to.

"Tracker," she whispered, twisting on the bed.

Another almost touch. "Anything you want, sweets."

"You. I want you."

"Where?" He breathed the question against her aching nipple.

"Here." She arched her back, pressing her nipple against the softness of his lips. They parted, tempting her further. His breath bathed the nub in heat, preparing it for the moist possession of his tongue. Soft against hard. Wet against dry.

"Tracker!"

She moaned, he laughed, and his hair brushed against her breast. Another sweet caress, ripe with tenderness, and just like when he kissed her mouth, she heard the *I love you* in his touch. And when his lips caught the tender bud between them and pressed before sucking slowly, easily, she also heard the *I want you*.

And that was beautiful.

His hand slid over her stomach and then farther. She gasped.

"Easy, sweets," he whispered against her breast. "Just more pleasure."

His finger nudged between the thick folds of her labia, finding her clit. Lights shot from behind her eyes as he pressed.

"Oh!"

"What? Too much? Do you want me to stop?"

It was a struggle to find her voice as his finger circled over the slick bundle of nerves, but she did. "If you do, I'm going to fetch that damn knife."

Her reward for her impudence was another flick, followed by a light pinch that had her whole body jerking.

"Oh, my heavens!"

"If you like that, you're going to love this."

"This" was a string of biting kisses down her torso, over the softness of her lower stomach and below. By the time she figured out what he intended, it was too late. His mouth replaced his finger, and all she could do was grab the pillow behind her head and hold on as wave after wave of searing joy rocked her body.

"Tracker."

"Too late to protest, sweets." He burrowed his tongue deeper into her folds. "I've got the taste of you now."

The pleasure rose hard and fast, spiraling through her center, tangling in her pussy, gathering in a knot in her womb, growing with every pass of his tongue, expanding until she couldn't bear it, but she had to, because he wouldn't let her go.

"Don't. Stop. Don't stop." The chant went through her mind, fell from her lips. He pushed her thighs open, slid a thick finger into her pussy. She spread her legs wider, the tension in her like a wild thing, clawing for release.

Another pass of his tongue. Another unbearable rake of pleasure. "Tracker!"

She was so close. So close.

"Come, baby. Come hard for me."

His teeth closed over her clit. She tensed, caught between fear and anticipation, which only made her quiver more. A second finger joined the first, thrusting in and out.

"Now," he growled, covering his teeth with his lips and drawing her clit out in a quick tug, at the same time he added another finger.

Her world exploded. Lightning slashed behind her eyelids, shot through her veins, seared through her pussy, sending her into paroxysms that had her screaming with an overwhelming joy. Before she could recover, his cock replaced his fingers. Delicate muscles struggled to stretch around the broad head. She bit her lip as the pleasure bordered on pain.

"Relax." Like velvet, the order slipped under her fear, stroking it away. This was Tracker. He would never hurt her.

Taking a breath, she did. Resistance faded and then he was in her, pushing forward in a slow, steady rhythm that opened her gradually, completely. Perfectly. Lights danced behind her lids, but there was no chaos, only good. He pulled out and thrust in again. Slowly and steadily. Oh, dear heavens. So good. The lights expanded, finding the dark corners inside her that had grown with the return of her memory, and bathing them in light. This was making love. This was the difference.

"That's it. Take me. Just…like…that," Tracker growled deep in his throat.

She moaned and lifted in counterpoint, driving his cock a fraction deeper. Oh God, he filled her perfectly. "Oh!"

He ground his groin into hers in small circles. "Good?"

"Yes!" Very, very good. This time, when he pulled back, his thumb was there, rubbing and stroking her clit, bringing back the burning that was so much more than desire. So much more than pleasure. And this time, when he returned, it was harder, but just as deep. Oh, heaven, so deep. The lights grew brighter, her breath shorter. She needed, needed…

"More!"

"Oh, hell yes!" Without breaking that driving rhythm, he pushed her knees up to her chest, opening her further, fucking her harder. She was so close, so close.

"Tracker!"

His answer was a growl and a thrust so hard it jarred her forward. "Come for me, baby. Come on my cock."

"You, too," she managed to gasp.

"I'm trying."

She opened her eyes. His were closed. The same passion that had her ripping at the pillow was there in his expression, but in the lines by his eyes, there was another emotion. A sadness that didn't belong there. Her wonderful, sexy man, giving even when he didn't need to, not asking for what he needed in return because he thought such things weren't for him.

We both know what it's like to be made love to for all the wrong reasons.

Yes, they did. But this wasn't one of those times, no matter what crazy notion he had in his head now. Tracker opened his eyes. Reaching up, Ari placed her palm against his cheek, the way she had before. She watched the understanding hit, the passion take over, the pleasure break, saw him struggle to contain it, to hold on to control. With a stroke of her thumb and a simple order, she stole both. "Come for me, Tracker."

13

"Damn, woman, I think you broke something."

Ari rolled over and propped herself up against his chest. "Nothing permanent, I hope."

Her stomach rumbled embarrassingly. She was hungry. It seemed such a mundane thing to realize, when her world had just shifted on its axis. Tracker's big hand slid across her stomach. Heat from their skin bonded them together. She placed her hand over his.

"Sounds like somebody's hungry."

She raised an eyebrow, trailing her fingers over his chest. "And you're not?"

As if on cue, his own stomach rumbled. He smiled and pulled her down on top of him. Her legs fell naturally to either side, and just as naturally, her pussy cradled his cock. He hummed in his throat before slapping her ass.

"None of that, now."

A sweet heat spread to her pussy, which didn't have the sense to be exhausted.

"I need food, woman."

"So do I." She slid off the side of the bed and stood, belatedly realizing she didn't have a wrap. And without the haze of passion to give her courage, she felt exposed. The edge of the sheet angled off the side of the bed. She tugged, but it didn't release. It was caught under Tracker's hip, and darn it if he didn't sprawl there like a pagan god, legs slightly spread, cock slightly engorged. She couldn't look away from his cock. Even at rest, it looked huge. She remembered how it had felt inside her. Thick and hard as he claimed her, harder at the end, just before he came, throbbing inside her as he flooded her pussy with his seed.

Even now she was wet from him, with him. With them. He'd offered her a towel, but she hadn't wanted to erase the moment just yet. His cock gave a little twitch. She wondered how it would feel against her tongue. Would it feel as good to him as his tongue had to her? With her past, it wasn't something she ever thought she'd be considering, but the man was just so mouthwateringly handsome in a purely uncivilized way. Pure strength of body, of purpose. A wild creature, tame for now. For her.

Tracker laid his head back on his folded hands. His crooked smile daring her to keep trying to get the sheet undone. She followed the trajectory of his gaze. Yanking on the sheet was making her breasts shimmy.

"Lecher!"

With an arch of a brow he upped the dare in his eyes. "Deep thoughts?"

It just burst from her. "I was wondering how you'd taste."

His cock went hard in a slow stretch. She watched it happen, marveling at the miraculous change. He caught her looking and laughed.

"Oh, my God." She spun with the sheet, using her body weight to yank it out from under him, covering herself as she went. With a suddenness she wasn't expecting, it released. She stumbled a couple steps. Tracker caught her hand, using her momentum to pull her back to the bed.

She fell against him, bracing herself on her hand and one knee. He still had that mischief in his gaze. She met and matched it, the novelty of laughing with a man in bed too unique to resist. "That isn't what I thought you meant when you said you were hungry."

"Me, either, but you've convinced me."

"How?"

"Lying there all sexy, flaunting your...your maleness."

"Maleness? Is that what we're calling it?"

"Do you have another word?"

"None fit for your lips."

Concern crept up beside the passion and humor in his gaze. It was for her. He never worried about himself. He was always so convinced that he could handle any pain that came his way. She touched a finger to the deep, circular scar on his shoulder. A bullet wound? Whether it be physical or emotional, he just went through life collecting scar upon scar.

"You don't have to do this."

But she wanted to. He knew everything about making love to her, while she knew nothing about him. "I want to know everything about you."

"Everything is a tall order."

So cautious. She sat back. "I want to start with this."

Leaning over, he lit the lamp with one of the sulfurs on the bedstand. The glass shade settled back into place with a soft rattle. He motioned to the impromptu wrap. "Then why the sheet?"

The scent of smoke drifted over, covering the scent of cloves. "I was embarrassed."

"After all we've done?"

"A belated attack of modesty."

Hooking his finger in the fold over her breast, he pulled. "What will it take to defeat it?"

She toyed with the end, holding it against the pressure he applied, her breath coming faster. Flirting with a naked man was not the horrible thing her mother had warned her about. She gave him her best coquettish smile. The one she'd practiced in front of the mirror. The one her mother said was guaranteed to land her the husband of her choice. "Why?"

"Because I'm going to want to be fondling those breasts while you're finding out how I taste."

Oh. She shivered. Tracker took advantage of the distraction to tug the sheet free. It fell around her hips without her giving even a whisper of protest. She slid off the bed and onto her knees. His cock flexed. Her mouth watered.

He cupped his balls and cock in his hand. The head was large and fat, darker than the rest. Beautiful. She remembered that intimate discomfort as she had taken him that first time. He was a big man and he'd been inside her. Now she was going to take him again. In a different, more intimate way. She stroked his thigh, her hand inching higher. Level with his cock, she had a bird's-eye view of the effect of her touch. His erection flexed again in invitation. Just a little closer and she'd be there. She'd know how he tasted. Meeting his gaze, she licked her lips.

"Are you ready?" she asked, desire and an odd sense of power flowing together.

"Goddammit, sweets, you're going to kill me."

She shook her head, her smile feeling as soft as her emotions. "No, I'm going to love you."

He angled his cock down so it was perfectly aligned with her mouth. "Then stop teasing me before I come just from the anticipation of how it will feel."

Could she really tease him to the point that he could come without being in her? Did she really have that power?

Tracker hooked his hand behind her neck and dragged her forward, laughing as he did. "Not this time."

"What?"

"I can see you toying with the idea." Kissing her softly, he whispered, "And not this time."

"You want my mouth."

"Yeah. Just a little."

He was a horrible liar. He wanted her mouth a lot. He'd pleased her without reservation and without restriction. Now she wanted to please him the same way, before it was too late. He had to leave her in two days. Another gift from Vincente's lie. She already knew the torment of living with regret. She'd spent months mourning all the things she couldn't remember doing with a husband she couldn't remember. She'd been in this country long enough to know there were no guarantees.

Good men died every day for reasons that made no sense.

In two days Tracker was leaving to settle a score with Harold Amboy, her father's solicitor, the man who hunted her and Desi. If Tracker never came back to her, she wanted every memory she could cram into her brain, so that in the years to come she'd be able to pull them out and relive the moments that were so special. Because there'd never be another man for her. She understood that now. This was why she'd trusted

Tracker from the moment she saw him. This was why he'd been able to touch her when no one else could. This was why she felt as if she'd come home when she stepped into his arms. He was the miracle she'd prayed for. The man meant for her.

She stuck her tongue out and touched it to the tip of his penis. Holding his gaze as she swirled her tongue around the sensitive head. Taking her cues from how he had loved her, she skimmed her fingers down his cock, gaining her pleasure from his. She did it again. He moaned and caught his breath.

"You like that."

"You liked my tongue on your pussy, too."

Cupping his balls in her hand, she shook her head at his slight defensiveness. Did he think she found him any less appetizing than he did her? "No. I *loved* that. And I think I'm going to like this, too."

This time she rubbed the flat of her tongue over the head, judging from his reaction whether he liked it enough to repeat. His hips bucked and his cock prodded her lips in tiny pulses of demand. She didn't grant entrance. He'd taught her that anticipation made the pleasure that much keener. She wanted every bit of pleasure for him.

She made another pass with her tongue, blowing lightly on the broad surface. He cursed. She smiled. On the next pulse of his hips, she opened her mouth, keeping her tongue flat so there was no impediment to his thrust. He moaned as his fingers tunneled through her hair, curling in the strands as his cock slid over her tongue. He smelled of cloves and man. He tasted of life and possibilities.

Pulling her down on his cock, he thrust almost helplessly. She gagged, and for a split second he held her there, suspended in his pleasure, as her throat worked. Breathing through her nose, she controlled her gag response, waiting as he found his own control. He pulled back, relieving the pressure, leaving her with the pleasure.

The stroke of his hand down her cheek soothed as much as his words. "I'm sorry, sweets. So sorry. I should be shot."

"No." She tried to hold him to her, but he was too strong. His cock slipped from her mouth.

She pulled, wanting him back. It was like trying to move a rock.

"This wasn't a good idea."

"I disagree."

She could imagine how she looked to him, still kneeling there, her lips wet with saliva, still parted, as if anticipating the next thrust.

"I can't control myself when it comes to your mouth."

"You want it that badly?"

"You could say that."

Letting go of his thighs, she changed her hold and her tactics. Curling her fingers around his cock, she milked it slowly, drawing his thoughts away from retreat and into pleasure. "I want that, too. I want to know how it feels to hold you against my tongue as the desire builds. I want to know how hard you can get. How wild you can be. How much heat you can show me. I want to taste your pleasure."

His hips pumped in counterpoint to her pumping. "Dammit. Stop."

"No. Not until I taste your pleasure." She met his gaze dead on. She wasn't a scared girl hiding from her past. She was a woman who remembered everything, and one of the things she remembered was that she hated being afraid. "Like you did mine. I want to know all there is to know about you this way."

"Ari?"

"Let me make love to you, Tracker. Let me give you the pleasure you want. Let me touch you with love just in case."

His cock jerked up and then down, coming to rest heavily in her hand. She gladly took the weight, took responsibility for his pleasure.

"Just in case what?"

In case the unthinkable happened. "If I lose everything again, I want the memories."

His thumb stroked over her mouth, sliding easily on the moist flesh. It was her turn to shiver. "It won't be some tentative thing. I could lose control again."

"Who said I wanted you to have control?"

"I did."

She added a second hand to the first. There was still more left over than she could take in her mouth. "Well, this is my memory, and I'm building it for us and I'm going to do it my way." To emphasize her point, she lowered her head on his cock, taking it deep, holding it deep.

His hands went back to curling in her hair, holding her in place. With a gentle push, he gave her that much more. "Just how much control do you think I have?"

More than her. There was something so seductive about pleasing Tracker this way. Something so hot about dragging those hoarse moans from his lips. She kissed his penis. Softly. Gently.

But this time she didn't pull away. Instead, she opened her mouth, covering her teeth with her lips, and made love to his cock. The way she wanted to make love with him. Without inhibitions. Without regrets. And according to the swear words being rattled off in a guttural explosion of sound overhead, without a lot of common sense. Tracker picked up the pace, shuttling his cock in and out of her mouth, tunneling

it deeper and harder. All it took was following the directions
of his hands and accepting as much of his cock as she could.
Relaxing her throat, she took what he offered, hearing the
need behind the curses, feeling the want, hearing the *I love
you* he didn't speak but always showed her.

She worked the base of his cock with her fingers as she
sucked the swollen head, running her tongue over it in rapid
swirls.

"Goddammit, Ari. I can't hold back."

Tracker's hips bucked out of rhythm. His cock became diamond hard, pressing back against her tongue as she tested his
readiness. He tried to stop. It was his nature to be in control,
but in this she was in charge. Every time he tried, she'd rub
her tongue in a different spot, rake her teeth a little harder,
scrap her nails along his balls. She wanted to destroy his illusions, take him to a place he'd never been before with any
other woman. She shifted and rubbed her thighs together,
trying to control her own passion.

He pulled back, leaving just the tip of his cock resting on
her tongue.

"I'm going to come."

She cupped his balls in her hand. They were heavy and full,
drawn tightly to his body. "Yes."

Her whisper fanned across the swollen crest. He shivered
and speared his cock back into her mouth. She sucked hard,
giving him as much as she could, caressing every inch when he
thrust deep, sucking hard when he withdrew. Giving, taking—
it all blurred together.

"If you're going to run, run now."

The words were harsh. The truth sweet. He was trying
to hold back for her. To spare her from the fullness of his
passion. She was beginning to believe he thought too much.

She nipped along the underside of his cock before nibbling over the smooth head. His fingers clenched in her hair almost compulsively.

Holding his gaze, she licked her lips, smiled and put her hands behind her head, pushing her breasts out, inviting a caress. She wasn't running.

"Shit." Pleasure followed the curse as his fingers closed over her nipples, pulling, tugging, twisting, drawing her into the storm, layering another texture on top of the ones already painted.

"That's good, baby. Oh, that's good."

The words flowed over her in dark encouragement. Her breasts throbbed with each tug, each twist. She wanted more. Needed more.

"More, sweets. Damn, you've got to take more."

She tried, but it was too much. He was too much. But so good. She gagged and held on, shifting her grip to his strong thighs. Her jaw ached. Her tongue burned; her pussy flowered and wept with need. As the passion built, she dug her nails into the back of his thighs and pulled herself farther onto his cock with each thrust. He hit the back of her throat again. She was better prepared this time. She didn't gag as much. He pulled back. His thrusts picked up speed but never force. Despite what he'd threatened, he was careful, going only so far, never too far.

It wasn't far enough. She wanted to take it all, wanted to swallow him whole, but he was just too big, so she took as much she could, pumping in tandem with her hands in counterpoint with his thrusts, following the rhythm he set—faster, harder, deeper. She wanted more. Oh, God, she wanted it all. Who could've known that something that had been so degrading before could be so pleasurable with Tracker?

"I'm going to come."

He tried to pull away. She did not let him. She'd known many men this way against her will. But it was different with Tracker. With Tracker it was good. She shook her head, opened her mouth wider and relaxed her throat, giving him just that much more of herself. She could feel the desire cresting within him as the pleasure built to the bursting point. She wanted it. For him. For herself.

She held on to his cock when he would have withdrawn. Her throat muscles worked as he pressed against them.

"Son of a bitch." It was a curse, a blessing, a compliment. His hips bucked in her hands. He stopped pushing her away and started dragging her closer. He came hard and sweet, challenging her to take him all. She tried, but he was too much. It was good, though. Pleasing Tracker was good. She swallowed one last time before dragging in a hard breath. She didn't need to ask if she'd pleased him. The answer was in the breath he couldn't finish, the fine tremor that ran through him.

He didn't immediately withdraw. She was glad. He was hers. This time was hers. Suckling his cock, she gentled him even as he gentled his hands on her nipples. They were so sensitive. Almost bruised after the hours of lovemaking. They needed soothing. She wanted the touch of his tongue, the softness of his kiss. She wanted soothing. She wanted to be loved.

As if understanding, Tracker brought his hand to her cheek, tracing her lips around his cock as if he, too, needed proof of the connection. A shudder went through him. He cupped her chin as she circled her tongue around the head of his cock one last time. "Are you all right?"

She was more than all right. For the first time in a long time she felt whole.

14

They were still hungry. Stealing across the yard like thieves in the night, they sneaked into the kitchen. Tracker, dressed only in a pair of leather pants, held the door open. As Ari stepped through, he pinched her butt.

She squealed. He held his finger to his lips. "Shh. You don't want to wake the house."

She giggled. Actually giggled.

He lit the lamp on the table. A soft, yellow light illuminated the room.

"Or do you?"

He wanted to know if she wanted to see Desi and Miguel. "Not yet." She wasn't ready for that yet. Desi, because she was so angry, and Miguel, because she was just beginning to feel clean. To feel worthy. She smiled at Tracker over her shoulder as she went to explore what was in the cupboards. "I need to eat."

"Can't say that I want to see your strength fail."

Unbelievably, she blushed.

A china clock sat on the cabinet. She picked it up and tilted it to the light. Ten o'clock. Dinner was probably still good.

Trucker walked over to the stove. She watched the muscles in his back flex under his skin, followed his spine down to his tight buttocks. There wasn't an ounce of fat on the man. He was all lean flesh and warm skin. The narrowness of his hips drew her eye. He took a step and muscle flexed beneath the supple leather of his pants. She curled her fingers at the memory of how all that maleness felt surging against her palms.

"Looks like stew and biscuits. Will that do?"

She blinked at the mundane question, then smiled. His mouth took on the softness that told her he was thinking about kissing her. Weakness assaulted her knees. Good heavens, the man was potent.

"I could eat cooked rat right now."

He faked a shudder. "Speak for yourself. I don't think I could ever be that hungry."

She knew that wasn't true. In the quiet moments after making love, he'd given her a brief rundown of how the men of Hell's Eight had managed after their parents had been killed. It was by what he didn't say that she knew how bad it had been. They'd almost starved to death.

She didn't contradict him, though. Tonight was not the time for that kind of memory. Tonight was about letting go of the past and greeting the future. For both of them. And she wanted to begin this right.

Trucker lifted the lid of a small blue crock on the stove. "How would you feel about honey for your biscuits?"

"Oh, yes!"

He gave her another one of those hot looks that she usually missed because he was hiding behind his hat brim. He hid a lot behind that hat brim. "Damn, I think I'm jealous of the biscuits."

She found the silverware in a drawer. Closing it, she shook her head. He made her feel young and silly and very desired. "Well, if you're good, maybe later I'll see what else I like honey on."

Hooking his hand behind her neck as she passed, he pulled her to him. She loved it when he did that. There was such possession in the gesture. It said more clearly than anything else "this woman is mine." And if she was quick enough to look into his eyes before their mouths connected, she'd see the anticipation he felt.

He tugged and she went, leading with her heart, because with him, she'd never had a chance. His kiss was hot and hard. Her response was just as hot, just as hard. He let her go, a smile on his lips. "Stop distracting me, woman. I'm hungry."

"*You* kissed *me*."

"Hmm, and what did you expect, when you're flaunting those pretty breasts at me?"

Looking down, she gasped. Her impromptu wrapper gaped open. She quickly clutched it closed.

"Don't bother on my account."

She rolled her eyes. "What if someone saw?"

"There's no one around to see."

"What if someone comes in?"

"I'd hear them first." He took the plates over to the table. Pulling out a chair, he stood behind it and waited. For her, she realized. It was a display of manners men reserved for ladies. And he was doing it for her. A smile lit her from the inside out and the niggle of doubt that he only wanted her for sex died.

She sat. As he walked around the table to take his own seat, he said, "You've got to have more faith, Ari. You're married to one of Hell's Eight. We have the hearing of wolves."

"Another trait is the inflated impression of their abilities."

Ari would recognize that voice anywhere. It was an exact duplicate of her own. She turned and glared at Tracker. "You didn't hear *that*."

Or had he? He didn't look surprised at all. As a matter of fact, he looked a bit satisfied.

"Damn you. When did you plan this?" she demanded.

"Ari…"

She ignored Desi. Tracker didn't flinch from the accusation. "When you were asleep."

"Why?"

"She's family."

And family was everything to him. "It was none of your business."

"Maybe not."

There was no maybe about it.

"I asked him to do it." Desi stood in the doorway, a white silk wrapper tied around her slender body. Her expression was strained, her eyes anxious.

"So I shouldn't be mad at him, because he betrayed me, too?"

"No one betrayed you."

"I trusted you."

He took a forkful of food. "And you still do. You're just mad because I forced your hand."

She wanted to throw her plate at him.

"Don't." The warning was so low that only she heard it. "Give her a chance, Ari."

"Please," Desi whispered. "Talk to me."

Tracker nodded. "Talk to her."

"Fine." Ari glared harder at Tracker and said to Desi, "That's a nice robe."

Desi tightened the belt of her wrap. Another sign that she was nervous. Ari looked around the rough-hewn kitchen. The wrapper was certainly more expensive than her surroundings would suggest Caine could afford.

Desi fiddled with the ties and looked away, a flush touching her cheeks. "Caine has it in his head that I have to have nice things."

"He knows what you gave up," Tracker said. "He doesn't want you to regret it."

"It was an easy trade. When it comes to a choice between love or money, the only choice is love. When are you going to understand that?"

"Maybe when love starts putting food on the table."

Desi rolled her eyes. "Fine. I'll check back with you then."

"Deal. In the meantime, you just go and let Caine spoil you as much as he sees fit."

"I do," Desi said. "I just worry that the ranch will suffer."

Tracker shook his head. "There's no way. No matter how much Caine wants to spoil you, he won't put the ranch at risk. It's your livelihood, his dream, your future. He knows that."

Desi nodded and continued to stand in the doorway like an intruder in her own home. Ari waffled between pity and anger. It took her a moment to realize why. She was jealous. Of her sister.

She pushed the food around her plate. Darn it. Life was simpler when it was a lie.

Tracker touched her foot under the table. She glanced up.

Both he and Desi were staring at her. Waiting for her to say something. She didn't know what to say.

She settled for, "It's good that he loves you."

Desi's smile was a mere stretch of her lips.

Tracker looked disappointed. "You haven't seen your sister in over a year. Is that the best you can do?"

"You didn't ask my permission to start this. You don't get to complain when it doesn't go the way you want."

"Ari!"

This time she glared at her twin, the feeling of being trapped growing. "Stay out of it, Desi."

"He just wanted you to be happy."

"He can't control everything."

Tracker's chair scraped across the floor as he stood. "I'm sorry, Desi. This was the wrong place."

"Not to mention the wrong time," Ari muttered, feeling small after the surge of anger faded. She'd wanted to talk to her sister in her own time, in her own way, when the rage had subsided. When she could do it without breaking down.

Tracker grabbed his plate and silverware. "You two have things to talk about. I'm going to leave you to it."

If he thought he was leaving her with this mess, he had another think coming. Grabbing her own plate, she caught up to him in four strides.

"Where are we going?"

"On a picnic, I guess."

"It's night."

"I'm still hungry."

Her appetite had long since fled.

"The picnic basket is beside the door," Desi offered. Ari admired her for the self-control that allowed her to make the suggestion. Ari was afraid if she tried to speak, she'd burst either into tears or screams.

Tracker picked up the basket with his free hand and nodded to Desi. "I'm sorry."

"I don't need you to apologize for me," Ari told him.

"Apparently, you do."

The censure hurt. "She's my sister."

"And my friend. You got a point in there somewhere?"

She did, but one look at Desi's face killed the impulse. She was suffering.

Desi ran her hand through her hair. "Don't let what you think I did come between you two. I'm not worth it."

I'm not worth it.

How many times had Ari felt just that way? How many times had she had those same thoughts? How many times had she let that feeling of being so low she wasn't worth noticing make her decisions for her? Most recently, when they'd taken Miguel away. She hadn't fetched him back because she'd thought he deserved better. She was his mother and she loved him, but part of her couldn't shake the belief that by keeping him with her she was dooming him to a life of hell. She wanted him to have a better life, so she'd been prepared to sacrifice herself.

Looking into Desi's eyes now, she saw the same sacrifice. She and her sister had come so far, but parts of them were still out on the plains, lost and looking for a way home. She wanted to hug Desi. She wanted to run. She didn't do either. She just stood there, her thoughts turning in her head.

Tracker opened the back door. Humid night air entered the room. Finally, she shook her head. "I'm sorry. I didn't want it to be like this."

"I understand."

SARAH McCARTY

The hell of it was, she probably did. Ari asked, "Is Miguel all right?"

"He misses you."

"I miss him, too."

"I'll bring him over tomorrow."

She had to start moving forward sometime. Tomorrow was as good a day as any. "Thank you."

Ari's hand was cramping from holding the plate. She didn't want the food, didn't want the confrontation. She didn't want to be this way with Desi, but whenever she looked at her twin, she couldn't forget that when it'd come to the moment of truth, Desi had saved herself. And after saving herself, she hadn't sent help. Ari had counted on that help. Prayed for it. Believed in it as she'd been passed from man to man, sold and used. Rescue had never come.

And now she found out that while Ari had been suffering, Desi had been falling in love. Getting married. Having a baby. Part of her was happy for her sister. The other part was bitterly resentful, and there wasn't any apparent way of resolving the two. What Desi had was what Ari would have wished for her if she'd had a choice. It was not having the choice that burned like acid.

Tracker nudged her arm with his elbow. "Let's go."

If she had any guts at all, Ari would kick him in the balls. It was because of Tracker's highhandedness that her night of new beginnings had gone to hell. She glared at him. He cocked an eyebrow at her.

"I'm not hungry."

"You've got to eat. You've got a child to feed. You know that."

"My milk dried up. You know *that*." She refused to blush when she recalled how he knew.

246

"It might come back with some good food and relaxing."

"And it might not."

"Borrowing trouble, sweets?"

Yes, she believed she was.

Tracker nodded and motioned for her to go through the door. "Thank you for dinner, Desi." To Ari he said, "Let's go."

Tracker's face looked as grim as the reaper's. It was dark outside. Hardly inviting. She hesitated. He jerked his chin again. "Come on."

As soon as she got out the door, he stopped and pushed his plate into her hands before putting the basket on the ground.

"What are you doing?" she asked.

"I forgot the lantern."

Two minutes later he was back.

"Where are we going?" she demanded.

"To someplace special."

"What could be so special that I need to go see it in the middle of the night?"

"Trust me."

"I did, and look where it got me."

He let that slide. Taking her elbow, he guided her around the house, the bouncing light from the lantern illuminating a faint path. As they went down a small slope, she could hear water running over rocks, but she couldn't see past the pool of light to where it originated. She looked back over her shoulder. A light still shone in the kitchen, but there was no sign of Desi. Ari shook her head against the onslaught of emotion that brought. Sadness. Loss. Too much of everything, when she felt as fragile as glass.

Tracker stopped. She had the impression of openness.

"We're here."

"The tone of your voice doesn't imply being *here* is going to be much fun."

"I'm not in the mood for fun."

"Well, neither am I, so why don't we just go back home?"

"I'm not happy with how you treated Desi."

"Then you shouldn't have ambushed me with the meeting."

"You're right." He sighed and took something out of the basket. When he snapped it in the air, she realized it was a blanket. "I guess I just thought you'd see each other and find the closeness again."

"Maybe the problem is we're too close."

"Can't be too close with family. When all is said and done, they're all you have."

"I know, but, Tracker, you can't rush me."

An expression she couldn't decipher flitted across his face. "I'm sorry."

She didn't want to talk anymore about the things she couldn't fix. She sat. "Why are we here in the dark?" she asked, slapping her shoulder. "Besides providing dinner for the mosquitoes, I mean."

Tracker squatted beside her and cupped her chin in his hand. His expression was deadly serious. "A chance to talk."

Oh, God. Not more talk. "About what?"

"The day after tomorrow at the latest, we'll be settling accounts with Amboy."

"*We* being you and the rest of Hell's Eight?"

"I'm not anticipating any problems, but you never know. I doubt your Mr. Amboy will be coming alone."

"You have to be careful."

"I'm always careful, but chance is a fickle thing. If something happens to me, I want to know you're safe. I want to know you've got your family."

He was talking about Desi. Ari shook her head and fisted her hands. "I look at Desi and I see her walking away, leaving me behind. No matter how much I want to forgive her, I can't."

"It might be easier if you heard her side."

"I know, but what if I do and I still can't forgive? What do I do then? I don't want to lose my sister forever. I don't."

"Then you come back and you try again until you do find the forgiveness. You've got a big heart, Ari. You forgave me for the way I look, for the way I behave. You're even halfway to forgiving Josefina and Vincente."

"What makes you say that?"

"You've lost the anger when you say their names."

"In a way, their lies were a blessing. They allowed me to know you without the scars of the past."

"I can understand that, but if you forgive them, why not Desi?"

"It's different with her."

"Because you love her."

"Yes."

"I want this settled, Ari."

"I can't."

A twig snapped behind her. He held her chin when she would've looked.

"I want it settled now."

Tracker didn't reach for his gun. She knew who was behind her.

She couldn't go through this again. "Don't ask this of me, Tracker."

"I'm asking."

"It's not fair."

"I never said it was, but I'm still asking." His thumb brushed her lips. "Just remember, she's hurting, too."

Ari could see that. Desi walked into the lamplight. Her arms were wrapped around her abdomen, as if she'd taken one blow too many. Tear tracks stained her cheeks. Her eyes were red, her face blotchy.

A crack appeared in Ari's anger. So much pain. For both of them. "Oh, Desi."

Tracker stood. Desi came to the edge of the blanket. She stopped dead, as if it were a border that couldn't be crossed.

Tracker held out his hand. Ari put hers in it, feeling as if she was about to step off a ledge. "Listen to her, Ari. At least do that."

Ari nodded.

"I didn't leave you," Desi whispered.

"I was there. I saw what happened."

"I know how it looked—"

"I'll get over it."

"Ari," Tracker warned.

She turned on him. "Why should I believe whatever she says?"

He squeezed her hand and dragged her off the blanket into the middle of the open area. The ground was soft and springy under her feet. She could see flashes of white as the lantern swayed. Tracker halted. "This is why."

He held the lantern high. Little white flowers dotted the ground. In daylight the leaves of the flowers would be green, but at night they appeared black, making the contrast even more startling. Tracker let go of her and bent down and plucked a flower. Ari knew what it was before he shoved it into her hand. It was a daisy. Just like the ones in the meadow back home behind the summer house. The meadow where she and her sister had played, dreamed, made promises to each other. Fanciful ones made with a child's belief that they could control life through sheer force of will. Where they promised to always protect each other. Where they promised to always stand up for one another and never let anything or anyone come between them.

"I don't know much about what your home life was like when you were little." He pointed to the flower. "But I know what that is."

"What?"

He waved his hand to encompass the meadow. "This is a hard land, Ari. It takes a toll on everything that tries to put down roots. By rights, not a single flower should survive here. But they're not dead. And neither are you."

He shone the lantern in Desi's direction. "And neither is your sister."

Desi sobbed and her hand covered her mouth.

"I may not know everything I should, but I know what that is in your hand. It stands for a promise from your sister to you. A promise kept."

And we'll protect each other forever.

"How did you know?"

"I didn't, but no one works that hard to make the impossible happen without a reason. These flowers are alive because they mean something to both of you. Something so important, Desi wouldn't let them die, despite the backbreaking work it took to keep them alive."

Ari covered her mouth and stared at her sister, the daisies and then back at her sister. "Oh, God. Desi."

Tracker cupped her cheek. Taking the flower, he tucked

it in her hair. "When you go, remember that moment of betrayal. But you might want to remember all this, too." He handed her the lantern, then took her by the shoulders and turned her in the direction of her twin. "Go talk to your sister. I'll stand guard."

She started walking. So did Desi, and the hope in her expression tore Ari's heart. Tracker was right. This was a hard land that took a toll on everything, but her sister had taken on the challenge and made it beautiful.

Nothing will ever come between us. Sisters forever.

Ari pulled the daisy from her hair and stared at the petals— so many coming together to make something simply beautiful. Whatever happened that day, she knew Desi hadn't left her willingly.

She handed the flower to her twin. "We promised to always be there for each other."

"I was."

"How?"

"If it had been you instead of me, what choice would you have made? What would you have done?"

"I wouldn't save myself, leaving you to suffer."

Desi crushed the flower in her hand. "What the hell makes you imagine I did? For heaven's sake, Ari, *think.* We did everything together, were everything to each other. What makes you think anything could possibly lead me to leave you like that?"

"I cried for you to come back. For months I waited for rescue. I held on, and I believed in you. No one ever came."

"That's not true. I sent Tracker. I sent them all."

Yes. She had. She couldn't stop the flow of words. They'd been trapped inside her for too long. "I didn't save myself, Ari. They said whomever I chose would be saved. I chose you, but then they turned around and said it didn't matter what I wanted. And they took me. It wasn't a rescue. They bought me for their personal use. Chained me naked to the bed when I escaped too often."

Her hand shook when she reached out. Ari grasped it, feeling Desi's pain as if it was her own. The trembling spread to her, and her own tears choked her voice, a harsh gasp of sound.

"I didn't know."

"How could you know anything? You were a prisoner."

"So were you."

"But I knew what you thought. Knew what you suffered. For almost two years I've had one goal—finding you. I sent the Hell's Eight after you even though I knew it would jeopardize Caine's dream, because the men couldn't be here, at the ranch. Even though I knew others would suffer because without the Eight there's no law. You were my sister. You needed to come home."

Ari couldn't stand it anymore. She hugged her. The tears poured harder. Hers, her sister's—who could tell? What did it matter? "I thought you were happy and free."

"I was. Eventually."

"Thinking that kept me sane."

"But you resented it."

"I hurt so much. I had to put the pain somewhere."

"So you put it into hating me."

Ari hugged her harder. It hurt so much to admit that, knowing how much it was going to pain Desi. "Yes." Her sister flinched. "But only because I knew there was nothing I couldn't forgive you for," she hastened to add.

Desi took a step back, still holding Ari's arm. "Tell me you forgive me."

"There's nothing to forgive."

Desi gripped so tightly that her nails bit into Ari's skin through her clothing. "Tell me so I have that memory, too."

The words came easily. "I forgive you." It wasn't so easy to ask for herself. "Can you forgive me?"

"Oh, yes. That's the easiest thing I've ever done. After years of not knowing if you were alive or dead, I've finally got my sister back."

Desi wiped her face with her sleeve. "When the note came from Zach that Tracker had found you, I just collapsed. I'd sent you that letter so you'd know who he was. I planted this field of daisies so you'd have a place to return to." She wiped her face again. Ari wiped hers. The tears wouldn't stop, for either of them, but the pain was subsiding.

"Tell me about Caine."

"When Caine found me, I was little more than an animal fighting and running, tempting death and defying it. My world was such chaos that some days I didn't even know who I was. Caine stepped into that chaos and did what he does best—sorted through it. When the padre backed him into a corner and told him he couldn't take me from the man who had me then, without benefit of marriage, Caine agreed. In one fell swoop he gave me respectability and a future. It took him a long time to get through to me. Even longer for me to believe that he wasn't tricking me, too, and that I was worthy." Desi shook her head. "It took a long time. But all that time I never stopped thinking of you and looking for you."

"I know." Ari believed her. When her sister's arms came around her, Ari started to cry again. "I'm sorry, I'm sorry."

"Me, too."

Desi shook her head. "Sometimes you need to be angry to stay alive. I know that."

"I'm so glad Caine found you."

"I'm glad Tracker found *you*."

She scrubbed her cheek. "He's high-handed."

"But a good man. You'll forgive him?"

Already her anger was fading. "Apparently I have a big heart."

"You do." Desi crossed her hands at the wrists and held her arms out in front of her—a memory lingering from childhood. Ari crossed her own wrists and held on tightly to her sister's hands. She didn't know whether she started to move or if Desi did, but suddenly they were spinning the way they had back in the old days, faster and faster, until the stars in the sky blended together into streaks of white.

For a brief moment, they were ten again and it was just her and Desi against the world, playing in a magical place where nothing could touch them. Where they were immortal. Where their parents were still alive.

She stumbled. "Mom and Dad…"

"Are dead."

"I know."

The sob came out of nowhere, wrenched from deep in her gut. Oh, God, would the tears never end? She'd never had the luxury of grief before, but now, under the stars in a meadow created from hope, she couldn't stop. She fell to her knees. Desi went with her, holding her close, crying with her, sharing the pain that both of them had bottled up for so long.

"We didn't even get to bury them. We just left them out on the plains."

"I put a tombstone up for them," Desi said quietly.

"Where?"

"The graveyard here. We can visit the site tomorrow."

"I'd like that." Ari wiped her eyes again. The tears were

finally slowing. On the other side of the pool of lamplight she could see Tracker watching. But he didn't come near. She held out her hand, but for the first time, he didn't come.

"I placed it beside the gravestones that represent the other Hell's Eight families. Caine's parents, Tia's husband and baby."

"So much death."

Desi nodded. "Yes, but there's also so much life." She smiled. "I have a son."

"I'm an aunt."

"Yes. His name is Jonah and he's a hellion, just like his father."

"Don't let Caine hear you say that," Tracker called over. "That's one man who dotes on his boy."

"He does." Desi smiled and wiped at her cheeks.

"I have a son," Ari stated.

"I know. He's the sweetest child."

Desi didn't mention his beginnings and neither did Ari. She preferred not to think of it. Miguel's life started with her.

"Thank you for taking care of him for me."

"You needed time to heal."

Ari shook her head. "Maybe. There were just so many memories coming at me so fast, so many bad things, I couldn't find the good anymore. In me or anything else."

Desi took her hand. Ari couldn't help but wish it was Tracker's.

"No matter how he came to be, Miguel is good."

Ari nodded, but bit her lip. "I worry because he looks so Indian."

"That'll be a problem if you go back East."

Ari looked over at Tracker. He didn't say a word. Had he changed his mind about her staying?

"I don't know what I'm going to do yet."

"You're welcome to stay here."

"Thank you." Ari swatted at her leg at the same time Desi slapped at her cheek.

"Are you ready to go in?"

"Yes, I think I am."

"Jonah's probably hungry. He and Miguel are already best buddies. When one wakes up, so does the other."

"Thank you for accepting him."

"He's my nephew."

Another mosquito bit her arm. A third went for her ankle. She swung at both. Desi was swatting them, too.

"Time to go." Desi picked up the lantern, hooked her arm with Ari's, the way they had many times before, and walked back with her to the house.

"The one thing that I found out here is that it's easy to start over. No questions. No explanations. You just go forward."

Ari looked back to where Tracker stood, watching but not following. "One step at a time."

"Yes," Desi agreed. "One step at a time."

15

"Looks like she's home," Shadow said, stepping out of the dark beside him.

Tracker watched the two women walk off, oblivious to anything else, anyone else. The sense of doom came crashing down.

"It took long enough," he muttered.

"She was well hidden." From her sister, from herself.

"Yeah. But she's back now."

"Does this mean we're finally going to get back to what we do best?"

The best thing he'd ever done was bring Ari and her son home. His methods might not have been the most highbrowed, but they'd got the job done. Desi had her sister and they were going to be all right.

"Looks like Ari got over hating her?"

"Ari never hated Desi. She was just hurt."

"You'll defend her to the grave, won't you?"

He probably would. "Yes."

"And Desi?"

"She got what she wanted."

Shadow reached into his pocket, handed Tracker a flask. "Special occasion," he said wryly. "Their finding each other is what everyone wanted, but it doesn't make it any easier for you."

Tracker shook his head. "I'm fine."

"Hell, man, she's not even looking back."

No. She wasn't. Tracker snatched the flask from Shadow, popped the cork and took a drink, welcoming the bitter burn as the alcohol made its way to his gut. "I got what I wanted."

Shadow took the flask back and took a swig. Tracker was surprised. Shadow wasn't much of a drinker, either.

"Shit. What you got was a taste of a heaven you'll never have."

"Since when do we need more than a taste?"

"Since you fell—"

Tracker cut him off. He didn't need it put into words. "You going to hog the whole thing?"

"Nope." Shadow handed the bottle over. "But you might want to hold off on drinking."

Tracker paused with the flask halfway to his mouth. "Why?"

"We got word from Caden."

Tracker put the cork back in the flask. "What did he have to say?"

"Harold Amboy came in with the army."

"How many men?"

"Not an army. *The* army. He's got the fucking U.S. Army guarding him."

Shit. "How did that happen?"

Shadow shrugged. "The man's got friends in high places."

"I don't care if he's the devil's own. He's not leaving San Antonio alive."

"That's what Caine said."

Tracker wasn't surprised. Desi had suffered as much as Ari, and Caine had a few scores of his own to settle. "He's going to have to get in line."

"I'll let you two work out who kills who, as long as in the end the bastard is dead. He's got too many contacts here, and now the stakes are too high. Now he's got to remove the women and the children. The next time he makes an attempt, he'll likely succeed, for the simple reason he can't afford to lose. His plan is getting too complicated to pull off."

"We won't allow it."

"No, we won't." Shadow's expression took on a calm that translated that "we" to an "I."

Tracker eyed him warily. "You're not planning anything stupid, are you?"

"Nope."

Tracker knew stupid was a subjective term to Shadow. Others might think taking on seven *Comancheros* alone was stupid. But to Shadow, who likely knew the families in their raiding path, it was stupid not to. The sad truth was that Shadow didn't fear death. Tracker wasn't even sure he didn't court it. He'd thought he'd accepted that part of his twin's personality, but watching Desi and Ari's reunion, he wasn't so sure anymore. He didn't want to lose his brother. But he didn't know how to stop it. Unlike Desi and Ari, they didn't have a field of daisies to fall into. They only had each other. And their demons.

"Just don't do anything rash. I'd hate to have to drink alone."

"No worries. Like a bad penny, I always turn up."

"Well, do us both a favor and don't turn up dead."

"I'll keep it in mind."

"What does Amboy know?"

"He doesn't know you have Ari. He's coming for Desi."

"Desi's married."

"Apparently he's got papers to set the marriage aside, claiming she wasn't in her right mind."

"I'm surprised Caine hasn't gone after them already."

It had been a year since Caine's marriage. The man still hadn't gotten over the miracle of Desi's love. She and their son were his greatest treasures. And woe to the man to tried to take them from him. The entire U.S. Army wouldn't be enough.

"He's working on it. The army complicates things. Plus, he needs to be sure Amboy is the one. He wants the threat to the twins removed once and for all."

"We need to keep Desi and Ari in the house."

"I'll tell Ed and Tia."

Tracker passed the flask back to Shadow.

"Are you all done?"

Yeah, he was. Ari was where she belonged, so half his promise was fulfilled. The second half would be finished when Harold Amboy was dead. The rest of Ari's life would be up to her. He wasn't worried whether she could handle it. She had her sister to help. If Ari stayed on Hell's Eight, Miguel would be accepted. If she went East, he'd still be accepted, because Ari would see to it. She might not see her strength yet, but Tracker could. She was Hell's Eight in the way she loved.

There was a pause and then Shadow said, "I'm sorry, brother."

"For what?"

"You lost the girl."

"But I got the prize."

"And was that enough?"

He'd been touched by love. "Yeah." He'd make it be enough.

"Well, I've got to tell you, if I can't have the whole, I don't even want to taste the part."

"You'll fall in love someday."

"If I do, feel free to bury me in that lot you've got reserved up at the cemetery."

"You serious?"

"Yes."

"Remind me when the time comes."

Tracker looked back at the meadow, all but invisible as the moon faded and darkness took over. He remembered Ari's trust, her tears, the way she'd walked away complete, with her sister, the way she'd never been with him.

It was time to go. He started walking. Shadow fell into step beside him. "You just going to leave the picnic stuff?"

"Someone will get it in the morning."

"All right." Shadow paced him for a few more steps. "If you don't mind my saying so, you've got the look of a man who's planning on doing something stupid."

Tracker moved to pull his hat down over his brow. It wasn't there. Shit, he'd left it at the house. He angled his steps to the right. "Just going to get my hat."

"Uh-huh. And then?"

He was going to hunt down Harold Amboy. "*Then* I'm going to do something stupid."

"Then I guess I'm tagging along."

The stage stop was one day outside San Antonio, but only four hours from Hell's Eight. A miscalculation on Amboy's part. Tracker was familiar with the station. It was the last in a long line of uncomfortable stops. And probably the worst. The wall boards had gaps between them, and the water tended toward briny rather than fresh. Inside there were two beds, one chair and quite a few families of mice. Usually the stage pressed on, preferring an open camp at a clean water hole a couple of hours west. The change this time was more than likely due to the Easterner. He'd probably shot off his mouth and Foul-Mouth Hank, the stage driver, had decided that was where he would sleep. The army might have wanted to change the location, but they didn't have any say over Hank, and he was an ornery cuss when pissed.

Tracker mentally reviewed the location. The hut was set at the bottom of a small hill. The horses would be in a separate corral to the right. Depending on how many men the army had sent with Amboy, they'd either be complacent because of numbers, and have minimal guard, or the guard would be heavy. Either way, Amboy was going to need more than an army to keep him safe.

Tracker opened the tack-room door. The hinge squeaked. Shadow picked up the can of oil from the ledge and oiled it.

Tracker grabbed ammo and guns from the boxes lined up against the wall and started shoving them into his saddlebag.

Shadow looked at the amount and cocked an eyebrow. "We going to war?"

"With the U.S. Army, if they're stupid enough to protect that son of a bitch."

Shadow tossed some dynamite into the mix. "Never been real fond of the army. Too many people given too many orders from too far away."

"So maybe, while they're sitting and waiting to figure out what they need to do, we'll slip in and invite Amboy over for a visit."

"We're not killing him?"

"No. Not until we know for sure he's the one."

"It'd be easier just to go in and kill him," Shadow said, packing his own supplies. "Stealing an unwelcome guest from under the army's nose isn't going to be easy."

Tracker cocked an eyebrow at his brother. "Since when do you worry about it being easy?"

"Since you've got something to live for."

"I thought we agreed that my time with Ari was just for a moment."

"I lied."

"We don't lie to each other."

"I slipped." Shadow swung his saddlebags over his shoulder. "You've got a chance with Ari, Tracker. Why don't you let us handle this, and you stay here with Ed, Tucker and Luke and protect that?"

Tracker hoisted his own saddlebag to his shoulder and headed to the horses. "It's my woman's parents who were killed. It's my woman who was raped and beaten." He met Shadow's gaze. "It's my woman's honor that needs to be restored."

"That's our father's way of talking."

"Maybe the man wasn't all bad."

"He was rotten to the core."

"Yeah, he was. But I'm thinking lately, it doesn't mean we have to be."

"Hell, Tracker, hating him keeps us going. No sense messing with it now."

"You've got a point." He cinched the saddle tight and lowered the stirrup. Buster snorted and tossed his head.

"You going to leave a note for Ari?"

Tracker shook his head. He would never forget that moment when she had walked away arm in arm with Desi, glancing back only that once. Independence from him was what he wanted for her, but the moment when she'd exercised it had been a knife to the gut.

"I'll explain when I get back." *If* he got back. He had a bad feeling about this ride.

Shit. Since when did he worry about the return?

He swung up into the saddle.

"You ready?"

Tracker slid his rifle in and out of the scabbard. Secure but ready. "Yes."

"Then let's ride." Shadow touched his hat and wheeled his black in a tight circle.

Buster was fresh and ready to run. Tracker gave him his head, letting the faint moon light the trail, pushing harder than was safe. But they'd never have a better opportunity to eradicate the threat to the twins. It couldn't be missed.

Four hours later he could see the rise. His pulse picked up, but his brain went calm. Over that hill was the man he'd come to kill. Just as soon as he found out for sure that he was the head of the organization.

When he got to the scrub at the foot of the rise, Caine stepped out of the shadows, his hat pulled low over his eyes.

Tracker pulled up his horse.

Caine pushed his brim back, revealing those green eyes that saw too much. "Going somewhere?"

"Likely the same place as you." Tracker nodded toward the hill. "They still there?"

"Yup. Stage isn't set to head out for five hours."

"How many men?"

"Twenty-five."

Twenty-five men cost a lot of money. "Just how rich *is* your wife?"

"Filthy rich, to hear her tell it."

"And she stays with an ugly-ass son of a bitch like you? Shit."

Caine shrugged. "What can I say, the woman has taste."

"Or a hole in her brain."

Caine smiled. "Either way, she makes me a happy man."

"Good."

"What about you? Zach said Ari has a soft spot for you."

"Just a temporary thing."

Caine shot him a look but didn't pry. "I'm sorry, Tracker."

"Water under the bridge." He swung down off his horse.

"Yeah, I guess it is."

"What's the plan?" Caine always had a plan. It's what made him such a good leader.

"Well, I was in favor of going in guns blazing, but Zach talked me out of it."

Caine never did anything rash. Zach, however, was another story. "We need Amboy alive."

"I know," Caine agreed.

"Is that why you didn't tell me about this little plan?"

"That, and Ari needed you."

"She and Desi made up," Tracker said.

"Good."

"So about that plan…?"

"Zach and Shadow are going in. Zach's found some chloroform he's eager to experiment with."

Shit. Why did it have to be Shadow?

"How are they going to get Amboy out?" Dead weight was hard to move, and depending on Amboy's size, it could be a tough haul. Past twenty-five army soldiers? A damn impossible one. Even for Zach and Shadow.

"We're going to launch a frontal attack." Caine moved back to his horse and lifted his canteen off his saddle. "Provide a bit of distraction. It'd be easier if we didn't have to worry about killing the guards." Caine took a drink before capping the canteen again. "But technically, the army is on our side."

"What good will a distraction do? The cavalry will come after us as soon as we leave. Everyone knows Hell's Eight. It's not hard to tell when we swoop in."

"Yeah, if Hell's Eight goes in."

Caine pulled out a rough-looking wig made of coarse black horsehair, attached to a sombrero. "Want to play Comanchero?"

The plan went to hell within ten minutes of inception. So fast, Tracker had to wonder if it was a trap.

"Are you sure Amboy is even in there?" he called to Caine over the sound of gunfire.

"He's in there."

"He knew we were coming." Tracker ducked as a soldier took aim. The bullet ricocheted off the rock beside him.

Caine fired back. He looked ridiculous in his hat and wig. "I'd say he was counting on it."

"Why? To get Desi and Ari alone?"

Caine shook his head. "Hell's Eight is too well fortified. My guess is he plans to discredit us."

"Discredit?"

"Think about it. Why get his hands dirty when he can use the law against us?"

Tracker looked at the blue-and-gold uniforms with new understanding. "Or the army."

Caine spat. "No one spins a tale better than an Easterner."

"And the tale would only have to hold until we played into his hands."

"Like attacking a stage guarded by the U.S. Army."

This time Caine ducked. "Yeah. Like that."

"Any sign of Zach and Shadow?" Sam called from his position to the right.

"Not yet," Tracker called back. The sick feeling that had been growing in his stomach all day got worse. "Not yet" wasn't good. It wasn't bad, either, especially considering how many soldiers were swarming around the hut.

"They'd better haul ass. Caden's swinging around back to provide cover, but I'm not sure he's going to be able to get there before they figure out we're covering for something."

Tracker searched the brush and hollows, and murmured, "Move your ass, brother."

There was no sign of any action for a few minutes, but then to the right something moved. He raised his spyglass. "Ten o'clock, near the left corner."

Caine shielded his eyes. "Got them."

It was only a matter of moments before the soldiers would see them, too. Tracker took aim at the men most likely to spot Shadow and Zach. In a volley of bullets, he pinned them down. The rest of the Hell's Eight took notice and soon had six guns trained on that section of terrain, pacing their efforts so a steady hail of bullets bought Zach and Shadow time.

"Move, damn you."

Zach and Shadow worked their way around the house, moving into the temporary bullet-free zone, ready to sprint up the hill. A soldier stepped out from behind a rock, took aim.

"Shadow!"

His brother was too far away to hear. Tracker couldn't get a clear shot. He watched in agony as the man leveled the gun.

Sam's big rifle barked. The soldier went down.

Tracker felt weak with relief.

"Son of a bitch, that was too damn close," Caine muttered.

Tracker sent another spray of bullets down the hill. The soldiers weren't going to stay pinned for long. Zach and Shadow crouched low, watching, waiting for that one-in-a-million opportunity, that break between bullets that would enable them to get back into the ravine they'd crawled down. It would be easier to cover them then. Once they got there, they had a chance.

"That seals it. If that Amboy character comes within range, I'm killing him. We can find out what we need to know another way," Tracker said.

"He's smarter than we thought."

Tracker lay back against the rock and reloaded while Caine took his turn. "Shouldn't have judged him so laxly, just because he's Eastern."

"That's a mistake we won't be making again."

But it could be a costly one to have made now, with Shadow's life on the line. Caine's gun barked.

The soldier at a strategic corner clutched his shoulder and spun around. He went down. It was the opportunity they'd been waiting for. Tracker let out a war cry that echoed down the valley. Zach and Shadow bolted forward. Shadow's answering cry flowed back up the hill.

Bullets exploded from above and below. The air was thick with the scents of gunpowder, sweat and determination.

"Goddammit, Tracker. Duck!"

He did. Bullets hit the dirt all around the rock he crouched behind.

"They've got you marked."

Shit. He'd have to change position. "Moving!"

He rolled to the left, grimacing as rocks dug into his side. A bullet splatted into the ground an inch from his head.

The sound of a rifle report immediately drowned it out. "All taken care of, Tracker."

He lay on his back, drawing three deep breaths as he waited to see if there would be any more shots. "Much obliged, Ace."

"Get that shot off a bit faster next time, Ace," Caine snapped.

"Will do, boss man."

"Damn fool took one to the leg," Caden announced.

"He all right?" Caine called back, a bit less gruffly.

"Bleeding like a stuck pig, but he'll live."

Tracker sat up against a small tree.

"Going to need more than that to cover your ass," Caine told him over the steady volley of gunfire.

"Working on it." Just as soon as he saw what was happening with Shadow.

Tracker cautiously leaned around the tree. A lot had changed in the few minutes it'd taken him to switch locations. Shadow and Zach had made it to the ravine directly below. They were climbing fast. The soldiers were catching up just as fast. There was something odd in Zach's gait. Tracker pulled out his spyglass. Through the lens, he could see the dark stain on Zach's side.

"Son of a bitch, Zach's hit."

"How bad?"

"Side."

"Shit."

Shit. Tracker seconded the sentiment. A side hit could be a flesh wound or mortal. There was no telling from here. Shadow grabbed Zach's arm, looped it around his shoulders and kept climbing.

"Got to be bad if Zach's letting Shadow carry him."

Shit again.

They laid down another spray of bullets, providing as much cover as they could. "Come on, Shadow."

Tracker checked his ammunition. He was getting low. Not enough left to do much good up here. Shadow wasn't making enough time carrying Zach. They couldn't control the soldiers down there much longer. There were too many and they had too much cover. Reloading his rifle, he eyed the fastest path down. Zach stumbled, taking Shadow to his knees. They weren't both going to make it. Not without help. And Shadow would never leave Zach.

Slinging his rifle across his shoulder, Tracker leaped over the log and ran down the slope, slipping and sliding. Caine's "Cover him!" trailed in his wake.

Shadow and Zach looked up. So did about a half-dozen soldiers who all started running toward Tracker. Whipping the rifle off his shoulder, he gave them something to look at. The men behind Shadow and Zach dived for cover.

As soon as he got close enough, Shadow shouted at him, "What the hell are you doing?"

Tracker slid his arm through the rifle strap and shifted the gun over his shoulder. "Saving your ass."

Coming up on Zach's other side, he took his arm. "How are you doing, Zach?"

"Had better days."

That Tracker could see. The side of his pant leg was red with blood. His skin was unnaturally pale and his breathing was labored.

"Well, let's see what we can do about getting you out of here."

"*Gracias.*"

Tracker exchanged a glance with Shadow behind Zach's back. His brother shook his head. With every step Zach grew heavier. By the time they were a third of the way up, he was dead weight. Behind them, the soldiers were gaining ground.

If it weren't for the twist and turns of the ravine, combined with Hell's Eight sharpshooters, all three of them would already be dead.

"Don't they know when to give up?"

"U.S. Army, Tracker." Shadow grunted. "They're not known for their surrendering attitude."

"I'm thinking they should get into the habit."

"Would be handy tonight."

"Did you get Amboy?"

"He's a greasy son of a bitch."

"Slipped out of our grasp," Zach gasped.

"Damn snake in the grass."

The moon was setting. Tracker couldn't see shit. His foot

slipped off a rock, and Shadow went down behind him. Zach groaned and listlessly struggled to regain his feet.

"He's the one who shot Zach," Shadow explained. "Had some fancy pistol stuck in his sleeve."

"Did you find out anything?"

"No."

"You will have to kill him," Zach moaned.

"Save your strength for walking."

Zach's head lolled on his chest. "He is desperate. This is why he shot me."

"He shot you because you broke into his room and attempted to kidnap him."

The path was getting steeper, narrower. It was harder to carry Zach between them.

"No. He is a very clever man with *mucho dinero*. The web he builds is very complicated. If he is not stopped, Hell's Eight may not win."

"No one can beat Hell's Eight," Shadow countered.

"This man, he can."

"You really think he's a match for Hell's Eight?"

"He intends to kill the women and children."

"He needs them."

Zach shook his head. "Not anymore."

"Why?

"I...don't...know."

"What do you know?"

Zach didn't answer.

Shadow swore. Tracker joined in.

"We can't get to him tonight?"

"He's surrounded by guards. The only way to get to him is if we could find a way to draw him out."

Son of a bitch. Tracker reached up and grabbed Zach's hair

from behind. There was no resistance when he pulled his head back. Zach had passed out.

Tracker's shoulder hit a rock. When he shifted, his other shoulder bumped the other wall.

"We're going to have to go single file," he said.

"I'll hold Zach while you get set."

Tracker took his rife off his shoulder and let Zach slide down. Shadow held him up with an arm around his waist. Blood spilled over his fingers in a black wash.

"He's in a bad way."

"Yes. That bullet was meant for me."

"He's a hell of a good friend."

"Don't let him die."

Tracker frowned. Shadow wasn't usually overly sentimental.

"We won't." Bracing his rifle against the rock, he hoisted Zach over his shoulder. The man didn't even moan.

Tracker could hear the soldiers scrambling over the same rock they just had. Hear them stumble over the same log. They didn't have much time.

"Take my rifle."

He let it go before he realized Shadow wasn't there to catch it. For a moment he could only stand uncomprehendingly. Shadow was always there.

Don't let him die.

"Shadow!"

"Get him home, Tracker."

That came from below. His brother was heading back down.

"What the hell are you doing, Shadow?"

His cry of "Evening the score" was almost lost beneath a

volley of shots, the sudden acceleration of violence that always happened when men finally spotted their target.

"Shadow!"

No response.

Zach moaned and shifted. For a moment, Tracker was torn. He had two choices. Leave Zach and follow Shadow. Or leave Shadow and get Zach to safety.

That bullet was meant for me.

Shit. He didn't have a choice. He left his gun and started up the trail, knees aching under the weight, pushing himself past the pain, climbing faster than he thought possible.

"Damn you, don't you die!"

"Who are you talking to?" Ace asked, coming down the path.

"No one, apparently, who's listening."

Tracker eased Zach off his shoulder. Ace caught him.

"He took a bullet for Shadow."

"He's a tough one."

"He's Hell's Eight." Tracker wanted that understood.

"We'll take care of him."

"Good." Tracker spun on his heel and headed down the path, twice as fast as he'd come up it.

"Where are you going?" Ace called.

"To get my brother before it's too late."

Tracker was too late. By the time he'd worked his way past the sentries to a small rock fall, dawn was breaking on the horizon, illuminating the yard of the stage stop in a feeble light. Fifteen soldiers surrounded Shadow. The commander stood in front, hands locked behind his back, the stripes on his sleeve catching what light there was.

"It's a hell of a pickle you've got yourself into, brother."

Tracker trained his gun sight on the colonel. His finger tight-ened on the trigger. Such an easy shot, but wasted. The officer was too far away from Shadow to be an immediate threat. Tracker angled the barrel an inch to the right and a quarter inch down. All he had to do was pull the trigger in quick succession and the soldiers on either side of Shadow would go down. He sighed and tipped the barrel up. For all the good it would do. Tracker eased his finger off the trigger. Bullets weren't going to get Shadow out of this situation. They were outnumbered.

Amboy was very well connected if he warranted a detail with a colonel. Tracker couldn't see all of Shadow's face be-cause of his position, but from the set of his chin, he was giving the colonel hell. Tracker could almost feel sorry for the man. There was nothing more aggravating than Shadow in a mood.

Tracker slid a little to the left. Shadow didn't appear to be injured. He still had his hat and he wasn't shackled. How the hell had they caught him without a fight?

The colonel barked an order. One of the soldiers snapped off a salute and went into the stage house. Tracker tensed. The door opened.

Distinguished. That was the only word that came to Track-er's mind to describe the man who stepped out. He was tall, with smoothly combed hair, a neat handlebar mustache, an impeccably fitted suit. He didn't have an ounce of fat, and it wasn't likely he had an ounce of muscle, but there was some-thing about the man that said he wielded power.

The soldier directed him to the colonel. Amboy crossed the yard with a measured stride. Everything about the man was measured and controlled. The colonel asked him a question. Amboy pulled a watch from his vest pocket and checked the time. It was a blatant display of power. One that didn't sit well with the colonel. After putting the watch away, he answered. Tracker was too far away to hear the words, but he could read expressions. The colonel hadn't liked what he heard. He turned to Shadow, likely to ask him the same question. This had all the earmarks of a get-to-the-bottom-of-things discussion.

Amboy stood, legs slightly apart, and surveyed the crowd of men. The colonel was dwarfed by the Easterner's height and presence. The smallest of smiles touched Amboy's lips when he saw Shadow. He locked his hands behind his back and turned to face Tracker's brother. His attitude said he didn't appreciate the colonel disturbing his morning. The colonel's attitude said he didn't give a shit.

The hairs on the back of Tracker's neck stood up as Shadow shifted his weight to the balls of his feet. It was a subtle transition from *waiting* to *ready*. Fighting beside a man for twenty years made him easy to read.

Tracker took a step forward and breathed, "No."

It was suicide to attack Amboy.

This time it was Shadow who asked a question. Amboy didn't flinch, but he also didn't answer right away. The colonel looked uncomfortably from Shadow to Amboy. It couldn't be easy for the officer to be the caught between a Texas Ranger and a high-placed Easterner.

The colonel motioned sharply. Two soldiers came forward, the clank of metal accompanying every step. Irons. They were going to put Shadow in irons. No way in hell.

Shadow glanced over his shoulder. Behind his back he made a sign. Tracker squinted against the sun.

Only one.

He was telling Tracker that Amboy was the man in charge. That they didn't have anyone else to worry about.

Tracker's fingers itched to sign back. It wouldn't matter if he did. Shadow was turned away, couldn't see.

Shadow's fingers moved again. This time the sign was chillingly clear.

Ride to Hell's Eight.

Amboy had sent assassins to Hell's Eight. Damn him to hell. It didn't matter that they'd anticipated an attack. Or that the place was rigged for defense and guarded by three of his best men and seven of Zach's. There was always a chance for the unexpected to sway the outcome.

The soldiers were getting closer. Whatever Shadow planned, he'd have to act soon. Tracker took aim. He might not be able to save his twin right now, but he could help him. Shadow took off his hat and wiped his brow with his sleeve. Rifles came up, and he held his hands wide. The colonel nodded. Shadow straightened the brim before settling his hat back onto his head. The soldiers moved in. Either Shadow used that small hidden knife he'd just taken from his hat now, or the opportunity would be lost forever.

Evening up the score.

Don't.

Shadow's hand whipped forward. Silver flashed in the sunlight tracing the knife's lethal path. Amboy grabbed at his neck. Blood sprayed red as he dropped to his knees, clutching the knife buried in his throat.

Four soldiers jumped Shadow, dragging him to the ground. As Tracker watched them put the shackles on his brother he had his answer as to how the army had managed to capture Shadow without a fight.

He hadn't ever planned on giving them one.

Tracker backed up slowly, inching his way to the ravine. Rage burned like fire in his gut, burning out reason, burning out caution, giving him strength. Which was more than he could say for that crazy son of a bitch Amboy had sent to Hell's Eight.

Tracker made it to the ravine. Slinging his rifle over his shoulder, he started running. A war cry ripped from his throat, filling the morning air with the promise of death. From the station came an answering cry. From above, the Hell's Eight battle cry began with Caine, joined in by Caden, Ace, and Sam. It rose in volume and strength, building in unity, getting louder and louder until the promise it contained was the only thing to be heard.

Whoever Amboy had sent to Hell's Eight was going to be in for a hell of a fight.

16

There *had* been a hell of a fight.

Tracker slowed Buster and picked his way with the others through the yard. To his left a man lay on the ground, his throat slit, his expression almost peaceful. Tracker recognized Tucker's work in the efficiency of the kill. To his right, two men sprawled. The neck of one was broken. The other had a stab wound to the throat. For such a big man, Tucker could move as silently as a ghost, and when he caught up with his victims, all that muscle pretty much guaranteed it wasn't going to be a fair fight.

"Doesn't look like they were caught by surprise," Caine said, his expression grim. Tracker knew how he felt. His woman and child were here, too.

"No. But it's damn quiet."

It was that. No hounds bayed a warning. No one stepped out of the house to greet them.

"Where the hell is everyone?"

More bodies littered the ground. None of them Hell's

Eight or Montoya. From his pen, the rooster, Cantankerous, crowed.

"Stay here with Zach," Caine told Ace. "I'll check the place out."

"Will do."

Sam reached for his smokes, reconsidered and laid his rifle across his lap, pulling his pistol instead. Tracker did the same. A pistol or knife was better for up-close fighting.

"I'll check the barn," Caden said.

Caine nodded.

"They're fine," Sam said.

"What makes you so sure?"

"None of these bodies are our men," Tracker pointed out.

"And none of them have holes as big as Texas blown in their guts." Sam smiled. "Bella's grown right fond of her shotgun."

"Would she be out here?"

"I'd like to think she'd stay put when I told her too, but…" He shook his head. "With the babies, I don't think she'd be able to let them get that close." He smiled a smile that didn't reach the blue of his eyes. "Bella's right fond of babies."

"Bella's right fond of *you*," Tracker countered. "She knows to wait for you."

As she had before. Hanging on until her Sam came, and when an explosion would have sent him over the cliff, she'd been there to catch him, holding on, pitting her determination against gravity and the fate that would have taken her Sam from her.

"Yeah, she does." Sam's smile faded. "When she remembers."

"She's a hell of a woman. Have some faith."

"Working on it."

There were more bodies near the main house. These were less uniform in placement. There had been an extended battle there. A closer inspection revealed the windows had been shot out, and bullet holes peppered the wood.

Tracker swore and turned his horse to the right, where Ari's little house sat.

The front door of the main house opened. Maddie stood there, her hair loose about her shoulders, her sheer wrapper barely covering her impressive breasts. Maddie was sweet but not quite right in the head. She'd been raised in a whorehouse and it was all she knew. Her mental problems and complacent ways made her the perfect whore, always doing what she was told, never understanding that not everyone was nice. Never understanding why she got hurt. Always coming back for more. She hadn't asked Tracker to save her, but Tracker couldn't have left her behind to be continually abused. The saying "God looks out for fools and idiots" hadn't held for her. Tracker didn't know how God could have overlooked Maddie.

No matter. Though she was near twenty by her count, she was like a sweet child trapped perpetually in the optimism of youth. Ever since Tracker had brought her in from Alguiero, Tia had been trying to teach her proper manners. The result was that Maddie still greeted everyone as if she were the hostess at a cathouse, though she did it with impeccable correctness.

"Hello, gentlemen."

No one said anything. The moment stretched out.

"Is this your first time to Hell's Eight?"

Maddie was having one of her flighty days. Anxiety did that to her.

"There's no need to be shy. Our ladies are the finest in the state and guaranteed to make a man feel welcome."

Caine swore. "Shit."

"Easy," Tracker warned. "She's the only one who knows what happened here."

"I don't have time for this."

"Make time," Sam snapped.

Tracker nudged Buster closer. "Hello, Maddie."

Her round face melted into a genuine smile. "Tracker, how wonderful to see you again. I assume you'll be wanting time with Ari." Her voice dropped to a conspiratorial half whisper. "She's one of our favorites. Very much in demand. Why, just last night several of her suitors got into a tussle as to who would win her favor."

Translated, the first part meant Maddie knew he'd been with Ari, and that Maddie liked Ari. The last made his stomach sink. For the first time in his life he felt true fear.

"So I see."

Maddie glanced around. "They did make a mess. Tia wasn't happy. She hit one over the head with her rolling pin."

A wave of fresh unease went through the men. The attackers had gotten into the house.

"Hurry it up, Tracker," Caine hissed.

"Where is the one Tia hit?" Tracker asked.

Maddie looked concerned. "He hasn't woken up yet."

Tracker wasn't surprised. Tia's rolling pin was made of stone.

"I'm sure he will soon. Could you let Ari know I'm here?"

Maddie's face fell. She hated to disappoint anyone. "I'm sorry, but all our ladies are currently occupied."

"The hell you say." Caine kneed his horse forward up onto

the steps. Maddie screamed and fell back. Tracker jumped down and grabbed her before she could run. His own impatience made it nearly impossible to hold a civilized tone.

"Sally Mae isn't going to like that," Maddie whispered, holding on to Tracker's arm while Caine hollered for Desi. "She told me horses don't belong in the house, ever."

Tracker didn't want to know what had brought up that discussion.

"Where is Sally Mae?"

Maddie shook her head. "She's at the cemetery with everyone else." She blinked, wide-eyed, as if surprised he didn't know. "Today's the funeral."

"Caine!" Tracker hollered. Sam was already riding out, Caden following suit. Ace came forward with Zach.

"What?"

"They're at the cemetery."

"Son of a bitch."

"Who died, Maddie?"

"One of Mr. Zach's men. And Mrs. Desi's mom and dad."

They were lucky they'd lost only one, and not the women, but still, one was too many.

"Maddie, I've got a man who's hurt. Can you care for him until Sally Mae comes back?"

Sally Mae was as close to a doctor as they had, and truth be told, Tracker had yet to see a real doctor equal her skills. It made her pacifist views tolerable.

"Oh, yes. Sally Mae has been teaching me what to do. She says I have a real knack for doctoring."

Ace smiled and dismounted. "Good, then you can practice on Zach."

Maddie hurried forward, her whole demeanor changing. "Zach is hurt?"

"Yes."

"What are you waiting for? Bring him into the parlor."

Tracker dropped the reins and went to help Ace with the unconscious Zach. Damned if she didn't sound just like Sally Mae right then.

"You got this, Maddie?" he asked as they carried Zach onto the porch.

She stood soldier straight, a confident smile on her face. "I've got this."

Tracker shook his head. He'd never understand women. Things that should make them cower gave them confidence. Things they should face without batting an eyelash sent them screaming for cover. For Christ's sake, Maddie got hysterical at the sight of a spider!

They carried Zach between them into the house. The first room on the right was the sickroom. Desi had dressed it up with some blue-and-white curtains, but it still carried the scent of carbolic, which removed any sense of cheer. Zach moaned as they laid him straight. Right away Maddie started stripping off his blood-soaked shirt. She didn't flinch as blood stained her hands.

"Get me some hot water, Ace."

"On it."

Tracker fetched the cleaning cloths and basins. Maddie looked up. "You need to leave."

"You think I can't stomach a little surgery?"

"I think Miss Ari waits for you."

Shit.

"She needs you right now."

"She's got her sister."

Maddie shook her head and unbuckled Zach's belt. "It's not the same. You're the one who understands her." She glanced up at Tracker, looking so sweet and intent, it was hard to believe she'd been whoring since she was twelve. "That's important, you know."

"Desi—"

"Miss Desi has Caine. He's the one who understands her."

"I'll go in a—"

She took the pan from his hand. "You need to go now. Mr. Zach would not like you to see him this way."

"Better me than you."

She shook her head and placed her hand gently on his stomach. "No. We have an understanding."

He guessed they did, if unconscious could be considered consent.

Ace came back into the room, carrying the pitcher of hot water. "Mr. Ace will help me."

Ace's smile was gentle, covering the worry in his gaze as he glanced at the exposed wound.

"Sure will. At least until Sally Mae gets here."

The others had likely already reached the small cemetery and relayed the need to Sally Mae.

"I'm sure she's on her way." As he should be. He had his own goodbyes to say.

It was a solemn circle at the cemetery. Desi, Tia and Ari stood in the center of the half circle of people surrounding the headstones set under the spreading branches of the elm tree. Caine stood beside Desi, who held Jonah. Ed beside Tia. In the middle, Ari stood holding Miguel, sheltered from the threats by Hell's Eight love. Sheltered in his absence. Protected. By her family. In front of them all, Father Bernard stood, Bible in hand before the freshly turned earth marking a new grave. Obviously he'd been leading the memorial. Desi must have been planning the family funeral for a while to have the father out here so quickly.

He pulled Buster to a stop. Buster snorted and stomped his feet. Ari looked up and smiled, and Miguel squealed with pleasure. Ari stepped out of the semicircle. She looked beautiful in her borrowed black dress with her braided blond hair shining in the sunlight and her blue eyes sparkling with tears.

"Tracker."

His name was her breath on the breeze.

He dismounted. "Sorry I'm late." He took off his hat. "Who'd we lose?"

"Juarez," Caine said.

A good man. "Zach will be pissed."

"Yeah."

Too many battles. Too many deaths already, but more to come. He watched Ari as she approached. He wanted so much more for her and Miguel.

"Caden told us what happened." She caught his hand. "Are you all right?"

Tracker closed his fingers around hers, part of him expecting her to pull away, to give some sign that she didn't need him anymore. Instead she stepped in closer, tilting her head back, lips pursed waiting for a kiss. The damn woman didn't have a lick of common sense.

"I'm filthy." From the trail. His choices. His life. And she had to stand there looking so pure.

She opened her eyes. Her right hand cupped his cheek. "You're perfect."

Miguel grabbed his hair and pulled it to his mouth, drawing Tracker closer to Ari. Closer to temptation.

"Hardly."

She smiled softly and the understanding in her eyes made the hair on the back of his neck stand on end. Her smile spread. "Tracker Ochoa, are you refusing, before your family and mine, to kiss me?"

He didn't know what the hell he was doing, let alone what *she* was doing. "Maybe."

"Oh." She blinked and the tears that had been drying freshened. She took a step back. A gun was cocked in the sudden silence.

He looked up. Caine smiled. "You get much more stupid, Tracker, and I'm going to have to plug you just to let some of it out."

He would, too. Tracker didn't care. "Stay out of it, Caine."

"Can't do that, Tracker. That's my sister-in-law you're trifling with."

"I'm not trifling with anyone."

Ari stomped on his toe. His boot took the brunt of the hit. Miguel pulled his hair.

"That's not what it looks like to me."

"Nor to me." The soft thump of a Bible snapping closed punctuated Father Bernard's statement.

Caine chuckled. "Now you've done it."

Tracker shot Caine a glare before turning it on the priest. "I didn't ask for God's input."

"Tracker!" He ignored Ari's protest, keeping his eyes on the priest. The man might be of God and might wear robes that resembled skirts, but he was a wily adversary.

Father Bernard shook his head and stepped closer. "That

always was your problem, Ochoa. Always thinking God didn't have you in his sights."

"Hell, Padre, I've never doubted being in his sights. I've just been waiting on him to pull the trigger."

"Hijo!" Tia exclaimed.

"Tracker!" Ari gasped. "You can't swear at a priest."

Tracker looked down into her face, that sense of doom building. "I already did."

Ari turned, placing her slight body between him and the padre. Defending him, he realized. "I'm sorry, Father. He's had an upset."

His brother under arrest for murder. A four-hour ride compressed into three because he feared Ari taken hostage or killed. *An upset.* He guessed she could call it that.

Father Bernard's "So I understand," was a bit dry.

Taking Ari by the shoulder, Tracker moved her aside. When she looked back over her shoulder at him, he explained. "I don't need you taking up for me."

He expected more tears, not a sharp "Well, you're not doing a very good job on your own."

Caden laughed. Caine snorted. Sam and Bella chuckled. Desi covered Jonah's ear and pressed his head to her chest. Looking around, Tracker got the sense everyone knew something he didn't. He hated that. "Good job of what?"

"Making a good impression."

"Father Bernard already knows me."

"As a Ranger, not a—" She bit her tongue.

The hairs on the back of his neck stirred again. Everyone went quiet as Ari exchanged an anxious glance with Desi, who nodded. "A what?"

Ari bit her lip and hoisted Miguel up on her hip. Miguel wiggled and squirmed before holding his arms out to Tracker.

Tracker steeled his heart and pretended not to notice. He didn't want to hold the boy. Didn't want to get any closer than he was. Didn't want to feel any more pain than he had to when Ari took him and went back to the life she was meant to have. That he was determined she have. Watching them put Shadow in shackles had driven home how tenuous a life with him would be for her. The little boy's face fell. Tracker lasted all of one second before swearing under his breath and taking Miguel from Ari.

"He's getting too heavy for you," he muttered.

Ari touched his arm when he would have stepped back. "Tracker?"

"What?"

Not looking away, she accepted his dare, finishing the thought he'd tried to kill. "He only knows you as a Ranger, not as a husband."

Damn it, the woman was tenacious. Why couldn't she let it go? Why did she need to make him want too much? "Why does he need to know that?"

She took a step that closed the distance between them, resting her breasts against his forearm. She stroked Miguel's head. "Because we deserve peace. Because our children deserve peace. For that to happen we have to make *our* peace with the past."

"Our children?"

Her jaw set. "Yes. Married people usually have children."

Now was the moment he'd been waiting for. His opportunity to sever her dependence on him. All he had to do was mock her belief that he'd ever intended to be honorable.

"Cat got your tongue, Tracker?" Caine asked, more than a little mockery in his own voice.

"Shut up, Caine."

Caine gave him a look that said he knew the words trapped on Tracker's tongue. "Don't do it."

"Do what? Point out we were never legally married?"

Desi grabbed Caine's pistol. "You deceitful lecher!"

Caine sighed and shook his head as Desi pointed it at Tracker. "Yeah, that."

Ari snatched Miguel from Tracker. The baby squalled. Ari shouted over the noise. "Shoot him, Desi."

"Gladly."

The pistol in Desi's hand wavered dangerously. Tracker felt a twinge of uncertainty. "She's going to hurt someone, Caine. That pistol's too heavy for her."

"You've got a point." Caine took Jonah from his wife. "Use two hands, angel."

"Shoot him now, *hija*," Tia ordered. "And aim low."

The muzzle was level with his groin. Tracker got the uneasy feeling the women weren't joking. "Tia!"

Tia huffed. "I did not bring up a son of mine to be a user of women."

"Control your wife, Caine."

"Why? I think she's doing just fine."

"Only if Ari wants to be married up with a eunuch."

"Well," Father Bernard interrupted, "maybe you should have thought of that before taking advantage of this sweet woman, making her fall in love with you when all you wanted was sport."

Tracker cut Father Bernard another glare. "I'm not above shooting a priest."

The aggravating man just smiled. And why not? He did have God on his side.

"Enough, Tracker."

And apparently Ari.

He arched an eyebrow at her. "You're giving me orders?"

She drew herself to her full five-foot height. "Yes."

"Why?"

"Because we don't have much time. Because I want to be married to you in truth as well as word before you ride out after Shadow. Because I love you and always will, no matter what wild hares you latch on to on any given day."

Shit.

She took a breath. "No matter how much you doubt me."

"Aw, hell." Reaching out, he cupped her face in his hand and with slight pressure on the nape of her neck, he drew her to him. She came willingly, leading with her faith, offering him the love he'd always been taught would never be his. Thigh to thigh, belly to belly, heart to heart. "Ah, damn, sweets, you make it hard to do the right thing."

"I think she's making it darn easy," Ed called.

Ari rolled her eyes and rested her forehead against his chest, turning slightly so Miguel wouldn't be squashed. "You have a very intrusive family."

Despite the confidence in her tone, he could sense the tension in her. She wasn't sure of him.

"Look at me."

She did, the shadows in her gaze reflecting the apprehension she was trying to hide.

"I'm an all-or-nothing man, Ari."

"I know."

"If we do this, one year, two years, ten years down the road, you'll be stuck."

"Sure you want to wake up to that ugly mug every morning?" Luke called.

Ari ignored Luke. "Do you promise?"

"Luke's got a point. I am an ugly bastard."

Her fingers caressed his scar, and it didn't matter whether he had feeling there. The emotion came through. "You're my beautiful man."

"You need glasses," Caden offered.

"Desi?" Ari said.

"Yes, Ari."

"The next person that tries to talk me out of marrying Tracker?"

"Yes?"

"Shoot him."

Desi lifted the gun and smiled at Caine, who obviously had a comment hovering on the tip of his tongue. "On it."

Caine didn't even flinch. "You might want to reconsider where you're pointing that," he told his wife. "This is our last night together for a bit. We ride in the morning."

Desi exchanged one of those looks with Caine that left no one in doubt as to what the two would be doing tonight. "Can I just shoot them in the toe, Ari?"

Ari's gaze never left Tracker's. "To start."

"Where do you think she's going to finish?" Caine asked.

"I hope we don't have to find out."

That was from Ari. She stood there, his world, offering herself up as if the sacrifice was nothing, but out here her pale skin would weather. Her soft hands would callus. And for her choice of husband, she would be spit on. His hand went to the hilt of his knife. He'd kill anyone who offered such an insult to her. Skin and gut them slowly before letting them rot in the sun.

"You were meant for better things."

Her hand covered his, lifting his fingers away from the hilt.

"I've had these better things. And I've had much worse. What I was meant for was you."

Miguel grabbed his hair. He wanted to be rough and yank his hand away, but as soon as he touched that tiny fist, the impulse died. Miguel gave him his gummy smile. There was a bit of white.

"He cut a tooth!" He leaned in for a closer look. Miguel grinned more broadly. Ari inched closer. His hair fell over her shoulder, cocooning them in the intimate moment. She looked up at him, her eyes darker, more mysterious, holding promises he wanted to accept.

"He's got thirty-one more to go, my love. Don't you want to be there for each and every one?"

Taking his hand, she placed it over her heart. The softness of her breast seared his palm. The softness of the gesture seared his resolve.

"Damn it, Ari, I'm trying to do the right thing for the first time in my life."

She stomped her foot. "Well, who asked you to start with me? You promised me all or nothing. Told me to make a choice. I did."

Yes, he had. He let his hand slip down her back, skimming the delicate ridges of her spine until his fingers settled in the hollow, pressing until she had no choice but to lean against him. Her lips were inches away. Full, red and tempting. "You chose all."

"Yes, I did." She said it with no hesitation. No regret. "And you said you'd give me anything I wanted."

"I'm more likely to die young than not." It was a fact.

"Tracker, I'm not asking for guarantees. I just want every second the Lord gives us together."

Every second.

Tracker watched Ari's lips shape the words, heard her voice caress each syllable with love, let them settle on that part of him that just couldn't believe he was more than expendable. Let them cover it, smother it, kill it. Felt the death he'd been dreading and then the joy. The freedom. The rebirth. He leaned in a little closer, savoring the emotion as it washed over him even as Ari's breath mingled with his. His life, his soul. His Love.

"Son of a bitch, Tracker. You going to make the woman beg in front of us all?" Sam asked.

No, he wasn't. "Come here, sweets."

She went up on her tiptoes, making it so easy for him to mate his mouth to hers. Her lips parted. He didn't take advantage. Passion burned, but this wasn't about sex. This was about them.

"Bad enough she had to do the proposing." he heard Sam mutter distantly.

Tracker kissed Ari gently. Sweetly. Tenderly. Once, twice. Ari sobbed and pressed against him. Miguel tugged on his hair. From beyond the circle a horse stomped his hoof.

"Is that a yes?" Desi asked.

Father Bernard cleared his throat. "Since I'd be hard-pressed to slide the marriage papers between them, I'm declaring it one."

Tracker smiled against Ari's lips, kissing her once more because it was too hard not to before replacing his mouth with his thumb, pressing gently on her lower lip, hiding nothing from her searching gaze. He was hers and with four words he confirmed it for everyone else. "That's definitely a yes."

"Great," Caine said, taking his pistol from Desi and moving her closer, away from the shade and into the sunlight surrounding Tracker and Desi. Out of the past and into the light.

"See," Ari whispered, watching as the rest of Hell's Eight followed suit. "How can you doubt this was meant to be?"

He couldn't. Not anymore. He believed in signs, and this one was too big to ignore. The old ways were dying, but the future was shining brightly. Just waiting for those brave enough to step into it. "I guess I just needed a shove in the right direction."

Ari chuckled. Father Bernard stepped up in front of them, his bald head reflecting the sunlight, his old eyes reflecting his satisfaction. "Glad to see you came to your senses."

"I usually do."

"Had my doubts this time." Tracker didn't believe that for a minute. The priest had that inner calm that came from being at peace with himself and his world. "And you're supposed to be the one with the faith."

Father Bernard smiled. "I'll pray on it."

He and Ari were going to need all the prayers they could get. Tracker held out his hand. "Thanks for coming."

The priest shook it and smiled. "Wouldn't have missed bragging rights on this for the world."

Everyone laughed. The priest opened his Bible.

"Just a minute." Tia hurried forward. In her hands she had a small bouquet of white flowers. Daisies.

"Every bride needs a bouquet." She handed them to Ari. "Welcome to the *familia, mi hija*."

Ari sniffed back a sob, her gaze locked on the flowers, a soft look of wonder on her face he wanted to ask her about. "Thank you."

"Are we all set now?" Father Bernard asked.

Ari's "yes" was tear-wet but sure.

"Then let's have this wedding before we lose the opportunity," Caine ordered. "No telling how much mischief Shadow will get into if we leave him to cool his heels too long."

17

Three hours later Tracker strode out of the study in Caine's house. They had a plan to rescue Shadow. It wasn't much of a plan, but at least they had one. There were only so many plans one could come up with to defeat the U.S. Cavalry and live. And the one thing they all wanted to do was live. Especially Tracker. Tonight was his wedding night. He intended to make the most of it, create as many memories as he could before riding out at dawn. He settled his hat on his head and opened the front door. When he came back, he'd start on a few more memories. Like Caine, Tucker and Sam, he was determined that his woman would never regret a moment of her decision to gamble her future on him.

Maddie grabbed his arm as soon as he cleared the door. "You're not supposed to go to your house, Mr. Tracker."

Had Ari already had regrets? "I'm not?"

She shook her head. "Miss Ari was very specific."

Tracker breathed a sigh of relief. Ari being specific was good. Ari being specific meant she had a plan. "How so, specific?"

"Just a minute."

The woman made him wait while she struggled with her memory.

"Maddie…"

"I have to say it right."

It wouldn't do any good for him to push. Tracker bided his time, frustration rising right along with his temper.

"She said to tell you that she knows what the daisies mean."

That told him nothing important. He wanted to know where she was. His wedding night was waiting. "And?"

"She's waiting for you with the daisies."

Ari was at the meadow. The smile started deep inside.

"Thank you."

The meadow was beautiful in the sunlight—a green-and-white oasis set amidst the darker backdrop of the pines. In the center of it sat Ari, her long hair draped across her torso. A crown of daisies rested on her hair. When she saw him she stood and smiled. Daisy chains wrapped her neck, her wrists and her ankles. She wasn't wearing anything else. Sunshine and smiles. That was his Ari.

Lust slammed through him with painful intensity. He bit back a moan when she stepped forward and her breasts swayed.

"Tracker."

No one else said his name in that particular combination of disbelief and wonder, as if he were a dream come to life. He couldn't imagine wanting anyone else to.

She crooked her finger. "I've been waiting for you."

"You damn well better not be waiting for anyone else dressed like that."

SARAH McCARTY

"Do you like it?"

How much he liked it throbbed in his pants. He couldn't look away from the symbolic placement of the daisy chains. "I like your jewelry."

She held up a long length of daisies strung together. "I've got more."

"What's that for?"

"Come here and I'll show you."

Show, not tell. Damn. "Sweets, I should tell you, I'm a bit on edge."

"Me, too."

"I've got a lot of questions." With all that had happened, he hadn't had a chance to discuss with her what had happened the night before.

Even the wave of her hand was seductive. "Ask away."

"It looked like there was quite a battle here last night."

Try as he might, he couldn't detect concern in her voice. "We handled it."

"So I see." He took a couple steps forward, not understanding her mood. She didn't act like a woman who'd just had her worst nightmare revisited. "Are you all right?

"I'm very all right. Better than all right. I'm strong." Without batting an eyelash she said, "I killed a man last night."

He stopped. "You bragging on it?"

She shook her head. "No, it was horrible. But I did what you said. I hid my pistol in my skirts and acted terrified until the last moment."

"You weren't?" He took another step forward.

"Maybe. But mostly I was mad." Her eyes narrowed. "They had no right to invade our home. Threaten our child. No right at all."

"No, they didn't." None at all.

300

She shuddered. "I'm letting you scrub the bloodstains off the floor, though. I don't think I can do that."

"I'll handle it." She was watching him, waiting for him. He had no idea what she wanted from him. Uncertainty wasn't his friend.

"Baby, I need you to tell me what we're doing here."

"Isn't it obvious?"

"No."

"We're getting married again."

He looked around. They were alone. "Thought we did that this afternoon."

"Yes. That was for everyone else. This is for us."

"Sweets, you are going to have to explain."

"Later."

"No. Now." It'd been a hell of a day. He'd just come from a battle and three hours of hard riding with nothing but worry for his companion, a wedding and now the planning of what would likely be a suicide mission. His emotions were running hot, needing an outlet, but he still needed some things said before he could start his wedding night. "Shadow killed Amboy."

Ari paused for two breaths. "I'll thank him later."

"It'll have to be a long while later. The soldiers arrested him."

"I know, but you'll get him back."

Such faith in him. "That's the plan."

"They won't kill him, will they?"

Not unless he did something particularly aggravating, and knowing Shadow that was a possibility. To Ari, though, he gave hope.

"Not likely. He's a Ranger gone bad. There will have to be

a public trial. To save the Texas Rangers' reputation. It will be public. That will buy us time."

"But you will get him back?"

"Absolutely." When he did, Shadow would be an outlaw, but that was better than dead. And knowing Shadow, he'd enjoy the challenge of staying one step ahead of the law.

"Good."

Tracker took her in his arms. She felt good against him, a sweetly scented angel from his dreams. Good and alive. "I never want a ride like last night again, Ari, not knowing if you were alive or dead. Whether you needed me."

"You taught me well. I wasn't afraid."

He still found that hard to believe. "Just pissed."

She nodded. "Very, very pissed."

She was finding her strength but losing more of her innocence. He had mixed feelings about that. "I'm proud of you, sweets, but I'm sorry you had to go through that."

"I'm not." Her attention was no longer on the topic, if the placement of her hands was to be believed. "It's good to know I'm not always helpless."

Yes, it was. For him, too. "Yeah. I can understand that."

Her fingers worked the buckle of his gun belt. He caught it, along with the knife tucked into it, and set them aside carefully before they could fall. Ari tugged up the tail of his shirt. He smiled when she grunted in frustration. She was too short to do it in one smooth motion the way he did.

"Looks like you need a bit of help there."

She pinched his side. "Then help."

She had no patience. With a grin, he tugged the shirt off. Her sweet hands were on his torso before he got it over his head. Her lips found his stomach, dropping a hot little kiss just below his belly button before working their way up his chest in a string of nips that danced over his skin like flame.

Her thigh slipped between his, pressing against his cock and balls in rhythmic pressure. Tilting his hips forward, he gave her better access, moaning as his balls pulled tight.

"What are you doing?"

"Seducing you." She glanced up. "Is it working?"

Cupping her head, he held her mouth to his chest, growling in his throat when her nip spread like fire through his system. "All too well."

"Too well?"

"I'm never at my best, coming off a battle."

She stepped back and took his hand in hers. "You don't want me?"

He shook his head. "I want you too much."

Wrapping the daisy chain around his wrist, she tugged him closer. "Not possible."

"I'm not feeling civilized, Ari."

"You want to make love to me."

"I want to fuck you. There's a difference."

"Are you telling me any woman would do?"

"Hell, no."

"Then explain." She wrapped the other end of the daisy chain around her wrist, binding them together.

"I want to take you hard and wild."

She bit her lip. A shiver went through her. "All right."

"You don't know what you're saying."

"I was in a battle last night, too," she reminded him.

"I'll take you in ways you won't be comfortable. Ways you're not ready for."

A blush mounted her cheeks. "Desi gave me some cream. She said you could say thank you later."

Shit, there was only one thing a man used cream for. The thought of his thick cock slipping between Ari's creamy ass cheeks, touching her there in a gentle kiss before pressing, parting that tight rosebud for the first time, hearing her cries as she accepted him totally, drove him crazy. "Did she tell you what it's for?"

Ari shook her head. "But I can guess."

"And you're not afraid?"

"I'm yours, Tracker. I always have been, even before I knew you. I am not a stranger to the ways a man wants a woman. What I am a stranger to is how it feels for a man to take a woman in those ways, with love."

"Ari."

Her hands tugged at the drawstrings of his pants. If he didn't want to break the daisy chain that bound them together, he had to keep close. The knot came undone. His pants fell to his ankles. His cock fell into her grasp. Damn, Ari's touch felt good. Smooth, soft. Tracker looked down at her very white hands against his skin, the contrast highlighting the differences between them. She was a lady, from the top of her head to the tips of her toes. He was an outlaw, flirting with respectable. In the eyes of many, a filthy Indian who deserved castration just for looking at her. She'd never be able to go back East with him and show him off.

"You deserve better."

"Desi warned me you'd start that again."

"You should listen to your sister."

"I am." She squeezed his cock. "That's why, when we finish the wedding, I'm going to lie down on that blanket over there and you're going to make love to me however you want, everywhere you want."

His cock jerked. Pre-come leaked from the tip. He could picture that. "Son of a bitch."

Her thumb swept that betraying little bead away. "If you last that long."

Oh, he'd last. "If I don't, you'll just have to get me hard again."

He could see from her expression that she liked the thought of that.

"You mentioned something about a wedding?"

"It's not the real one, of course. Father Bernard already performed that, but I figured since you got to marry me your way, I should get to marry you mine."

"You do?"

"Absolutely. It's only fair."

"I'm all for fair."

"Good." She took a step back, indicating with a tap of her hand that he needed to bring his up. He didn't need her to tell him to turn his hand over and hold hers. That came as naturally as breathing.

She met his gaze squarely. No matter how he searched, he couldn't see any uncertainty in hers, but there was a question. He didn't have to wait long to hear it. Placing her fingertips on his cheek, she warned, "Be very sure, Tracker. Because once I do this, there's no going back. I'll never let you leave me, and if you try, I'll pack up all our kids and follow you across the plains until you give up out of sheer exhaustion."

"Anyone ever tell you a man does the threatening?"

"Nope, but even if they had, I'd tell anyone that they didn't understand you like I do. That they don't understand that your need for me to have the best makes you miss the fact that *you're* the best thing I could ever have." Her hand opened over his heart. "I'd tell anyone that they don't understand how beautiful

I always feel with you. How wonderful and free I feel when I'm in your arms. How perfect your kiss feels against my lips. How you make me smile and laugh, how happy I am to see you. How you make me feel strong, important, valued. If they had, I'd tell anyone that when a smart woman is lucky enough to find the man who completes her, she holds him close to her body, to her heart. Her soul." She took a step forward and slipped her hand over his cheek. Touching him with love. Son of a bitch, so much love.

Tears filled her eyes, roughened her voice. "And she thanks God every day for the opportunity to do so."

His own voice wasn't that smooth. "You love me like that?"

"How can you doubt it?"

Because when a man grew up knowing fairy tales were for others, it was hard to believe anything different. And to have his own personal happily-ever-after handed to him on a silver platter? How did a man tell a woman who gave him everything how much that meant?

"Tracker?"

He slid his hand around the back of her neck, pulling her up into his kiss. Kissing her slowly. Gently. Before resting his forehead against hers. "I don't have the fancy words you deserve."

"Then show me. You're very good at showing me."

"You think?"

"I always feel the love in your touch."

"Good." He rubbed his thumb against her mouth. "Is the ceremony over?"

"Do you promise to love and cherish me forever, to always hold me close, and never send me away?"

Clever of her to address her worries in the vows. "Tying my hands?"

"Absolutely."

He did like a clever woman. And this one he loved.

"I, Tracker Ochoa, promise to love you, Arianna, for all the rest of my days. I promise to cherish you with my heart, my soul and my body. I promise to always hold you close, and to never let you go. In this life and the next, sweets, and all the lifetimes to come, I'm yours."

Tears filled her eyes and the tip of her nose turned red. Her breath caught. Even blotchy, she was beautiful to him. She threw her arms around his neck. "Oh, God, I love you."

"I love you, too." He lifted her. She wrapped her legs around his waist and he held her close, breathing in the scent of crushed daisies and Ari, hugging her with the same intensity. She was his greatest treasure. His only love. The one he'd always hungered for. And she'd just given herself to him, without reservation. Son of a bitch.

The blanket was three steps away. He made it in two. Dropping to his knees, he laid her on the ground. The tip of his cock tucked into the well of her vagina. She was wet and ready. He was hard and throbbing. Her legs tightened around his hips. "Don't worry. I'm not going anywhere."

She gasped out, "Good." He rotated his hips in small circles, teasing her with the possibilities. "I'd better warn you, though, I'm feeling pretty wild."

It was his turn to say "Good."

He needed to hear it again. The daisy chain broke as he slid his hand behind her neck and tilted her head back.

"Tell me again how you want me."

"However you want, whenever you want." She licked her lips, leaving them moist and parted. "I'm yours."

Yes. His. He'd meant to tease, but ended up possessing. With a hard thrust he tunneled his cock through the tight folds of her pussy, watching her eyes widen in shock as she absorbed his possession. *His.* The thought ricocheted around his head, inspiring lust, joy, disbelief. He dropped his thumb to her clit, finding it swollen and wet. He rubbed it slowly, gently, coaxing her desire to rise to match his. He needed her to match him in everything. Love, lust, determination.

"Oh."

Her eyelids lowered until he could just make out the glitter of her irises behind the fan of her lashes. The muscles of her channel fluttered about his cock in blatant invitation. "If you're going to run, do it now."

"Shut up and love me, Tracker."

"How?"

"Hard. Oh, God, hard."

"You won't be afraid?"

She wiggled beneath him, forcing his cock deeper. "No."

He pulled back, gritting his teeth as her pussy clung to every inch of his cock, letting him go just one inch at a time. "Good."

He forged back. She was tight, so tight. *Damn.* He rubbed her clit harder, watching pleasure replace surprise, lust replace need. It wasn't enough that she wanted him—he needed to see it.

"Do you want me, Ari?"

"Yes."

"Show me."

"How?"

"Pull your legs back."

A blush colored her cheeks again, but she didn't hesitate. Reaching down, she caught the back of her thighs and pulled her legs apart, tilting her pussy up, leaving herself open and vulnerable to his thrusts.

"Like this?"

"Exactly like that."

He took a moment to appreciate the view. Her pussy was stretched wide around the width of his cock, the pretty pink inner lips drawn flat from the pressure. Bracing his weight on his hands, he pulled all the way out until her pussy hugged just the tip in a silken kiss, before tunneling back, pushing past that last bit of resistance until his groin was tucked up tight to hers, so close that not a whisper could slip between. So close there was no telling where he ended and she began.

Her head whipped side to side on the blanket as he pumped slowly and steadily, giving her all, taking all, and still it wasn't enough. For him or for her.

"More!"

The huskily moaned demand slid along his nerves, finding the wildness inside him, bringing it forward. Yes, she needed more. He needed more. The jar of cream caught his eye.

A gentle slap on her thigh opened Ari's eyes. He leaned in, kissing her mouth, gently, softly. "This isn't enough."

She blinked. Her lip slid between her teeth, letting him know she knew what he meant.

"Are you ready to be mine?"

She blew out a breath and just as quickly sucked it back in, her head turning until she could see the jar of cream. "Yes."

Kneeling, he lowered her thighs, first the left and then the right, before bracing his hands on her bent knees and slipping free. Her moan of regret matched his.

She tried to close her legs.

"No." He picked up the jar of cream and uncorked it before setting it beside them. "Stay just like that."

"Why?"

"Because I want it."

Leaning forward, he pushed her legs apart with his chest as he kissed her mouth, running his tongue along hers before lightly nipping her full lower lip, her throat, her chest, her stomach, her clit. The last drew a small scream that dissolved to a hoarse, sexy moan as he soothed the sting with the hot pass of his tongue. The next pass brought another moan. The next another small scream. He loved her with his mouth, breathing in her scent, savoring her taste as he scooped some cream onto his fingers.

Sucking her clit into his mouth, he stroked in quick succession, hearing the rise of her passion in a soft spill of his name from her lips, feeling her joy in the fingers twisted in his hair, tasting it in the honey that coated his tongue. When she was panting and bucking against him, he rubbed the cream into her anus. The muscle clenched against him. He rubbed a bit more, pressing gently as he circled the tight rosebud. Gradually the muscles relaxed and parted the tiniest bit.

"That's it, sweets. Relax."

He repeated the procedure again and again until his fingers and her ass were slick with grease. This time when he pressed, she opened, taking him easily to the first knuckle. "That's it, baby," he whispered against her clit. "Just like that, nice and easy."

Ari gasped as Tracker's finger parted her ass. Nice and easy. Oh, God, how was this going to be easy? His tongue flicked her clit. Her pussy spasmed. She was close, so close.

He pressed deeper. She tensed, old memories intruding.

"Too much?"

No, not enough. It would never be enough until there was only Tracker in her head. Only Tracker in her bed.

"More."

His mouth left her clit to string a line of kisses down her thigh as he straightened. "Turn over."

She knew what he wanted. She wanted it, too. She rolled over slowly, the way he liked to see her move, so he could look his fill, tucking her knees under her torso, lifting her ass. His "son of a bitch" was the sweetest compliment.

She wiggled her butt. He chuckled. She smiled. Loving Tracker was always so sweet, so nice.

From the corner of her eye she saw him scoop more cream from the jar and slide it along the dark length of his cock. She licked her lips as he palmed the fat head. Anticipation rode side by side with apprehension. He was a big man.

"Tracker?"

"What?"

"Tell me again you love me."

His big body came down over hers. His fingers tucked between her legs, finding her hungry clit, stroking it, kissing her shoulder when she shivered. His cock settled between her ass cheeks, sliding down until it notched against her anus. "I'll love you, Ari, for all the rest of my days." He pressed, opening her body and her heart with that gentle persuasion he'd always given her. She gasped as the pressure built.

She slid her hand over until it was on top of his, weaving her fingers between his, holding on as she struggled to accept the enormity of the moment. "Tracker..." Another kiss on her shoulder. Another stroke across her clit.

"I promise to cherish you with my heart, my soul and my body."

Tears burned her eyes, even as pleasure seared her body. "I love you."

He squeezed her hand, holding her as she took him this

first time, stroking her clit, balancing the pain with pleasure, taking her past the difficulty to the pure joy of loving him. Of being loved by him. Taking her to the place where there was nothing but them in this moment. His cock slid deep, filling her with lust, with him. Filling her past the point of no return. So good. So good. And she was so close.

"Oh, God. More."

He gave it to her with a slow, careful pump and a hard stroke to her clit and a promise as solid as he was. "In this life and the next, sweets, and all the lifetimes to come. I'm yours."

She came, crying his name, her body spasming around his, clinging to his. Her climax triggered his own. His thrusts got longer, stronger. She pushed back, relaxing her muscles and taking him deeper wanting to give him everything he wanted. Needing to be for him what he was for her. Everything.

His cock jerked within her, filling her with a hot warmth, sending shards of lightning skipping up her spine. As sweet as his moan of her name was the knowledge that she'd pleased him.

"Ari!"

His weight came over her, pressing her down. She slid forward. He followed her, still holding her hand, still thrusting, still loving her. She lay on the blanket, feeling him in her, all around her. Her vision filled with daisies.

Tracker rolled them over to their sides.

"You all right?" he asked, his palm pressed low on her stomach, massaging her through the discomfort as he worked his cock free.

Turning into his embrace, she cupped his cheek in her hand and kissed him gently. The daisy chain slipped down to her forearm. "I'm better than all right. I'm yours."

Emotion flared in his eyes as he brought her wrist to his

mouth. It had taken her a long time to recognize what that emotion was, but she knew now. It wasn't flashy. It wasn't overt, but it was as powerful and as deep as the man himself. It was love.

"Do you know what the daisies mean, Tracker?"

He shook his head, his dark gaze holding hers as his tongue touched the pulse in her wrist. A shiver went down her spine.

"They're forever." She took the chain from her neck and wrapped it around their hands, binding them together. "Like us."

★ ★ ★ ★ ★

SARAH McCARTY

He is everything her body craves…and everything her faith denies.

Tucker McCade has known violence his whole life: orphaned in a massacre, abused as a "half-breed" child, trained as a ruthless Texas Ranger, he's learned the hard way that might makes right. So even he is shocked when he falls for Sallie Mae Reynolds, a Quaker nurse.

Every night they spend together exploring new heights of ecstasy binds them ever closer, slowly erasing their differences…until the day Tucker's past comes calling, precipitating an explosive showdown between her faith, his promise and the need for revenge….

Tucker's Claim

Available now wherever books are sold!

Spice

From *USA TODAY* bestselling author

kayla perrin

When money is no object, life truly is cheap.

Their romance was a modern-day fairy tale: handsome older millionaire falls hard for struggling young waitress. Robert swept Elsie off her feet—and into his bed—put a huge diamond on her finger and spirited her away in his private jet destined for happily-ever-after.

Eight years later, Elsie Kolstadt realizes the clock has finally struck midnight. The five-star restaurants, exclusive address and exotic vacations can no longer make up for Robert's obsessive desire to control everything about their life together. From her hair color to her music playlists, Robert has things just the way he wants them. No matter what.

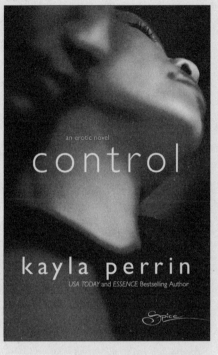

But it's Robert's ultimate, unforgivable manipulation that finally shocks Elsie into action. Though divorce would strip her of everything, she can't live under Robert's roof any longer. Making her decision easier is Dion Carter, a high-school football coach with a heart of gold and a body of sculpted steel. Suddenly Elsie is deep in a steamy affair that could cost her everything—because Robert will stop at nothing to keep Elsie under his thumb.

control

Available wherever books are sold!

ALISON'S WONDERLAND

ALISON TYLER

Over the past fifteen years, Alison Tyler has curated some of the genre's most sizzling collections of erotic fiction, proving herself to be the ultimate naughty librarian. With *Alison's Wonderland,* she has compiled a treasury of naughty tales based on fable and fairy tale, myth and legend: some ubiquitous, some obscure—all of them delightfully dirty.

From a perverse prince to a vampire-esque Sleeping Beauty, the stars of these reimagined tales are—like the original protagonists—chafing at unfulfilled desire. From Cinderella to Sisyphus, mermaids to werewolves, this realm of fantasy is limitless and so *very* satisfying.

Penned by such erotica luminaries as Shanna Germain, Rachel Kramer Bussel, N.T. Morley, Elspeth Potter, T.C. Calligari, D.L. King, Portia Da Costa and Tsaurah Litzsky, these bawdy bedtime stories are sure to bring you (and a friend) to your own happily-ever-after.

"Alison Tyler has introduced readers to some of the hottest contemporary erotica around."—*Clean Sheets*

Spice

www.Spice-Books.com

SAT60545TR